The Sunset Assassin

The Sunset Assassin

Book Three of
The Siranoush Trilogy

Stuart Campbell

This is a work of fiction. Names, characters, businesses, places, events, locales, and incidents are either the products of the author's imagination or used in a fictitious manner. Any resemblance to actual persons, living or dead, or actual events is purely coincidental.

Third paperback edition [i], 2023
Published by Stuart Campbell
www.stuartcampbellauthor.com

ISBN: 978-0-6457198-2-6

Contents

About The Siranoush Trilogy

The Siranoush Trilogy comprises the novels *Cairo Mon Amour*, *Bury me in Valletta*, and *The Sunset Assassin*. The three stories are stand-alone episodes in the tribulations of reluctant British spies Pierre Farag and his wife Zouzou Faris. The couple are exiled from Cairo to London in 1973, and then to Malta in 1975, ending their quest for freedom and anonymity in the northern Australian tropics in 1978.

Siranoush, meaning 'sweet love', is the stage name of a legendary Armenian actress who began her career in Constantinople, but left Turkey after the banning of Armenian plays. Her acting and operatic career continued in Yerevan, Tiflis and Baku. She died in 1932 and is buried in Cairo. Pierre is Armenian on his mother's side; like Siranoush, he is forced to make a life in exile.

I used Siranoush as the codename of the espionage operation that Pierre and Zouzou are enmeshed in during the 1973 Yom Kippur War. By literary chance, Pierre's great-aunt saw Siranoush perform at the Cairo Opera House in 1928.

The novella *Ash on the Tongue*, is a prequel to the trilogy, introducing the main characters in the run-up to the Yom Kippur War between Israel and Egypt. *Cairo Rations* is a collection of essays that I wrote to jog my memory before embarking on the trilogy.

Chapter 1: A Barbecue Lunch

Pierre Farag was woken by a thump and a clatter. He put his hand out of the sheets to touch the wall of the tiny ground-floor flat. Their rented home was in a muddle of walk-up brick apartment buildings and the backs of dry cleaners and TV rental shops, four streets away from Manly Beach. The bedroom wall was still warm. It would be this way until April, when autumn released Sydney from the ravaging summer heat.

He padded out to the front yard. The Sunday paper—New Year's Day 1978—lay on the doormat where it had bounced off the flyscreen. The paper van slewed around to serve the other side of Rialto Close, the driver steering with his left arm and lobbing the rolled-up papers into the front yards with his right.

Zouzou was up.

"Did you sleep well, my heart?"

"Perfectly well." No 'darling' or 'thank you'.

"Is there something wrong?"

"Wrong? What could be wrong?"

"Zouzou, what is it?"

She turned towards him. "Pierre, *habibi*, please cancel it."

She'd spoken in homely Egyptian Arabic, the language they used in tender moments—and in serious ones. Which was this?

"Cancel what? The paper? The milk?"

"The barbecue of course."

"Cancel the barbecue, *habibti*? Why ever should I do that?"

"I had a dream, Pierre. A premonition. Please cancel it."

Well, that ended the conversation. You didn't argue with Zouzou's dreams, not with a former Egyptian film star proudly descended from a Circassian slave. Not with a woman who had lived three lifetimes in her thirty-seven years.

He made tea for both of them and sipped in silence. A premonition? Was one of his work colleagues to choke on a sausage? He allowed himself a chuckle at the thought of Dr. Bogovic, head translator of Serbo-Croatian, clutching his wizened throat. Nonsense. Of course he wouldn't cancel his first barbecue luncheon.

It had been Zouzou's idea, the barbecue. A chance for her to meet his colleagues at the State Translation Office, she'd suggested. Perhaps later in the year, when the weather cooled, Pierre had proposed. He was, he had long acknowledged, 'a man turned in on himself'. Barbecues suggested a degree of opening up, the risk of revealing secrets. But no, a New Year's Day barbecue it would be.

And now his wife had a premonition.

The morning sounds of Rialto Close brought him back to the present: Birdsong, if you could call tortured yowling 'birdsong'. The first time Pierre heard a local raven, he thought a cat was being tortured. Neighbours greeting each other with "G'day" and "how yer goin";

how he'd struggled to understand the ragged speech these people forced through the sides of their mouths; and there was always the faint thumping of the waves in the background.

Tyres squealed outside the house, followed by a metallic crash. Pierre's stomach lurched. Shouts rang out. "Oh, my God", "Is he dead?" He rushed outside. The paper delivery van straddled the pavement, while an unshaven man in shorts and sunglasses lay next to the driver's door. A shower of rolled newspapers covered most of his body, but one of his feet, still wearing a *shibshib*, poked from the pile. The paper-lobber babbled, "Oh Jesus, Oh Jesus, Oh Jesus". Pierre yelled to Zouzou through the front door, "Call an ambulance!"

A knot of bystanders in thongs and singlets tutted and wrung their hands. Pierre knelt by the injured man. The victim's forehead was grazed and he was half-conscious. His eyes were hidden by the dark glasses, which had somehow stayed on. Pierre pushed the rolled-up newspapers aside. No sign of injuries to the legs, and the man was weakly moving his arms. Pierre had done his first aid training during national service with the Egyptian army. There was hope for this fellow. He eased a *Sun Herald* under the man's lolling head. The bystanders mopped their necks, passed around cigarettes, and fretted until the police and ambulance arrived. Sirens blared from the direction of Sydney Road.

The sweating paramedics went to work. A tow truck crammed itself backwards into the cul-de-sac, but there was nothing going in the way of crash repair business; if the paper-lobber's old bomb had suffered any damage, you'd be hard pressed to find it among the dents and scrapes.

The sun had risen almost directly overhead. Rialto Close burned like the Valley of the Kings. Pierre went back into the house.

There was a knock on the door. Two police officers, no doubt wanting a witness statement.

During his three years in Australia, Pierre had avoided contact with the cops. Working as a court interpreter, he'd learned that police officers were either very good or very bad; the trouble was that you often couldn't tell which. If he was assigned a case at the Manly courthouse, five minutes' walk from Rialto Close, he'd try to flip it to a colleague. A man with a complicated past didn't need to be on nodding terms with his local police. He preferred to ply his trade at the courts in the city centre or the distant suburbs.

These fellows were perhaps one of each type. The possibly good one was about thirty, with blond hair to his collar and eyes as vacant as the surf. The possibly bad one was fifty and fat with an intimidating ginger moustache.

"Full name and date of birth, Sir," Ginger said in a voice you'd use for scrubbing the toilet.

"Kevin O'Donnell, 30 April 1938," Pierre said. Blondie started to write in his notebook, but Ginger stayed his colleague's hand.

"You havin' a lend of me?"

Pierre shrugged. The idiom wasn't familiar to him, but he preferred not to query it. No point in showing weakness. "You takin' the piss?" said Ginger. Pierre took a mental note; *a lend of you*—another new expression to file away; he was fluent in Armenian, English, French, and Arabic, and could make a fair impression in half a dozen other languages. But the victory over Australian English was yet to be won.

"Would you like to see my ID?" Pierre took his Australian passport from a drawer.

Ginger looked at the passport and back at Pierre. He passed the passport to Blondie.

"How come you've got an Irish name, then? You being . . . " Ginger hesitated.

"You being a New Australian, but," Blondie chipped in, not in a complimentary way.

"That's one way of putting it," Ginger said. "Yer not Irish, that's for sure."

"It's a long story," Pierre said.

"I bet it is." Blondie poked Pierre's chest with the passport and dropped it on the floor. "Oh dear, Sir. I seem to have dropped it."

So much for Pierre's judgment about good cops and bad cops. He stooped before Blondie's police boots to pick up his property.

"Will we ask him about the accident?" Blondie asked, pen poised.

"Huh?" Ginger asked. He'd taken a crumpled racing guide out of his pocket and was studying the small print.

"Will we take a statement from the gentleman?"

Ginger looked up from the geegees. "I don't see any gentleman." They sniggered and walked out.

Pierre went back into the street. The accident victim, a man of about forty, was sitting on the back deck of the ambulance. A paramedic was fixing a dressing to his scalp.

"Are you alright, my friend?" Pierre asked. The man's sunglasses had come off. He jammed them back on. Pierre shivered; something felt wrong, out of kilter. Pah! Zouzou's talk of premonitions! Pull yourself together!

"He'll be right, Sir," the paramedic said. "Concussion probably. Looks like the car clipped him and he bashed his head on the wall. We'll get him up to the hospital to get checked out."

The man was helped onto the bed in the back of the ambulance, but just as the doors were about to close, he called out, "Wait". The paramedics paused. The man pushed himself onto his elbows.

"Pierre," he said. The doors closed and the ambulance pulled away. Pierre glanced around. Had he heard correctly?

Zouzou had been watching the scene from the front gate, but seemed not to have caught the man's words. He was struck by her languid pose. She had, perhaps, been born languid.

"Have you cancelled it?" she asked.

"The guests are due in an hour. It's too late to cancel."

"So be it," Zouzou said. "I'm going to buy cigarettes." They went outside. She started down the hill towards the Manly ferry wharf, her hips swaying in her cotton dress, her thick black hair coiled high. His flicker of arousal faded when he looked down at the pavement at a fading trail of little brown smudges. Somebody's shoe—perhaps one of the onlookers'—had picked up a clot of bloody gauze, leaving the marks until the dirty scrap had fallen off. His stomach turned; too many memories of bloodied bodies. The words of the Lord's Prayer came to his lips from nowhere, in Armenian— his mother's language.

"*Hayr Mer, vor hergines yes,
soorp yeghitsi anoon ko,*"

He stopped. *Hallowed be thy name?* Pierre's faith was as faint as the blood smudges. He fetched a bucket of water from the yard and sloshed the mess away.

Had the man really called his name? Of course not. Pierre was known as Kevin, Kev , Kevo. Only Zouzou called him Pierre, and only out of the range of curious ears. "Beer". That was what the fellow had called out. A drunk, no doubt, still sozzled after New Year's Eve. These Australians drank as if there were to be a world shortage of beer within the hour. He'd taken a stroll along the Manly Corso last night and seen men openly urinating against the pub wall. "Beer." That's what the man had said for some confused reason only known to himself. Or had he?

* * *

Zouzou came home from the milk bar and announced she would take a brief nap in the spare bedroom before the guests arrived. She arranged a wet towel on a clothes horse with a fan behind it to cool the clogged air.

In the yard, Pierre poured a bag of ice into a brand-new Esky. He tore open a packet of charcoal, and arranged a pyramid of waxy firelighters in the rusty iron box under the hotplate, carefully following the instructions to pile the fuel on top. Yes, this was how it was done. Quite easy.

But it was an odd business, this Australian barbecue. "Tell them to bring their own meat and grog. Just make the salad," his colleague Hermann had said. Could this be true? It would be unforgivably rude in Egypt, laughable in fact. Why eat your own food in someone else's home? "Keep a few snags and some booze on hand in case you're a tad short," Hermann had added. So, the emergency sausages were in the fridge, along with a four-litre cardboard box of moselle.

Zouzou appeared after ten minutes, apparently refreshed; she could sleep at will. "How long does the barbecue take to get hot?"

Pierre had no idea. As a teenager, his family had spent their summers at Agami, near Alexandria. Zouzou's family rented the beach cabin next door, and their parents lit a brazier on the beach each night to grill brochettes. He remembered his father fanning the charcoal, the smell of grilled lamb, the adults laughing over bottles of Stella beer. But cooking *en plein air* was a skill he'd never acquired.

The contraption made a sullen puff of kerosene smoke when he lit the firelighter, then went out. Where was the Sunday paper? He tore off some pages, twisted them and poked them into the coals. *Nude bathers invade beaches*, he read just before the paper curled and blackened.

"They are here, Pierre, the guests."

He wiped his sooty hands on his shirt and eyed the barbecue nervously.

* * *

By two in the afternoon, the conversation had done twenty laps of office gossip, and was galloping into the rocky ground of politics.

A few months after his arrival in Australia in 1975, Pierre had watched the country tear itself apart over the dismissal of Prime Minister Whitlam. A *coup d'état*, some had called it. Ha!—he yearned to say to them. Come to my part of the world, and you'll see what a *coup* looks like! Come to Libya where I saw Ghadafi's maniac dunghill of degradation and oppression! No, these lunchbreak radicals wouldn't know a *coup* if it poked them in the eye with a prawn cutlet, as one might say.

But predictably, with the afternoon heat and the moselle—he'd had to break out the emergency supplies—the political temperature in the front yard was hot enough to roast a chop. The guests were divided on the Whitlam question; the Portuguese translator had to restrain the Turkish health care interpreter from slapping the Greek office manager. Politics, always politics. And that was when they were having a break from sport!

The mood hadn't been improved by the debacle of the barbecue contraption. The dozen guests had arranged their assorted koftas, steaks, cutlets and sausages on the griddle, but the feeble glow barely heated the items through. "A veritable multicultural feast," the Hindi translator, an ardent vegetarian, said without conviction. The crowd wolfed the salad down in seconds. Two Iraqi gentlemen, PhDs with impeccable manners and faultless English, had brought identical lamb kebabs but misidentified their property in their efforts to keep their *halal* meat away from somebody's pork chop; not knowing which kebab belonged to whom, each urged the other to serve himself first until they stood staring at the griddle in a deadlock of courtesy.

Now a litter of soiled paper plates bearing gnawed butchery items was witness to Pierre's foiled ambition to emulate the Aussies he lived among. The cardboard box would yield no more moselle. Conversation flagged and faded. The perspiring guests peeped at their watches. The head translator of Italian broke ranks and excused herself; the others shortly followed.

Zouzou stood by the front gate offering a farewell handshake and a "So pleased you could come" to each guest. When the last had gone, she lit a cigarette, surveyed the rubbish in the yard and said, "You should have cancelled it". She went indoors.

Pierre considered her words. They were unreasonable, of course. The barbecue was her idea; he could hardly have cancelled at an hour's notice. Some of the guests had taken two hours to reach Manly: A suburban bus to a train station in some far-flung inland suburb, an hour sweating on the plastic seats of a red rattler, a change at Central for the Circle Line to Circular Quay, and finally the ferry.

Her peevishness was of course connected with the matter of pregnancy. They'd both had unpleasant medical tests, both passed muster. "Just give it time," the doctor had said. "Relax, don't make a big issue of it." Easier said than done when lovemaking became a clinical obligation, repaid each month with no joy.

He took a broom and started to sweep. Someone had stepped in a dollop of tomato ketchup and walked a little trail of brown smudges on the concrete. As he tried to scrape it off with the edge of the broom, Pierre's mind returned to the blood on the pavement. He couldn't shake the sense of something being awry.

A picture flashed in front of his mind. The foot in the *shibshib*; it was missing a toe. A rush of clarity: The echo of familiarity in the voice, the trace of recognition of the face behind the sunglasses.

The accident victim was Mark Bellamy, he was sure. The last Pierre knew of his friend was that he had been abducted from Cairo to Moscow in 1973 suffering a gunshot wound to his foot.

* * *

It took Pierre just a couple of days to track down Mark Bellamy.

He'd met the man in Cairo during the Yom Kippur War in 1973. *Pierre Farag (Bachelor of Arts) Translator and Private Investigator*, it used to say on his office door in Arabic, English and French.

He'd crossed paths with Bellamy one night when the Englishman was being attacked by a bunch of street thugs. Bellamy, it turned out, was on a clandestine intelligence mission that had gone disastrously wrong. Within a week, all their lives had been turned inside-out. Betrayed on all sides, Bellamy was abducted to the USSR with his girlfriend Lucy, and Pierre fled Egypt with Zouzou on the last ship to leave Egypt before the war broke out in earnest.

Here in Sydney, his old skills as a private investigator in Cairo were more than adequate to the task. This wasn't a city of watchers, not a city where you were always glimpsing over your shoulder. This wasn't a city where a lie would better suffice than the truth. The faces of the people were as open as the sunshine that bathed their lives.

The lady at the local hospital had yielded the name and address of the gentleman who'd been brought into emergency, no questions asked. And why ask suspicious questions of such an ordinary man as Pierre? With his short dark hair, slim build, olive skin, and conservative suit he plied the reception counters and interview rooms of Sydney's courthouses and legal chambers almost unnoticed. If anyone were to remark on him, they might say, "Isn't he that translator fellow?", or "French isn't he, or am I thinking of someone else?"

The name Bellamy went by was unknown to Pierre, but this was no surprise. Over recent years, living under false names had become a way of life. Mark Bellamy would be no exception.

He took a sickie (how easily that piece of argot slipped off the tongue) on a day when Zouzou had a day job. Her work as an Arabic party singer generally took her in the evenings to the areas where she was in demand: The Egyptians in the immigrant suburbs around the airport, the Lebanese further west. Weddings were her speciality—Muslim, Maronite, Orthodox, Iraqi, Palestinian—she'd tailor her repertoire to the nuances of faith and allegiance. But today she was performing at a birthday lunch for a family of Moroccan Jews somewhere in the wealthy bayside suburbs near Bondi.

"I'll take an aspirin and stay in bed, *habibti*," Pierre lied. He needed to see Bellamy quickly, but he didn't want to expose Zouzou to anxiety until he knew why the man was outside his house and not in Moscow. Pierre could have gone to work and tried to make a detour to Mark's address, but his job rarely took him to the wealthier parts of the city; a sickie was the solution, although it pained him to tell her an untruth.

"See you this afternoon, my heart," Zouzou said. She'd been practising songs since dawn, filling the flat with languid melodies. The finale today would be *Miserlou*, which she'd sing in Greek and Arabic. They all loved *Miserlou*, with its melancholy oriental progression—Greek, Assyrian, Lebanese; it left all of them in a state of wistful longing for their homelands.

Pierre gave a sniff and a cough to farewell his lovely wife. He heard her kick-start the Vespa and waited twenty minutes.

The address he'd been given at the hospital had an 'A' after the street number. He wedged the UBD street directory in the panier of his Honda scooter, headed up Sydney Road to the top of the hill, then swooped down to the Spit Bridge trailing smoke. The traffic stopped as the bridge span was cranked open to let a yacht pass from one side of the basin to the other. Colonnaded houses clung to the hillsides that flanked this gleaming finger of Sydney Harbour.

Pierre turned off the Honda's motor and gazed at the hillside mansions and the marina of gleaming sailboats below. He manufactured a vision of himself and Zouzou looking down from one of those verandas, a gaggle of children playing at their feet. Ha! Not in this life, or the next for that matter.

The house he sought was in a North Shore avenue of great trees forming a green tunnel between grand bungalows with ornate wooden balconies and delicate brickwork. The pavements under the shade trees were deserted, but for an old man in shorts and khaki hat poking something in the gutter.

A distant memory sparked in Pierre's mind: Yes, burning eucalyptus; gum trees were everywhere in Egypt. He looked more closely to see that the man was tending a little bonfire of leaves and twigs. Pierre slowed to find the house number, and the man with the fire stared at him.

Here it was, a corner block, but occupied by an ugly duckling: A cement cube with metal-framed windows, and a garage door inset in the front wall. No gracious Japanese maples in the garden, no plantings of Bird of Paradise shrubs: Just a car tyre cut in half to cover the water meter protruding from a parched lawn.

24, it said on the front door, 24A on the garage door. Pierre tapped on the corrugated metal. Nobody answered. He knocked again, with no result, walked back to the Honda and sat astride it, foot on the kickstart.

"Wait. I heard you," said a faint voice—a British voice. Pierre waited.

"Won't be a sec." Yes, even muffled by the metal door, this was the voice of his friend Mark Bellamy.

* * *

Zouzou's sense of premonition had been correct, even if she had no idea how events would play out. Her dear Pierre was as foolishly naive as ever. Sick day? He looked healthy as a goose!

She'd met Mark Bellamy just once, in a villa near the Pyramids that Pierre had rented as a hideout; the man had walked in covered in blood, having just dumped a Mercedes and a corpse in the Nile. Despite the unshaven face and sunglasses, she'd recognised him— part of her premonition perhaps—when the paramedics helped him to his feet, but said nothing; consider before you act, that had been one of her survival strategies in life.

After she left for her singing engagement, she rode the Vespa around the block searching for a vantage point from which to watch Pierre leave the flat. There— a panel van with surfboards on the roof rack, a shirtless boy with long blonde hair waxing a board, oblivious to her. A coat hanger aerial bent into the shape of Australia stuck out of the front wing of the van.

And here was Pierre, bolt upright in his crash helmet, wobbling out of Rialto Close.

Forty minutes later she parked her scooter behind a tree from where she could see the house on the corner of the leafy street. Pierre was standing in front of the garage door. It swung up and Bellamy appeared. The two men shook hands. Bellamy stumbled. Pierre took his arm and led him into the garage. The door clanged shut. Zouzou looked up and down the avenue. Nobody to be seen except a man in shorts tending a little fire.

Questions assailed her: What was Bellamy doing in Sydney? Did he own the house with the garage? Where was his wife? Lucy, yes, that was her name. She wouldn't find answers standing under a tree.

Zouzou kick-started the Vespa and headed for the Pacific Highway, the main artery through the wealthy North Shore. There was still time to get over the Harbour Bridge and into the Eastern Suburbs to get to her lunchtime job.

She had more than Bellamy on her mind, but the man's appearance out of nowhere added urgency to a decision she must make.

She intended to leave Pierre and return to Egypt.

The idea of leaving him had been astonishing when it first occurred to her a few months ago. She remembered the moment precisely. She was singing at a wedding hall in Lakemba. The first set had ended when something—perhaps the aroma of a platter of Lebanese food—catapulted her back to Cairo. A father at one of the tables was dandling two infant boys on his lap; the man could have passed as Pierre. And so the two ideas became unbearably intertwined: Her compulsion to see Egypt and their inability to have a child. She was thirty-seven now. Perhaps it was too late. Although the doctor had cleared both of them as capable to produce a fertilised embryo, she suspected she was damaged; there had been a miscarriage in Malta after she'd been imprisoned on a ship and punched in the abdomen by her captor.

And Bellamy's appearance had opened a door she had prayed would be shut for ever. Exile in Australia was supposed to have severed the connection with the British intelligence agency that had played them like marionettes for years. But it hadn't worked that way.

To leave Pierre! Yes, it was monstrous, unthinkable, a bitter worm that burrowed through her thoughts. But it would be an act of love—to release him so he could find the woman who would give him complete happiness.

Her past life as a film actress nudged into her reverie. She'd starred in so many films, always the bad girl: The 'national bitch', the fans nicknamed her. But there had been one movie where she portrayed a virtuous maiden: *The Sweet Sacrifice*. Zouzou was a poor Christian country girl working as a servant in Cairo. A rich city boy fell in love with her, and she ran away to a convent in the desert to save his family's shame. The Cairo filmgoers shed tears by the litre. What was that English expression? *Art imitating reality?* Tears misted her eyes behind the motorcycle goggles.

A car hooted her back to the traffic. Concentrate! You don't want to end up in a grave at the far edge of the world.

Chapter 2: An Act of Love

Life's bloody good, Kerry Rich said to himself. The throb of the outboard, a cold can of Tooheys, the bow of the Mustang 2400 Sports slicing through the wake of the Manly ferry as it lumbered across the Sydney Heads. And stretched out in a bikini on the white leather bench in the stern—the lovely, no, the bloody gorgeous Liz Lanzoni. Yeah, life's fan-bloody-tastic.

So here was the plan. Moor off one of the little beaches near Mosman—maybe Obelisk—find a private spot, stretch out a blanket, open a bottle of bubbly and see if Liz is up for getting her gear off. See if he still had the famous youthful charm now he'd just turned forty.

They'd been out a couple of times—just bars around Circular Quay—and she'd put up token resistance.

"Your place or mine?" he'd said the second night they met, moving in for a kiss. He'd mentioned he had a penthouse with a Harbour Bridge view.

"My place, on my own," she laughed and skipped away to the taxi stand. The bloody little minx!

"Will we do it again?"

"How about New Year's Day?" she asked from the backseat of the taxi.

"Sure. Where'd you say you live?"

"Manly."

"I'll pick you up at Little Manly Beach at midday. Watch out for my boat."

* * *

It wasn't that Kerry was short of females. He could make a couple of calls, and in short order he'd have three girls in the boat, all gagging for it. A bloke like Kerry Rich got what he wanted when he wanted it. Usually. But right now he wanted Liz Lanzoni, and the lady wasn't making it easy.

She was there on time at Little Manly—waded straight out and slid over the side of the boat in a beach wrap that barely wrapped anything at all.

"I was about to come over and get you," he said.

Liz Lanzoni smiled behind the shades and let the wrap fall away.

"Make yourself at home." He pointed to the white leather bench seat in the stern.

They pulled out of the tiny cove and around the point. As they approached Mosman, he slowed the motor and steered in close to the shore. The ferry to Taronga Park Zoo chugged past them, packed with families. The wake rocked the Mustang and he slowed to avoid bumping against the rocks. He glanced back at Liz, pulled his stomach in. She'd tipped a straw hat over her face. He feasted his eyes on her tanned body.

"We've got it to ourselves, Liz." Bloody perfect. There might be a couple of poofs in the buff behind a rock, but a few choice words would send them packing.

Liz raised a hand in response without removing the hat. He nudged the prow into a patch of soft sand, grabbed the painter and jumped into the knee-deep water. His tiny shorts were wet. He knotted the rope through a metal ring set into a rock. Liz was sitting up now. He peeled the shorts off and tossed them into the boat.

"What did you say you did for a living, Kerry?" she asked.

"This and that. Real estate, import and export, resort in Queensland. You know, that kinda thing."

She took off her bikini top and slid out of the boat.

Yeah, Kerry thought, life's fan-bloody-tastic.

* * *

But Kerry Rich had a problem, he reflected later that evening, as he took a leak over Sydney. Well, that was how it seemed in the urinal of his penthouse, where you stood in front of a wall-to-ceiling smoked window overlooking the city. He got a huge kick out of directing male guests for a pee, even if they didn't want one. It had become something of a ritual for a selected few of his acquaintances—after a bevy or three—to line up against the wall and choose an imaginary target—usually a Labor minister or a union leader, or for variety a rich wog. That was the beauty of it: The enemies of the state could be having an innocent stroll along the harbour, completely oblivious to the fact that someone was—in a manner of speaking—pissing on them from thirty floors above. Of course you wouldn't ask any of The Impeccables to join in; not the Archbishop or the Major General, but they wouldn't deign to visit Kerry Rich in his penthouse anyway.

Kerry's problem was Liz Lanzoni. Things hadn't quite worked out on the beach. The minute they'd stretched out on the blanket, she had some kind of weird fit: Body all stiff and trembling, drool coming out of her lips, a weird groaning noise. It had completely put him off his stroke, even with those lovely tits on show. When she came around, he definitely wasn't up for it anymore; Christ, she might do it all over again. The last thing he needed was to pull in at a public wharf with a half-naked woman in a coma. At any rate, when he helped her off the boat at Little Manly, she was groggy but in her right mind.

"So sorry, Kerry. Maybe some other time. Hey, I could come up to the penthouse," she'd said weakly.

"That'd be great, Liz. Call me when you're better."

A problem, or at least a potential problem, that was Liz. Vigilance was The Impeccables' watchword, vigilance for infiltrators and spies. If they were to achieve their goal of installing a government of true Australian patriots, there was no room for loose talk or stolen secrets. Especially when strange women were involved. The honey trap, the Major-General called it.

When he thought it through, the signs had been there; he just hadn't seen them: She'd dropped her handbag when she was in front of him at a taxi stand at Circular Quay. When he picked it up, they found they were going the same way. Why not share the cab?

But who'd initiated the cab ride—her or him? He couldn't remember, but they found themselves in a taxi going to Double Bay with her thigh close enough to his to stir up some excitement down south. Then, she played hard to get, then this spazzo performance on the beach. And now she suddenly wants to visit the penthouse! Kerry might play the part of the rough and ready self-made millionaire, but he wasn't a bloody dill.

He knew he should report it to Sir Robert. But he didn't want to look rattled. The rest of The Impeccables looked on him as an outsider—not old money, not private school, not sandstone university. Oh no, Kerry had powered his way up the greasy pole through used car yards, labour hire, cash businesses, gyms, debt collecting, imaginative real estate deals. He knew more about patriotism than any of the high-ups, who'd never set foot in a scrapyard or a betting office. He knew first-hand how the culture of the true-blue working man was being corrupted by communists and wogs. Bugger Sir Robert. He'd fix Liz Lanzoni himself.

The phone rang twice and stopped: The signal to stand by. It rang again and Kerry snatched it from its cradle.

"Thursday, nineteen hundred. HQ." The voice was muffled.

"Copy." They had a mission for him. It was on. Worry about Liz later.

* * *

"I stopped at the corner store and bought honey and lemons, Pierre. I'll make you a hot drink."

"Thank you, *habibti*. I think I fought off the worst of it by staying in bed. But a hot drink will chase away the last of the sniffs."

Zouzou unpacked the bag that contained the blonde wig, cocktail dress and shoes she'd worn to sing for the Jews. It irked her that he lied about where he'd been, but she felt wretched that she'd followed him. What games they played for love.

"I brought *baklava*." There had been a groaning table of sticky Middle Eastern pastries at the party. Zouzou put the syrupy sweets on a plate and made Pierre his soothing drink. He blew his nose theatrically. She hesitated, and then decided to say her piece.

"Pierre. That man in the street yesterday. I thought I recognised him." She watched him stiffen, the forkful of pastry hovering between plate and lips. She prayed he would look up at her. Her husband put the fork down and splayed his fingers on the table as if he were about the play a piano. She held her gaze until he lifted his eyes to hers.

"It was Mark Bellamy," he said.

"Have you seen him since?"

"Yes, as it happens." Pierre made a flicking movement with his fingertips as if the details were mere crumbs. Yes, there were times when a lie would suffice for the truth, they both recognised. In London they had each secretly followed the other on occasions, and knew that trust was a delicate flower, easily crushed. Zouzou rested her knee against his under the table.

"Tell me."

"I found him living in a garage attached to a private house, in squalor. He sleeps on a camp bed and washes in an outhouse like a *bawwab*." The *bawwabeen*, the old doormen of Cairo, had been part of Pierre's network of spies and stooges.

"How long has he been here, Pierre, and why?"

"It took me a long time to get the story from him. The poor man is quite broken. He's obviously an alcoholic, and his speech meanders from one topic to another."

"*Miskiin!*"

"Yes, a poor thing indeed, Zouzou, but let me go on. He was completely frank, perhaps recklessly so. He told me what happened that day when he and Lucy were bundled off to Moscow by the *shaitan* Donald Waters."

"He was Satan indeed. It was the day before we fled Cairo." Her fingers subconsciously traced her jaw, finding the scar from the explosion that had blown Donald Waters' head off his shoulders.

"It was no coincidence that he was outside our house, Zouzou."

"I never believed in coincidences, *habibi*. Go on."

"He told me that he and Lucy—you'll remember, the blonde woman—were given jobs in a publishing house in Moscow. They weren't exactly prisoners, as I understand it, more bargaining chips. At any rate, Lucy accommodated herself to the situation. She learned Russian. They had a child, a little girl."

"Are they here with him?"

"No, Zouzou. It's a sad and curious story. Mark Bellamy took to drink. He suffered a variety of depression. And then last year an opportunity came up for one of them to return to England."

"What kind of opportunity?"

"A swap. An exchange of spies. But only one of them could go. I gather they each have a price, these spies, and letting both of them go was not an acceptable bargain."

Bargains.

Zouzou had endured a life of bargains: Her years as an actress in Egypt under the protection of old men with the highest connections and the lowest morals; the false papers they bore in Australia, payment for their involvement in a scheme that could have ended Pierre's life in a Libyan jail. And here was Mark Bellamy with a bargain.

"So Mark left Moscow alone? He abandoned the mother and child?"

"It was a heart-wrenching tale, Zouzou. It seems that Lucy begged him to stay. You see, she is happy there. She has friends. There is nothing for her in England except . . . "

"Except Ealing." The bland code name for the British intelligence agency they thought they'd escaped.

"Except Ealing indeed, Zouzou. But we have not left Ealing behind. They are here. We cannot escape those

23

British devils. In fact, Mark Bellamy believes that they send their damaged goods—people like us—here to Australia. There are more of us here, he believes."

"Why don't they just shoot us like broken-down donkeys? It would be kinder."

"Did you ever observe kindness among them?" Pierre asked. "We are sad pawns in their game of *shakhmat*."

Zouzou topped up Pierre's drink. Their destiny had taken a lurch in a distressing direction. Her own life faced a fork in its path: Should she confess her intentions to Pierre? Should she remain with him to face the trials that would no doubt enmesh them soon? But she needed to know more about Mark Bellamy and the awful decision he had made.

"Did they enjoy *Miserlou*, the Jews?" Pierre asked.

This was Pierre's way—to change the subject. She shrugged his question away. "Pierre, tell me. How could Mark Bellamy have left his family. What did he say?"

"He said it was an act of love, I recall. He'd drunk a mugful of his shocking wine—I accepted a few sips— so his state of mind was no doubt muddled. Yes, now I remember: He said that Lucy and the child would be better off without a broken-down drunkard, and that she should find her happiness with somebody new, one of her Russian friends."

"A peculiar variety of love, my heart," Zouzou said.

"To leave one's child . . . " His words trailed off and he looked down. They rarely spoke of the children they'd failed to have. The silence between them strengthened her resolve to release him so that he could fill the empty space in his spirit.

But all this could wait for now. She needed to know what Ealing wanted.

Pierre straightened up in his chair and lit a cigarette. "Zouzou, they have a task for us."

"A task? For you and me? And if we refuse?"

"What can we do? Where can we run?"

* * *

Thursday night found Kerry Rich in the study of one of the grand Federation mansions lining the road leading down to the zoo on the Harbour's edge. It had to be something big to get an invite to Sir Robert's place. He'd only been there once before, the evening he'd been inducted into The Impeccables. It had all been a bit juvenile, he thought at the time: Making the salute and repeating the Pledge. But the other fellows there took it quite seriously, so who was Kerry Rich to question them in their dinner jackets and medal ribbons?

Sir Robert shook his hand warmly and gestured towards a stiff-looking sofa with scrolly arms.

"Whisky and soda, I seem to remember, Kerry?"

"Spot on, Sir Robert."

"No need for ceremony. Bob'll be fine. . . " Sir Robert had the easy manner of old money. He was a fit bugger for his age—sixtyish, Kerry guessed—with thick silver hair, and everything in the kind of taste you didn't learn in the suburbs: The cufflinks, the paintings, the posh wife. He spoke in that rich educated Australian accent that would go down just as well in a shearing shed as on the bench of the High Court. Nope, you didn't learn that kind of poise at Westbridge Technical High.

No sooner had Sir Bob handed Kerry his drink than the door opened and a tough-looking bloke walked in. This one had the build of a weightlifter, a headful of curls that looked like a perm, and a bent nose. Men with perms—bloody stupid fashion. Kerry was a mullet man.

"Clem," he said, thrusting a hand in Kerry's direction.

"Well, I'll leave you two to get acquainted," Sir Robert said, and left.

Kerry and Clem stared at one another. Kerry sipped his whisky. Clem, he noticed, was holding a glass of milk in the other fist.

So that was the game; Sir Robert wanted something done under the table, and he didn't want to hear the details. Kerry had known all along that he hadn't been invited into The Impeccables for his drawing room manners.

"You're a man with connections, I'm told, Mr Rich."

"Depends on what you're after," Kerry said warily. Better watch your step with this one.

"We're after a bloke who can hold his nerve and keep his mouth shut. And get hold of certain materials."

"Materials?" Kerry's antennae poked up. This was crunch time.

"Y'see, Kerry—can I call you Kerry?—the Supreme Council is of a mind to create a bit of a diversion, a bit of a spectacle, if you get my meaning."

"Sorry, I don't grasp your meaning. Can you get to the point?"

"We want to blow something up."

"Fuck me." Kerry spluttered a mouthful of whisky. He'd never signed up for bombs. He wasn't a friggin' Arab. Clem stared at him. It was obvious that he was trying to get Kerry's measure. This was the moment of truth: Tell The Impeccables where to stuff it, or bite the bloody bullet. Go back to making money and screwing girls, or do something for Australia worth bloody doing. Honour the memory of his Dad, the poor bastard.

He chose the bullet.

"What do I have to do?"

"That's the spirit, Kerry. I knew you wouldn't let us down. I'll be sure to tell Sir Robert we made the right decision to bring you in."

So who was this Clem, who'd just popped up out of the blue and was all knowledgeable about him? There was so little he understood about The Impeccables, but then technically he couldn't complain. What was that line in the Pledge? *To obey without question the directives of the Supreme Council however oblique . . .* He'd had to look up *oblique* in the dictionary, but the general idea was crystal bloody clear.

Clem took a sip of his milk. "So Kerry, you're gonna get some explosives and make a little bomb—nothing too big. Just for the shock value."

"Yeah, I got that, but what are we blowing up?"

"Try the Bennelong Restaurant at the Opera House. Anzac Day."

Kerry's mouth went as dry as a shoe. Something throbbed in his temple. His eye fluttered from a childhood tic, shocked into action for the first time in years.

He heard some words that sounded like "I'm gonna blow up the Bennelong" behind the roaring in his ears. Kerry dragged himself back to the here and now.

"Well, you'll blow it up in a manner of speaking. The job's actually gonna be done by a New Australian."

"How's that?" Kerry asked.

"A New Australian's gonna make the bomb and let it off."

"So a wog gets the blame?"

"Got it in one, Kerry. But if you don't mind, we don't use the w-word. We wouldn't want to be accused of being racist or anything of that kind."

"Of course not, Clem."

Bloody oath, it was a thing of beauty: Blow up the Opera House and pin it on a wog.

"And how do I find a New Australian to help me?"

"All sorted, Kerry. We've got just the bloke."

Chapter 3: Kiss Me Quick

They were sitting on the sea wall at Manly Beach watching the weekend crowds eating ice creams and fried fish. This was Zouzou's favourite spot, a place where they found anonymity among the multicultural crowd.

The suburban visitors poured off the ferries all day, some lingering at the decrepit funfair on the wharf, some crossing the road to the Corso from where they wandered the hundred yards past the milk bars and T-shirt shops to the surf beach. The sign above the funfair said *Seven miles from Sydney, a hundred miles from care.*

"So Mark Bellamy didn't exactly say what we were to do, Pierre?"

Zouzou had asked Pierre the same question a dozen times in the last few days. He had shrugged the same reply: "He said someone would approach me with the password."

"Ouf. Passwords. Whatever next? Secret handshakes? A note with invisible writing? And why do they not approach you directly rather than sending an errand boy?" She spoke in English, as they tended to in public; no point in attracting unnecessary attention.

"*Errand boy* is a rather unjust epithet, my heart. Mark Bellamy is a true friend and a man of courage."

Zouzou couldn't quite see where the courage came in. The man was a drunkard who'd left his wife and child in another country. That seemed quite different from her own dilemma. Just look at the nubile girls on the beach! Pierre could have his pick. He'd forget her when the babies started coming. And as for being a retired film actress, Zouzou was still young enough to get parts back in Cairo. It was talent not age that won the day. Just look at Mona Mahboob, fifty if she was a day, and still playing roles half her age.

A gull swooped down and snatched a sausage roll from the hands of a man sitting next to them.

"Friggin' mongrel!" He took a swig from a bottle in a brown paper bag and nudged Zouzou with his elbow. "Ah, bugger it, eh love?" She winced under her sunglasses. Ouf, bugger this, bugger that, bugger everything. What went on in the sewers these men had for minds?

But she had to confess to a fondness for the place they'd called home the last few years. Manly was free and easy. A woman could pop out to the shops in *shibshib* and a ragged shift, just like a servant girl in Cairo, and nobody would raise an eyebrow. *Ma shaa Allah*, once she had gone to the milk bar for rolls on a Sunday morning and waited in line behind a woman wearing nothing but a transparent black negligée, and showing evidence of having been recently pleasured. And what about the homosexualists? They were to march in the street this year to press for their rights. Imagine, a *khawal* with rights! The poor creatures would be flogged if they dared such a thing in Egypt. The thought of leaving free and easy Manly left a pang in her breast.

"The reason for Mark's appearance, Zouzou, is obvious. It is to confirm that we are who they think we are. Mark can give a positive characterisation . . . "

"A *positive ID* is the proper term, Pierre. I remember it from when I played a New York detective in *Murder International*. I was seconded to Cairo to extradite a suspect and I fell in love with the judge. . . "

"The exact term slipped my mind for a second, but you do see my point. Nobody in this country knows me from a row of beans, as the local expression goes."

Zouzou pressed her shoulder close to his. Her heart surged with exquisite love for him. She'd miss him as she'd miss her own blood.

Perhaps they'd given up hope of a child too soon. She slipped a hand around his neck and pulled him close, kissing him in full sight of the beachgoers, free and easy.

"Let's go home, Pierre. It's surely siesta time." He kissed her back, the man 'turned in on himself', who she had opened up to the pleasures of life.

"Oh, what is Mark Bellamy's password, by the way?"

"*Kiss me quick*," Pierre said.

"I just kissed you, *habibi*."

"No, that is the password. *Kiss me quick*."

"I spit on his password."

* * *

Later in the afternoon they walked barefoot along the great arc of beach past the blocks of flats, the down-market Corso with its chip shops and day-trippers, and the beachside clinic where children from the bush came for medical treatment.

Pierre knew about this 'bush'. He'd been sent to Broken Hill once to interpret for a Syrian charged with swearing in public. The thousand-kilometre train journey was a torture of lumpy seats, lukewarm meat pies, and featureless scenery. The list of stations to come was announced at each stop in a funereal dirge: Condobolin, Eubalong West, Ivanhoe, Darnick, Menindee . . . There were families on the train—obviously hard up—their small children in dressing gowns and snoozing on pillows they'd brought with them. He listened to the slingshot speech of the adults, barely understanding a word. He thought they might be Aboriginal people but did not know how to ask politely. His other fellow travellers seemed to be mostly mental defectives.

When he arrived at Broken Hill, a detective met him at the station. The man was wearing tailored shorts and knee-length white socks. Pierre had been surprised to see men wearing this outfit when he first arrived in Australia; he'd last seen it when the British still ran Egypt.

"Sorry Sir, ye've wasted yer time. The gentleman's karked it overnight."

"Oh dear," Pierre said, disguising his puzzlement. Perhaps the police sergeant meant the Syrian had changed his plea.

"Should I have a word with him nevertheless?"

The policeman roared with laughter and slapped Pierre on the back. Pierre caught the cue and forced a guffaw.

"Good on yer, mate. If we didn't laugh we'd have to fuck'n cry." The detective blew his nose and swept an arm from red horizon to red horizon.

"Just look at it. Orange dust and bugger all else, with apologies of course to our indigenous brethren. I'm from the Gold Coast originally. D'yer know it?"

"The name is familiar. But what should I do now?"

The man looked at his watch. "The train back to Sydney's not for another four hours. Why not get yerself a feed at the Royal Exchange? Well, it's been a pleasure to meet a man with a sense of humour."

"The pleasure was mine, Sir," Pierre said, striking up a red-dusted street named after a noxious chemical—Sulphide, Chloride?—until he reached a low-slung building of vaguely colonial design, which served as a boarding house and tavern. Three children in *shibshib*, shorts and singlet—was it national dress?—listlessly kicked a ball on the porch. Like the porch rail, they seemed coated in brown dust. In the bar, he gnawed through a steak a foot and a half long, washed down with a schooner of Reschs, all the time watched by locals in national dress through side-aimed eyes.

Yes, it was surely an act of profound kindness to bring sick children to Manly from this 'bush'. But kind? Were they kind, these Australians? No, fair, perhaps. They never stopped declaiming about their 'fair go' and their 'mateship'. They projected a kind of insecure superiority over the British, and in this Pierre was with the Australians; Pierre and Zouzou had spent a miserable year and a half in seedy London digs only to be tricked into a gun-running mission, and cheated out of passports to the USA. No, he'd take the Australian 'fair go' over perfidious Albion. But his new countrymen puzzled him: He yearned so much to get their measure, to adopt their effortless demeanour, to sling and slap the words of their far-flung English like the Manly folk who ambled along the promenade.

Their walk continued along the cliffside walk to Fairy Bower, where a small crescent of calm beach nestled under a ragged outcrop of boulders and sea-swept trees. Up a steep path and they stood on the brink of a sheer cliff with the endless ocean before them: New Zealand ahead, the Antarctic to the right: The end of the world. And yet Ealing had found them.

He made a solemn bargain with himself that after this next mission, he would find a way for Zouzou and himself to truly disappear. The final bargain.

* * *

Pierre's week passed, a week shunting from one local court to another. The work was tolerable rather than enjoyable, but it suited his nature. His stock in trade was information, facts, words, names, titles, dates, every snippet stored away for future use.

His private investigation practice in Cairo had relied on intimate knowledge of who was who, who owed what to whom, and who was in a jam. And there was his *shabkah*, the network of informers and stooges and apartment janitors he traded favours and secrets with. True, Sydney was nothing like Cairo, but the basic principle was the same: Keep your head down, keep your ears open, and grow your *shabkah*.

He'd got the job at the State Translation Office by a fluke. He and Zouzou had booked into a cheap hotel when they first arrived in Sydney, jobless and in total ignorance about their prospects. When Pierre stepped outside on his first morning, a man had touched him on the shoulder.

"*Ya* Boutros," the man said in Arabic, "What are you doing here?"

"By God, it's you, Girgis. I can't believe it. What's the story?" It was a distant cousin, one of the many Georges who inhabited the dense family tree on his father's side—the Coptic side. Pierre was *Boutros* to his Coptic relatives, *Bedros* to the Armenian kin, and *Pierre* to anyone else—except when he was being Kevin O'Donnell in Australia.

"Didn't you hear? I emigrated. I'm working as an optometrist. Look, have you got time for a coffee?"

Pierre had all the time in the world. He listened to his relative's account of getting his Egyptian qualifications recognised, of buying a fifteen-square house, a block of land, and a 1975 Commodore. A fiancée had arrived from Egypt under a scheme to reunite family members, and soon there was to be yet another Coptic George on the planet.

"So what brought you here, Boutros?"

"Oh, a chance opportunity, contacts, you know," Pierre replied.

"And what about a job? Have you got something? I can't remember what you were doing in Cairo."

And that's how Pierre preferred things—keeping 'under the radar' as they said in Australia.

"Oh, you know, Girgis—I was in the bureaucracy, not really something I could talk about. But right now I'm looking around for a suitable *rukn*."

"Ah, yes, a suitable corner. I tell you what, a friend of mine picked up a job at the State Translation Office last year. That might suit a fellow like you. Just get the form and submit it with your diplomas."

Well, it hadn't been quite that straightforward. He'd last seen his diplomas in a flat in Camden Town; they were probably rotting in a municipal rubbish dump by now. But he concocted a history that included a rationale for his Irish name, and took a government test, which he passed with ease. Soon he was an accredited translator and interpreter doing the rounds of the courts.

Now he was on the train after finishing a dreary day at a local court in the inland suburbs. The first case was an elderly Lebanese man in the dock for exposing himself in a park. He maintained he was relieving himself.

"I was shaking my *zubr* afterwards, that's all," the man said in a dense rural dialect. He worked his fingers around a neck that was suffering the insult of a tie for the first time.

Pierre translated, carefully choosing the word *member* in English from among the many terms for *zubr* at his disposal.

"I put it to you, Sir, that you were engaged in an act of self-gratification in an attempt to attract the attention of an unsuspecting female member of the public," the police prosecutor said.

Ma shaa allah! These legal people could make a sentence run up the garden path and back again. Pierre translated more or less literally for the bumpkin, who responded with a slack jaw and a frown. The prosecutor put the question again, but Pierre turned to the magistrate.

"May I address the bench, Your Honour?"

The magistrate rolled her eyes and nodded.

"The accused is a simple man, possibly illiterate. I beg the court's indulgence to use a vulgar expression in my translation."

"A vulgar expression in Arabic?"

"Yes, Your Honour. It is approximately equivalent in English to the term . . . "

"Yes, I think we understand. Please get on with it," Her Honour said.

And so the day passed: On one side the police and the lawyers, confidently steering the well-oiled machinery of the court; on the other a procession of unfortunates in cheap suits who'd got themselves entangled with a legal system that might have been invented on Mars.

The 'meat in the sandwich': This was the English term that resonated with Pierre's place in this scheme: To the immigrants, he was untrustworthy, a countryman in the pockets of the Government; to the police, a wog who was too clever for his own good.

But right now he was Kevin O'Donnell, just another commuter sweating it out on a red rattler bound for Central Station. He changed onto the City Circle line for the three stops to Circular Quay, where the old wooden ferries chugged past the Opera House and on to the Harbour suburbs.

Pierre had downed three cans of Fanta during the roasting hot train journey—horrible stuff, but all a thirsty man could wrestle from the vending machine on Platform 2 at Blacktown Station. He glanced at his watch—ten minutes before the Manly ferry left, plenty of time to visit the lavatory. As he stood at the urinal in the Gents, he became aware of a man next to him showing excessive interest. Pierre sighed. In his line of work, he'd come across instances of this kind of behaviour. But at five-thirty on a Friday at a crowded station? Bold, indeed.

"Excuse me," the man said as they both zipped up.

"You must have mistaken me for somebody else."

Pierre looked him up and down. A man of his own age, dark hair, fit if a little paunchy, and dressed in tan slacks and a shirt with bold blue stripes.

"No, it's you I want," he said. "Kiss me quick."

Chapter 4: Worth a Shitload

He was a funny little bloke, not what Kerry had expected. But what had he expected? The photo Clem had given him showed an ordinary kind of face, a slightly woggy look, and an oily quiff. But up close the fellow had something in his expression—Jeez, Kerry had never been good with this kind of thing—but if he tried to put a word to it, it'd be *trustworthy*. A bloke who looked like you could trust him.

Which was a challenge. He was expecting someone shifty, someone he could screw over without feeling bad about it.

"'Not on your Nelly'," the bloke said, the correct answer to 'kiss me quick'. He sounded like a Pom, well maybe with a bit of something else mixed in.

"Right-ho. They tell me you call yourself Kevin."

"I prefer to be called Pierre, if you don't mind."

"Pierre? Fair enough. That's your business. A nod's as good as a wink."

"And might I be apprised of your name, Sir?" the little bloke asked.

"Beg yours?" Kerry said, trying to sort out what *apprise* meant.

"Your name. What do they call you, Sir?"

"Kerry," he blurted, then regretted it; elementary mistake, he should have given a false name, like this fellow. He'd have to watch his step.

"Look here, Pierre, let's find a quiet place for a chat."

"As you wish, Mr Kerry."

They walked around Circular Quay and up to The Rocks where the commercial artery of George Street ducked under the Harbour Bridge and came out as a village street. The tiny English-style pubs and cafés looked like something out of Windsor or Kent or somewhere. Kerry loved the place. It was just so bloody historical. Made a man proud to be Australian.

They climbed some winding steps and stopped at The Glenmore Hotel, where a packed crowd of city workers were celebrating the end of the week with brimming schooners.

"Here, this'll do."

Kerry fetched a couple of schooners from the bar and took them out to the pavement, where his new chum Pierre was looking a bit lost.

"Not used to the local customs, eh?" The New Australian shrugged and took his glass. "Now, listen, my friend. I'm told you're the man for a little job I need done."

"It is possible. Might I know the nature of the assignment?"

Kerry cupped his mouth: "I want you to make a bomb and blow something up."

The little bloke didn't flinch: No 'fuck me' or 'say again'. Just a nod and, "Go on."

Kerry went on: "Thing is, can I trust you? How do I know you'll do what I ask you to do?"

"I'd hazard a guess that you'll break my legs if I don't," Pierre said, poker-faced.

This wasn't going the way Kerry had expected. He'd expected some thick wog who'd shit himself when he was told what he had to do. But this one talked like a dictionary on legs and made out he was . . . he was . . . equal! That was it. He thought he was equal to Kerry bloody Rich.

What to do? Go back to Clem and say the New Australian didn't fit the bill? No, he wasn't going to question the judgement of The Impeccables. Someone higher up the food chain had picked this Pierre, and that was that. Deal with the hand you've been given.

"So what do you think, Pierre. Are you up for it?"

"Would you oblige me with a little background about the project?"

"Hang on mate, the idea is that I ask the questions and you give me the answers quick smart, got it?" Pierre was starting to piss him off.

The little bloke stared up at him and said, "Well, since you ask, yes I am."

"Yes you am what?"

"I am up for it. We will discuss the background later."

Kerry took a deep breath followed by a long swig on the beer. Party over. He'd have to watch this one.

"All right. You meet me here next Tuesday night at 8pm." He showed Pierre a piece of paper with an address. "Got it?" The New Australian nodded, and Kerry tore the paper to bits. He gave the bloke a long look, trying to figure out what was behind that expressionless face. Was he trustworthy, or a smart Alec? Kerry wasn't so sure now. He swigged off the rest of his beer and turned on his heel.

It was only a ten-minute cab ride to his apartment. He was at a loose end, not his usual style for a Friday night.

The concierge tipped his cap with a, "Good evening Mr Rich. Any plans for later?"

"A quiet night in, I think, Raymond."

"Are we expecting any visitors, Sir?" Raymond was well tipped for his discretion when it came to the professional 'girlfriends' who occasionally buzzed at the security door of Palladian Towers. The bloke might be an ABC, but he did his job right. Kerry's dad didn't mind the Australian born Chinese because they'd breed themselves out in a generation or two.

"No visitors tonight, Raymond." Truth be told, the only woman he wanted was Liz Lanzoni, and he didn't have a clue where to find her. She wasn't in the White Pages. All he knew was that she lived in Manly. He rang a contact who helped him with this sort of thing—bad debts, pests of one kind or another, finding people who didn't want to be found. The guy said he'd get back with the info the next day.

He took a shower and put on his favourite black kimono. Next he made a scotch and soda at the African blackwood wet bar, before sinking into the white leather recliner. The chair was angled so it took in the whole sweep of the city from the corporate towers, past the Harbour Bridge and the Opera House, on to Kirribilli and Mosman. An intense orange sunset turned the glass walls of the high-rise office blocks to molten flame. Traffic flowed north over the bridge and on to the Pacific Highway. An event was kicking off on the Opera House steps—a marquee, dancers, puffs of smoke. The Mosman ferry gave three hoots as it reversed away from the Quay. Kerry lay back and planted his feet on the genuine zebra hide footstool.

If only his dad could see him now. Worth a shitload.

The glassy eyes of Neville Rich stared out from a framed photo on the bar. Those eyes had a compelling effect on him when he was a kid. 'I'm counting to three,' the old man would say if Kerry misbehaved, the eyebeams penetrating his guilty skull. Dad never got past one. They were grey-blue, those eyes, cold as a catfish. Dad never belted him; he didn't need to with those eyes.

At dinner times, he'd read out articles from *Aim Straight*, the newsletter he got from the Southern Cross League. There were all sorts of subjects he'd pick up on and explain the ins and outs of: How the traitor Republicans wanted to cut the ties with Britain; the huge fees we had to pay to the useless United Nations; the Russian ballet companies bringing Communism into Australia by stealth; and the stupidity of swapping the British pound for the Australian dollar. For six months after the new currency was introduced in 1966, Dad had two price lists in the shop: One in dollars and one in pounds. Until some busybody from the Council threatened him with a summons. Talk about the nanny state!

Kerry soaked up those dinner time lectures, his dad telling how to put the world to rights if only the stupid buggers would listen to sense. Dad always had a bee in his bonnet about the end of the White Australia policy. It just didn't make sense to change the way things were, a white country with proper values. Nobody wanted a country of mongrels, that was Dad's line.

Neville Rich's heart had given out, broken by the migrants who ruined his business. Kerry's jaws ground as he remembered the day they'd called him from the fish and chip shop. Funny how his mum's exact words stuck in his head. 'Dad's had a turn by the fryer. You'd better come quick.' It was more than a turn. The poor sod lasted half a day.

When Mum and Kerry went through the books, they found unpaid bills and final notices. It turned out the rot had set in when someone opened a Mexican restaurant next door the year before. When the Lebanese place opened on the other side, Dad was finished. Nobody wanted Aussie fish and chips. He'd kept it to himself that the business was down the gurgler.

Kerry found the mortgage documents for the house, along with a bunch of old letters from an uncle who fancied himself as the family historian. The old bloke had drawn up a family tree that showed Dad was descended from a convict of Cornish stock. People used to say Kerry was a chip off the old block with his dark hair. Mum said she might be descended from convicts too. They weren't afraid to tell people, not like some people who tried to hide it.

Thank God Dad hadn't lived to see Whitlam change the law to let the hordes in.

Kerry was thirty when Dad passed on. He was just getting a start in business but had to work like a dog the next few years to clear the debts and pay the house off. Then just when they were sitting pretty, Mum died. There was a bit of hassle with the will because he couldn't find her birth certificate, and he had no idea who her family were; she'd had a big bust-up with them years ago, she'd said. Kerry had never met any of them. A bent solicitor he played poker with sorted it all out in the end.

Poor Mum—she'd never got over the heartbreak of losing Dad. And Kerry never got over the bile in his guts when he saw the country chucking its British heritage down the drain. The people from the Southern Cross League wrote a lovely obituary for Dad in *Aim Straight*, and sent Kerry a letter saying he'd been given life membership of the League and a free subscription to the magazine. They kept sending copies of *Aim Straight* in the mail, but Kerry wasn't much of a reader, so he put them in a sideboard drawer. It didn't seem decent to toss them out. It'd be disrespectful to the old man.

He had another whiskey and adjusted the recliner so he was almost lying flat, but he couldn't get comfortable. The trouble wasn't in his back but in his head. He got up and paced the apartment. Kerry's success in life was down to two things: His instinct for a deal, and his skill at fixing problems quickly. He didn't like loose ends, and he had two of them hanging around right now: Liz Lanzoni snooping around his private business, and a New Australian with the wrong bloody attitude.

It would wait till tomorrow. Maybe a woman would take his mind off this crap.

The escort agency was on speed dial for emergencies.

"Hello Zelda, who's on this evening?"

Reliable and discreet—that was Zelda's Escorts. They'd only ever slipped up once—sent a nice-looking lady around, and when it was time for action, the lady turned out to be a bloke. One glimpse of a Kransky and two dumplings, and Kerry had Miss Lesley into the fire stairs like a rat down a drainpipe.

"I'll just check, Sir. Yes, Miss Coco is available for an appointment."

"She's the little Thai girl who doesn't mind . . . "

"That's the one, Sir. And we also have Miss Rosalita."

"Is she new?"

"Yes, Sir, she's a bubbly Latin beauty."

He thought for a moment, licked his lips.

"Send the Thai girl."

Chapter 5: Two Sides of One Coin

Pierre dabbed at his chin with a napkin and pushed his plate away.

"Utterly delicious. Can I make you something to drink, *habibti*?"

"*Karkady*, please Pierre," Zouzou answered. Her husband's work guaranteed a flow of middle eastern delicacies from the Lebanese and Egyptian corner stores in the Western Suburbs: Roasted chickpeas, *tahina*, sticky oriental cakes, and the hibiscus tea they knew as *karkady*. This evening, he had taken from his briefcase a bunch of *molokhiya*, which Zouzou stewed up into a slippery green gravy to spoon over lamb and buttery rice.

"It is called 'Jew's mallow' in English," he said, handing her the glass of cherry-red infusion.

"*Kardady*, you mean?"

"No, *molokhiya* is Jew's mallow. The mallow of Jews, you could say, I suppose."

Zouzou smiled to herself. It was an old habit of Pierre's, the man 'turned in on himself', to remark obliquely and unexpectedly on the objects in his orbit, and to name them thoroughly in alternate languages.

Perhaps this was how a man with at least three names fixed himself in the shifting world they lived in, shunted from country to country, tossed into other peoples' messes.

Or perhaps he was delaying telling her some fresh news.

She sipped her drink. He opened a packet of Winfields. They lit up and sat back in their chairs. The hot air in the tiny kitchen hung like damp drapes.

"Shall we sit on the front step?" she asked. It was dark now, the air a little cooler.

The TV was on high volume in the house next door. Joss-stick smoke, loud laughter.

"Let's stay inside, Zouzou." There was fresh news, she was sure.

"I met a man today," he began. "Well, to be precise, the man approached me in a public toilet, and we went to a bar."

"A peculiar meeting."

"*'ageeb 'awi*, very peculiar." Pierre said.

"What kind of man?" Zouzou wasn't in the least interested whether the man was a Russian czar or a garbage collector, but she needed time to ready herself to hear of the bargain Bellamy had foreshadowed.

"A vulgar fellow, but seemingly wealthy. Australian *nouveau riche*, if I were to hazard a guess. My age. A tendency to bully, perhaps, but possibly nervous also. Yes, he seemed somewhat unsure about the situation."

"What situation, Pierre?"

"About what he asked me to do."

"And what was that, *habibi*?"

Pierre leaned forward and brushed a crumb from Zouzou's sleeve.

"He asked me to blow up the restaurant in the Opera House."

Zouzou choked on the drink. She felt herself blinking furiously, the pricking of tears behind her eyes.

"A bomb?"

"Yes, a bomb."

She lit a cigarette, took one puff and stubbed it out. She'd been in tight spots before—a price on her head in Cairo, imprisoned on a rusty ship off Malta. And bombs—she'd been standing behind Donald Waters when he'd killed himself with a grenade. But to blow up a restaurant in the Sydney Opera House?

The Manly ferry hooted once.

"We are up shitty creek without a paddle," she said in English.

Pierre stood up to clear the dishes. He seemed entirely composed, faintly amused perhaps. He replied in English.

"Indeed Zouzou, but we will find the paddle and we shall stick it up their arse."

* * *

Just as sleep lulled her seething thoughts, it bolted into the night again. Zouzou eased herself away from Pierre and slid from the crumple of bed sheets. The floor tiles cooled her feet. A feeble gasp of sea breeze parted the curtains and died. A car drove into the street, and its headlights swept the bedroom walls as it turned and pulled away. Pierre slept on, the man 'turned in on himself', still wearing that faintly amused expression.

The bomb business had knocked her sideways. The idea of leaving Pierre now seemed preposterous under the circumstances. They could be in jail or worse in no time. Her plan to leave Pierre would need to be put to one side, ready to activate when—if—they squeezed out of the current jam.

But an idea occurred to her that she barely dared consider: To leave him now, tonight. Yes, don't dismiss it, it's not crazy. What use would a wedding singer be to him in these latest troubles? She'd be in his way.

But even if she packed a bag and slipped away, where would she go? Her Australian passport was fake. She had just 452 Australian dollars in a passbook account at the Manly branch of the Commonwealth Bank of Australia.

Her investigations in the last few weeks had led her to the Egyptian Consulate in Sydney, where she'd peeked into the waiting room but fled when a nosy-looking clerk at the counter stared knowingly at her. Had he perhaps recognised her as Zouzou Paris, the film actress who always played the *sharmouta*? Ha—some slut! The *sharmouta* who had lost her virginity to her husband Pierre at the age of thirty-three.

She'd been wealthy in Cairo—shrewd enough to spot the crooks among her circle of professional 'friends', smart enough to read her contracts properly, to hire trustworthy lawyers, clever enough to trick her sugar daddies into thinking they'd visited fleshly paradise. She spat on their memory—old bullies in aviator glasses with withered prongs and puerile fantasies.

There was money in a bank in Lebanon, but getting her hands on it was as likely as winning the Opera House Lottery. An Armenian cousin of Pierre's in Beirut had offered to help extract it, but the civil war had raged since 1975. The relative could be dead.

There was only one solution: To throw herself on the mercy of the Egyptian Consulate:

"I am Zouzou Paris, star of *Spies Need Love Too*, *Nadia the Reluctant Assassin*, and numerous other artistic masterpieces. Surely you recognise me, Excellency? You see, I was kidnapped by Mossad five years ago and have been imprisoned in a secret location in Alice Springs as a bargaining chip for the return of Israeli criminal terrorists . . . ."

At this point the script demanded more work, but she was sure she could pull it off. They would welcome their lost kinswoman, fly her home to Cairo, where she'd give tearful interviews for the magazines . . .

"Zouzou, would you like a glass of milk?" It was Pierre, in singlet and pyjama shorts, standing in the shadows. She knew his expression without seeing it: Head pitched a little down and to the left, forehead wrinkled, concern and worry in his eyes. She stepped into his arms, stood there in the dark.

"Do you not think," he murmured, "that we are two sides of one coin?"

* * *

A hot west wind had been blowing all day, drying the eyes and the mouth, and sapping the soul. Pierre turned into Rialto Close, jacket over his shoulder, tie loosened. He checked his watch: 6pm. Plenty of time to meet the man Kerry.

His neighbours Jed and Sue lolled on folding chairs on the pavement drinking beers. They were in their twenties, and neither went to work. Jed took his surfboard down to the beach three or four times a day while Sue spent most of her time in the front yard on the phone, which had a special cord, long enough to reach from deep inside the house. According to Zouzou's eavesdropping, Sue was a drug dealer and Jed was on probation for stealing cars.

"Southerly'll be here around midnight, they reckon," sweaty Jed said, scratching something inside his shorts.

"Bloody oath, it's hot," red-faced Sue said, unpeeling her T-shirt from her breasts and flapping it to ventilate her stomach.

Hot indeed. Pierre had never known such heat as Sydney's. Certainly, the objective facts held that Cairo was as hot or even hotter. But in Cairo, the ceilings were high, the French shutters tamed the heat before it penetrated the fan-cooled column of air in one's apartment. A man could lie for hours on marble tiles watching a chitchat stalk a fly on the ceiling. Here in Manly it was like living inside a freshly fired brick, with the additional hazard of being stalked by lethal spiders.

But soon the Southerly Buster would come, presaged by an eerie stillness as the hot westerly gave up the fight. A flurry of gritty dust and swirling newspaper sheets, a rattle and whoosh in the trees, and the massive wedge of cold air from the south would sweep away the fatigue, the lassitude, the irascibility. Rubbish bins would tumble and spill prawn shells and beer cans into the gutter. As the temperature plunged, the mood in Rialto Close would snap to levity and energy with happy chatter and the clinking of plates and glasses.

But, bloody oath, it was still thirty-eight centigrade and Pierre had a night's work ahead. He went inside.

Zouzou was wearing a magenta summer dress that accentuated her curves and set off the light bloom on her ivory shoulders. The mass of glossy black hair was drawn into a dense bun atop her head. She was as delectable as the day when they'd met five years before: Childhood sweethearts reunited. She poured him a glass of *citron pressé*.

"Let us go over the plan again," Pierre said.

"We will travel in convoy as far as Bankstown," she said, opening the UBD street directory, "from where you will pull ahead by two hundred to three hundred metres."

"Precisely. And if you are caught at traffic lights, I will pull up after the lights and keep watch for you."

"And we will maintain two hundred metres separation until the turnoff at Milperra Road," Zouzou said, placing her finger on the spot in the UBD. "I will wait for five minutes and drive past your Honda, which you will have parked outside the premises. I will then find a hidden vantage point to observe the door."

"Very good. If I do not come out after one hour, you will go to the phone box on the corner of Atkinson Road and Travis Lane and call 999," Pierre said.

"Triple-zero, Pierre, this is Australia."

"My mistake, *habibti.*"

"And I will report a violent altercation to the police."

"After which you will get out of there swiftly . . . " Pierre said.

"By this route." She traced a zigzag of back streets.

"*Yalla!*" Pierre said, "We leave in half an hour."

* * *

Kerry kicked Miss Coco out after a lousy couple of hours. Maybe it was too much whiskey or the thought of Liz Lanzoni, but he just couldn't rise to the occasion despite the best efforts of the little Thai girl. In the end he yelled at her and she burst into tears and told him she wanted to do her best because she was supporting two kids in Chiang Mai. He gave her an extra twenty bucks, and then she asked for a cuddle. Well, he drew the line at that. Off you go, sweetheart.

It was ten-thirty next morning when he woke up, gritty eyed and sour-mouthed. The image of Liz

Lanzoni's tits floated into his mind and he was considering a restorative hand job when the phone rang.

"G'day. I've got the info yer wanted."

"Go ahead."

"The lady's a reporter for *The Australian Examiner*."

"Never heard of it."

"It's a bit out of left field. Doesn't have a form guide if you know what I mean."

"What else did you find out about her?" Kerry asked.

"Lives on her own on Eastern Hill, thirty-two, divorced."

"Anything else?"

"Yeah, well this is the weird bit, Kerry."

"Go on."

"Her ex is in jail for murder."

Kerry sat up straight. "Fuck me."

"There's more."

"Don't tell me it gets any worse," he said.

"Sort of worse depending on how yer look at it."

"Why, is there another way of looking at it?" Kerry snapped.

"Just a manner of speaking, mate. So here's the story. She was arrested as an accessory but the cops couldn't make it stick. Hubby got the shit sandwich—eighteen years. Thing is she went under a different name then."

"Jesus fuck'n Christmas cake. What name?"

"Liz Cruickshank."

Any last trace of desire died inside Kerry's pyjama shorts.

"Thanks mate, I owe you big time." He slapped the phone into its cradle.

Seven or eight years ago, it'd been. Yes, it was coming back, and it wasn't pretty. Andy Cruickshank had an upmarket landscaping business that had gone bung when a big client refused to pay his bills. Kerry couldn't remember the exact details, but there was a hit man involved. Yeah, that was it, the hit man crept into the client's house to shoot him, but aimed at the wrong pillow in the dark, hitting the guy's wife instead. Poor cow hung on for a month or two but then karked it.

Oh, shit a bloody brick. Now he remembered. His blood froze. A witness had claimed to see a woman break into the house. Liz Cruickshank was arrested, but she got off, and Andy went down.

What the hell had he got involved with?

Think, think, think. Call Sir Robert. Tell him everything. No, what if it was nothing and he made a dill of himself? They'd boot him out of The Impeccables.

Calm down. Yeah, she could be a nice girl who'd got mixed up with the wrong bloke, she'd started a new life, new job, nothing suspicious at all. That spazzo business at the beach—maybe she had some condition, epilepsy or Parker's Disease or something. Didn't they make people shake and go weird?

He had to know more about Liz Cruickshank, but how? Old newspapers, that was it. They kept them in libraries. Where was the library? Now he remembered. He'd had a discreet meeting once with a slightly dodgy character in the Sydney City Library. The library was down in the Queen Victoria Building. It was wintertime, and he'd seen the down and outs keeping warm reading the papers. But it had to wait. The morning was almost gone, and he had work to do.

It was a full day: Lunch with his accountant to talk about a tricky tax problem; a drive out to Kellyville to see a block of land he was hoping to snap up just before the bank foreclosed on the owner, who just happened to owe him fifty grand for the deposit. The block of land was located conveniently near a demolition business he part-owned, where he would find a bloke who would be able to help with the 'certain materials' Clem had talked about. And in the evening, he had a catch-up drink with a real estate agent about a tropical resort in Queensland. Apparently, the vendor needed to offload the property before he quietly offloaded himself from Australia.

And as for the meeting with the New Australian tonight, the arrogant little prick wouldn't find Kerry there. Mr Pierre could sweat it out for a few days, and appreciate who was boss.

He showered and dressed, choosing a worn denim shirt and some cheap grey pants; he'd take the Datsun rather than the Porsche. You didn't dress up when you were crying poor to the accountant. He made a slice of toast and Vegemite, but an image of Liz Lanzoni brandishing a gun popped into his head and he pushed the plate aside.

* * *

Zouzou followed Pierre, maintaining the agreed separation. The suburban traffic was thin at this time of year when most of Sydney was on holiday. Just as they hit the Liverpool Road turnoff to the South Western Suburbs, the Southerly hit, buffeting the Vespa with cold gusts and stinging grit. She saw Pierre's rear light wobble and straighten up.

A yellow VW Beetle overtook her and drew ahead to sit behind Pierre, blocking her view of the Honda. She tried weaving out to the centre line to catch a glance of his bike helmet. Yes, still there, with the Beetle behind. A bullhorn blast from a huge truck forced her to the left. The thing veered in front of her and blocked her view.

The UBD had shown a side route. She took the next right into a knot of mean bungalows and industrial yards. The smell of baking cookies reminded her she was hungry. There it was—the Arnotts biscuit factory, and then she was streaking along a near-empty backstreet, over a railway bridge, and back on to the main road. There was a glimpse of the yellow Beetle ahead. She was sure now that Pierre had a tail. Her job was to tail the tail.

The convoy was now approaching Milperra. Zouzou held back, just enough to see the yellow car in the failing light. Her back was stiff and her wrists ached from gripping the Vespa's handlebars. The Beetle's indicator light blinked and the car turned left at the street that led to the rendezvous. She prayed that Pierre was ahead of his tail. At the left turn she slowed but not enough. A woman walked off the pavement in front of her. The Vespa slid, Zouzou toppled, flopped onto the woman and knocked her down. She heard the crash of the scooter hitting the road. The smell of vinegar. The woman was getting up, cradling a paper bag of hot chips.

"You spilt half me fuckin' supper, yer stupid bitch," she said, and walked off.

No injuries, *al-hamdu lillah*. The chip woman had broken her fall. A ute pulled up and a man in a singlet and shorts got out. He picked up the Vespa, looked it over and pulled it onto its stand.

"Your lucky day, darl," he said, and was gone.

Lucky day, indeed! Her bitter luck to find herself in this wasteland of metal-clad warehouses and concrete hardstands and industrial waste bins. She stifled a sob. A signboard displayed the names of the businesses in the industrial park where Pierre was to rendezvous: *Gibbons & Sons Metal Fabricators, Marvel Sauces and Pickles, Paradise Adult Products, All Makes Washing Machine*

Repairs, Jap Clutch and Gearbox Service. She dabbed her eyes and laughed: Was she expecting to see *Milperra Bomb Factory?*

Zouzou scanned the road ahead for the next turn. The Vespa started after two kicks, although it made a rattle she didn't recognise. Straight ahead, left after thirty metres, brakes on hard as she saw Pierre's parked Honda, and the nose of the VW poking from a driveway opposite.

* * *

Zouzou lay back in the kitchen chair while her husband dabbed antiseptic on a miniscule graze that may or may not have resulted from the crash.

"Only an amateur would have made the rendezvous in person," he said. "These events were quite predictable."

Zouzou wondered why Pierre hadn't thought to mention this before they'd left. But as an authority on the male ego, she deferred to his judgement.

"Just press there, Pierre, with your thumb. Yes, ooh, I'm sure it will be like a balloon in the morning."

Her husband frowned. "But the tail was very amateurish. I spotted the Beetle just after we crossed the Harbour Bridge."

Touché. That would have been at least twenty minutes before she'd noticed it.

"And you say the car parked in Manly after I got home?" he asked.

"Yes, Pierre. She watched you go inside, and I followed her up Eastern Hill."

"You said 'she', Zouzou."

"Yes, a woman got out. A young woman."

"A woman of a young age," Pierre looked up, nodding.

"And what about the rendezvous, my heart?"

"Mr Kerry was playing games, putting us off our stroke. He will make contact us again soon, you can be sure."

"Of course, Pierre. Ooh, just there below the kneecap, please."

Chapter 6: She's Apples

The real estate agent was getting toey. He'd phoned four times, with variations on "Mate, I need a decision. There's another buyer sniffing around. You wannit or not?"

Kerry had enough balls in the air right now, but this needed fixing pronto. He'd only seen photos of the resort. There was an Ansett flight to Cairns in the morning. He'd stay a night or two, have a good look at the place and be back in time to get the New Australian down to work on the bomb.

This needed the old thinking cap, though. He didn't actually need a tropical resort, but it was the kind of thing that would 'broaden his portfolio' and 'raise his profile' according to his accountant. It just had a good feel about it. How many of The Impeccables owned a resort after all? Not many, he reckoned. And it was cheap as chips, mainly because the present owner had lost a big case against the Australian Taxation Office and was stuck with a bill that could only be solved by decamping to Manila and changing his name.

He called the agent. "I'll take it off his hands at the right price. How about a viewing tomorrow arvo?"

The agent almost shat himself with gratitude. He'd make sure the vendor himself was waiting at Cairns airport with a car. No, there wasn't an agent in Cairns due to one or two local sensitivities. But a solicitor up there had the paperwork ready. Sure they could agree on the right price over a beer or two. Cash sale of course.

Kerry called his travel agent, who promised to drop the plane tickets off later.

The penthouse safe was behind a framed copy of the poster for the 1966 Rolling Stones concert at the Sydney Showground. Jeez, what a night that was! OK, at 28 he'd been a tad older than most of the crowd there. But he couldn't be blamed if the hairdresser from Hurstville said she was already eighteen and on the pill. Or her friend from Kogarah. Or that he had sperm like a gorilla. Somewhere out there were two twelve-year old kids. The little bastards had cost him a packet—strictly cash of course. He left the poster in front of the safe as a warning—always use a rubber.

In the back of the safe was a fat wad of cash with a slightly fishy smell to it. It would cover about half the asking price for the resort, and that's all he intended to pay. He stuffed the notes in his washbag and packed it in his overnight case.

The concierge called on the intercom. There was a gentleman with an airline ticket. Should he have the maintenance man bring it up?

"Just leave it in my mailbox, Raymond." Better remember to slip him a few dollars.

Kerry couldn't settle. It was 6pm, too late to do any work, too early to go out for dinner and a drink. A jog might be an idea, get some of the tension out of him, work up a sweat. Might even be a good habit to get into. There was a pair of red Nikes around somewhere, still in the box. And a headband and shorts. No need for a shirt in this weather.

His run took him along New Beach Road with the bay on his right. In minutes the sweat was pouring off his chest and there was a sore patch on his heel. The shorts were bloody tight, and he needed to adjust his tackle.

A kid in a turquoise singlet thundered past, yelling, "Move over, Granddad". Kerry slowed to a hobble until he got to the Rushcutters Bay marina full of gleaming yachts and power boats. He glimpsed his Mustang 2400 at its mooring and had a soothing flashback of Liz Lanzoni's tits.

Locals were scattered around the park drinking wine and chatting in the late afternoon sunshine. Luckily he'd tucked his smokes into his waistband. He sat on a bench, lit up, looked around, then quietly eased his hand into his pants to sort things out. A couple of chicks in skimpy tops looked his way and laughed. He winked back. They gave him the finger. Fuck 'em. He ground out the cigarette butt on the grass.

Worth a shitload, that was Kerry Rich. Yeah, but he still felt . . . what was the word? Inadequate, that was it. Like there was something missing. That was why he liked being one of The Impeccables, he supposed. Made him feel he was part of something bigger, something that people would remember him for.

But the truth was that having a shitload of cash wasn't all it was cracked up to be when you . . . when you . . .

When you didn't have someone to share it with.

There, he'd admitted it to himself.

And then it occurred to him that the resort in Queensland was part of all this, part of this 'inadequate' business. He let his mind drift: Palm trees, the flip-flop of waves on a deserted beach, him and a lady walking hand in hand in the surf, a couple of steaks back at the resort gagging to be barbecued, piña coladas in frosted glasses. The scene widened: Kerry and the lady back at a circle of cute grass-roofed huts around a pool with a swim-up bar. Some of the locals and their sheilas— they'd use that word in Queensland—dropping by for happy hour, Kerry's arm around his lady's shoulder. G'day mate. Been fishin'? Yeah, byoodiful out on the reef today, mate. How's the family, Kerry? Here, grab a Fourex.

A voice broke into his daydream. "Can you stop doing that?" It was a podgy git with glasses.

"Doing what?"

"Playing with yourself, you filthy pig. There are children about."

Playing with himself? Jeez, he'd only been sorting out the meat from the veggies.

"Piss off, yer four-eyed dickhead."

Before the bloke could finish saying, "Mind your language," Kerry got up and slapped the side of his head. The arsehole fell over. Kerry strode up to the road and flagged down a cab.

"You got shirt?" the driver said.

"What'yer talkin' about? Course I don't have a shirt."

"You don't go my cab with no shirt, Mister." The car sped off. Bloody Lebo.

Kerry turned back towards the park. A dozen people were pointing at him. The podgy git had blood on his face. A little kid in his arms was bawling.

"Fuckin' losers!" Kerry yelled at them. He turned and ran back up New Beach Road, his blistered heel on fire.

A car slowed down beside him. A yellow Beetle— stupid looking thing. The driver was a woman with a hat and dark shades on. She looked straight at him, then accelerated away. It was her, he was sure, then not so sure. Bloody Liz Lanzoni was playing with his mind. What did the fixer say about her car? Nothing. Didn't mention it. Better call him and find out what she drove.

* * *

"Yep, boss. A yellow Beetle."
"Give us the rego, buddy."
Kerry wrote down the number plate and Liz's address.
"I owe yer."
He slapped the receiver down, went to the bar fridge for a cold beer, prised off the brand new Nikes and the tiny shorts. Jeez, he stank like yesterday's prawns. Long cold shower, another beer, then another, a big think, another beer, thinking getting too hard, another beer. How many beers was that now? Six empties. Feeling a bit spewsome as the water bed rippled under him, and then a fading picture of a naked Liz Lanzoni aiming a gun at his old fellow.

* * *

The next morning he had a bag of spanners in his head. And felt bloody angry with himself. He'd let himself down, as Dad would have said, by slapping the bloke in the park. Violence was for idiots. The smart ones let others do the slapping if it had to be done. The Impecabbles knew that; let the New Australian do the dirty stuff.

On the taxi to the airport he checked the weather for Cairns, but the paper only gave it as far as Brisbane, where it was 30c. Darwin had thunderstorms and 31c, so if you split the difference, it'd be hot and maybe rainy in Cairns. Far North Queensland was a long way down his list of holiday spots. When he took a vacation—and that wasn't very often—it'd be in a five-star hotel in Fiji or Surfers Paradise.

The plane was on time, and luckily half-empty. As soon as the seatbelt light went off he lit a ciggy, reclined his seat, and enjoyed watching a stewardess stretching up to dislodge something from the locker opposite him. Maybe he'd ask her for her phone number, see if she was staying over at Cairns. The breakfast trolley arrived, and he loaded up on sausage and omelette to settle his stomach. The drone of the engines and the nice meaty taste in his mouth nudged him into a half sleep, and soon he was unzipping Liz Lanzoni from an Ansett uniform.

"Seat upright for landing, please." The stewardess again. "Are you feeling OK, Sir?"

"I'm fine, why?"

"When you were asleep, Sir. You were . . . making comments quite loudly."

"What did I say?" Shit, he'd been out of it for three hours.

A man in the opposite row said, "Don't embarrass yourself anymore, mate".

Christ all bloody mighty. What was happening to him? He'd need all his ducks in a row when he met the fellow with the resort.

The plane lined up for the descent into Cairns. They drifted from blue sky into thick cloud. In a second it was like a horizontal waterfall outside, some sort of rainstorm, no land in sight. Tighten up the seatbelt, the sausage repeating on him, the plane's shaking, he's feeling sick, the wheels bounce on the tarmac, whack down again, and they're slewing along with the engines screaming.

He got some funny looks when he got up to lift the overnight bag from the locker. He looked down. Shit, his zipper was undone. Time to get a bloody grip.

Remember, you're worth a shitload. You're a member of a secret organisation that'll get this country sorted out. You're buying a resort today. Zip up. Walk proud.

The resort vendor was waiting in the arrivals area, biting his nails and gushing over-friendly. Tropical shirt, all palm trees and parrots, baggy shorts and a set of varicose veins like a Moreton Bay fig. He popped an umbrella and they ran through the puddles to a Mini-Moke with a canvas cover.

"Be 'bout an hour depending on the weather," the vendor said, grinding the gear shift into first.

This was a mistake. This wasn't rain, it was bloody Niagara Falls. No wonder the place was cheap. The rain was leaking through the gaps in the canvas cover onto Kerry's jeans.

"Look, mate," he said. "Maybe we'll pop up there in the morning. I'll get a feed and a good sleep in Cairns tonight."

The vendor dragged the gear stick into neutral and turned to Kerry.

"Mate, I'm in shit up to me friggin' kneecaps. Have a look at the place at least. Just name your price."

He pulled a dirty hanky out of his pocket and wiped his eyes. The poor bastard was crying. About the age Dad would have been when the fish shop went bung, Kerry reckoned, and there was something in the face, like a bloke whose pride had been taken away from him. A good man who'd been dealt a few low blows.

Business was business for Kerry. It was nothing personal when you got the advantage over the weaker man. But this fellow—well, it'd be like kicking a three-legged dog.

"OK, buddy, let's hit the road."

Two hours it took, two hours of sloshing rain, potholes, the Mini-Moke's gearbox moaning like a dying dog when they got stuck in a flooded stretch of road. Outside the plastic windows there was a blur of drooping trees, glimpses of an angry brown sea with no horizon, signs saying BEWARE OF CROCODILES. Tiny towns came and went. Now there were canefields marching across the landscape towards distant mountains that occasionally appeared through breaks in the cloud. The vendor wrangled the vehicle like a rodeo rider, calling out "Smoke!" every half hour, so that Kerry lit a ciggy and put it between the fellow's lips. It was hot as a sauna under the Moke's plastic roof cover. Kerry's clothes were drenched, and he itched all over, trying not to imagine what was biting him.

"Home stretch," the vendor said at last when they slewed right onto a narrow road that led between green walls of sugar cane.

"I need a flamin' leak," he yelled, braking hard.

They climbed out and unzipped. Kerry finished his business and looked up.

And then the sun came out.

He stood transfixed by the colours of the cane, and the bush and the sky and every bloody thing he could see. Greens and blues he'd never witnessed before. Light like no light he knew.

"God's own country, mate," the vendor said.

The road went for a kilometre or so until they saw the sea—it was blue now—through a strip of bush. The cane gave way to trees with dinner-plate sized leaves. They slowed by a clearing where four or five people were hanging wet clothes on a rope strung up between two poles. One was an old bloke with a scraggy grey beard, the others young fellows with long hair, wearing sarongs. Two women were breast feeding babies in the doorway of a shack. The men stopped their work and waved.

"Hippy colony, mate. They don't do no harm. Stonkered most of the time."

The road forked soon after, the left marked with an old car bonnet. CROCODILE FARM AND BOAT RIDES was painted on it, and POSITIONS VACANT underneath. They took the right fork, where another car bonnet announced YOU ARE ON TRADITIONAL ABORIGINAL LAND.

"What's that all about?" Kerry asked.

"Dunno, mate. Here we are."

They got out. The vendor took a couple of warm Fourexes from behind the seat and knocked off the tops on the bull bar.

There wasn't much to see. Bugger all, actually.

"So where's the resort, you know, the huts and the swim-up bar?" Kerry asked.

"Well, the pool was just over there, but after the cyclone, you know, there was a bit of clearing up to do.

"Cyclone?"

"Tropical Cyclone Keith of course. Last year. Didn't the agent mention it?"

"Are you taking the piss?" Kerry asked, but the bloke took on such a tragic look he had to walk away. Sure enough, there was an area of disturbed ground about the size of a backyard swimming pool. Splintered lumps of roofing timber and palm leaves stuck out of the rubble. The vendor scurried to his side.

"We bulldozed all the debris into the hole and ran the grader over the top. But the manager's residence is OK."

They walked to a fibro building beyond the pool. It had a tin roof, a water tank and a couple of big gas bottles strapped to the back wall. The vendor handed Kerry a key and stood back waiting with spaniel eyes.

"All right, champ. Go sit in the vehicle while I have a think."

The place was a dump. He'd been a fuckwit to listen to the agent in Sydney without asking more questions. That wasn't like Kerry Rich. When Kerry did a deal, it was usually the other bloke who was left with his arse out of his trousers. He should be furious, should be giving the bloke with the varicose veins a proper shellacking for wasting his time.

But there was something weird about the place—something calm, green, soothing. He had a funny, dreamy feeling in his chest, or maybe his heart, somewhere inside his sweaty shirt anyway. He looked back at the Moke, where the vendor was sitting on the mudguard with his head in his hands. On a normal day, Kerry wouldn't have a problem kicking a man when he was down; business was business and it wasn't always pretty. But this'd be like kicking his old man. In paradise.

The residence had a big lounge with some beat-up sofas and a zillion dollar view. At the back was a bit of a kitchen, a couple of bedrooms, and a kind of bathroom, sort of more a laundry with a dunny. Palm fronds nodded outside the window. Peace and quiet. The sound of breaking waves and squawking birds.

The front veranda faced the ocean, where gentle rollers broke on a beach that stretched to a milky green headland in the far distance. A strip of palms and squiggly black trees lined the beach. The impossibly blue blues and impossibly green greens struck Kerry dumb. He sat in a battered cane chair on the veranda, finished the warm Fourex and chucked the bottle on the beach.

Nah, that's not the thing to do. He picked up the bottle and threw it into a forty-gallon oil drum someone had used as an incinerator, took his shoes off, and walked into the surf.

A movement caught his eye. Two black kids in singlets and shorts standing on a tumbledown bit of dock made of logs, a place you'd tie a boat up.

"Hey, you," he called.

The boys jumped off the dock and came near. Skinny legs, one wearing a woollen hat. Aboriginals.

"You the new boss?"

"No mate. Just visiting. From Sydney. D'you live round here?"

One of them pointed through the trees to where the crocodile farm would be.

"Who's the owner, then?"

The other boy shrugged and they walked away.

Kerry locked up the residence. Instinct, that was what cut it in business, and he had an instinct for this place. Sure, he'd never make a buck from it. Kerry knew nothing about holiday accommodation, but it needed thirty seconds of mental arithmetic to see the income would never cover the expenses, and that was leaving to one side the costs of rebuilding the place.

No, this might come in useful one day when a shovelful of shit flew out of left field and hit the proverbial fan. A nice little hideaway with the right company and a well-stocked bar. The Ansett stewardess's backside floated past his inner eye.

"Watcha think, Mr Rich?" The vendor was savaging a cigarette in the front seat of the Moke.

Kerry looked back to the resort. Out to sea a bank of grey clouds was building. Better get this done before the weather changed his mind.

"She's apples, mate. Let's talk to the lawyer tomorrow."

* * *

The same stewardess was on the plane when Kerry flew back to Sydney the next day, but he was too distracted to enjoy a soothing eyeful. Liz Lanzoni was heavy on his mind: Why the hell was she interested in him? She must be after a story, but what about? The most bloodcurdling possibility was that she had a hunch about the bomb plan. Even more reason not to tell The Impeccables; they'd surely kick him out.

He cast his mind back over his business deals in the last couple of years, but nothing stuck out. Sure, he'd separated more than a few blockheads from their hard-earned, but it was all fair and square business, even if the Tax Office wasn't always in the picture.

There was no way she knew the story behind the cash for the resort. In fact, it'd been so complicated that he'd forgotten some of the details himself: A bloke in Blacktown owed a bespoke car dealer for a brace of vintage vehicles, and the dealer took a share in three lobster boats in lieu. But the lobster boats had an outstanding loan on them from a bent demolition contractor, and Kerry paid off the loan in kind using a thirty percent share in a macadamia farm. The demolition guy promised him a commission in cash 'for a rainy day'. But there'd been a bit of argy bargy about where the demolition guy got the banknotes, so Kerry had upped the commission . . . . At any rate, he ended up with a wad of cash he might have a job explaining away.

The part that really shrivelled the family jewels was the Cruickshank connection. The details were coming back to him now. Andy Cruickshank was mixed up with a bunch of detectives who were better avoided if you wanted to keep your wedding gear intact. Kerry had come close to their orbit a few times, but luckily swung away. He shuddered at the memory of closing the deal on a warehouse in 1976. Next day a bloke in a brown suit came up to him in the street and told him how much the contribution to the benevolent fund was.

"What contribution, and who the fuck are you?"

"I'm your fairy godmother, buddy, and here's my magic wand." He pulled his jacket open to show a revolver strapped under his arm. "See, it's not very safe in this part of town. That's where me and the benevolent fund come in. You can pay a year in advance or my associates can offer an instalment plan."

Three months later he offloaded the warehouse at a loss.

No, it couldn't be that. It had to be the bomb plan.

They made a slow circuit over Sydney waiting for a landing slot. It always felt good, his city, the place where he'd made the grade, made his shitload. Down they drifted over the red roofs of The Shire where he'd been brought up, across Tom Ugly's Bridge and the suburbs of Miranda and Sylvania Waters pushing into the Georges River—green fingers of land with mansions and swimming pools. The plane banked and straightened, Botany Bay, a glimpse of the Opera House, the flash of sunlight on his apartment block at Point Piper.

If bloody Liz Lanzoni thought she could piss in his pocket she'd regret it. No, that wasn't right. A chick'd have a bit of trouble pissing in a pocket. Anyway, fuck it, she'd better watch out.

Chapter 7: Evening Classes

They followed the same routine—Pierre two hundred metres ahead on the Honda, Zouzou's Vespa behind. The note in their letterbox had said SAME TIME SAME PLACE TONITE.

He forced himself to concentrate on the traffic. But he was tired, tired of maintaining an optimistic demeanour for Zouzou, tired of second-guessing, tired of the insecurity. Pierre would have happily spent the rest of his life as Kevin O'Donnell, the quiet chap at the State Translation Office, never having to explain himself, never having to watch out for watchers.

Forget Cairo, forget Ealing, forget all of it—just to be left in this remote corner of the planet with Zouzou. And a child or two if they happened along.

The Honda coughed and he forced himself to concentrate; a fellow could end up squashed like a cockroach under one of the immense trucks that thundered along the narrow traffic lanes of Parramatta Road. There were car yards on each side, Turkish food shops, grimy pubs. The bike coughed again; the spark plug fouled regularly. There was a spanner and a wire brush under the seat in case he had to clean it.

Twenty minutes to go. No tail tonight. Twenty minutes with his thoughts, and one troubling thought in particular.

He was convinced that Zouzou was hiding something from him. Two sides of one coin they may be. But that recent night when she had stood in his arms, he'd felt his words jar and her body stiffen slightly. The two sides of a coin may be inseparable, but those two sides could never face one another, without the destruction of the coin.

The turning into the industrial estate lay ahead. All the businesses were closed for the day. The roller door of one of the units was half-open. He parked the bike and glanced back to see Zouzou's Vespa disappear into an alley.

"Here, over here." It was Mr Kerry, dressed in mechanics overalls, rubber gloves and a cap pulled down over his forehead.

The man pressed a button to fully open the roller door, and turned a light on.

"C'mon."

Pierre entered. The roller door closed.

"You've got twelve weeks to make it," Mr Kerry said, pointing at a workbench stacked with brand new tools still in their packages.

"Are there some instructions?" Pierre had never made anything in his life. When he grew up in Egypt, nobody of his class knew how to make things. Making things was done by other people, mostly poorer people. He'd been bemused when they were exiled to London to learn how the British were obsessed with making things. In the newsagent there were racks of magazines for hobbyists: Cabinet making, wine making, scale model sailing boats, replicas of George Stephenson's

Rocket, bird cages, go-carts. And shops where a man could buy advanced fabrication tools to take home in his car.

The man nodded to a manila folder on the bench. "Look in there."

Pierre took a school exercise book from the folder. It was Egyptian Ministry of Education issue, poor quality paper and scuffed maroon covers. He hadn't seen one in years. He flicked through it and his stomach lurched.

It was a book of instructions in neat Arabic handwriting. He flicked through it. Dangerous words jumped from the pages: *infijaar*, 'explosion', *qunbula*, 'bomb'. There were wiring diagrams, mathematical formulae, intricate sketches of mechanical parts. The names of chemicals were in German; it must have been translated into Arabic, with the original terms left intact because the author couldn't find the Arabic word.

"Where did this come from?" Pierre asked. He'd read about German terrorist groups—Red Army Faction, Baader Meinhof.

"None of your business. But I'm told you can read it and you know your stuff."

Know his stuff? Whoever had chosen him for this job had been given the wrong information.

Or intentionally set up a rank amateur to do a professional job.

The more he learned of Ealing's methods, the more he marvelled at their capacity for deception. Two years previously he had been smuggled into Libya in the guise of a fake arms dealer called Cornelius Lamine. After surviving an encounter with Ghaddafi himself, Pierre ended up drifting in a lifeboat off Malta with a dead British Under-Secretary for company.

"I will need to study it carefully."

An idea occurred to him. How was the thing to be detonated? Memories of his army training in Egypt forced themselves to the surface. He'd done a course on land mines. He opened the exercise book at a random page and adopted what he hoped was a confident demeanour.

"For example, Mr Kerry, there are numerous options listed here. Is the device to be activated by a timer? Or are we talking of radio control? A pressure plate? These are vital questions for a professional."

The man rubbed his chin, crossed his arms.

"Look here, fella . . . "

"And the material—gelignite, nitro-glycerine, dynamite?"

"Just get working on it and I'll find out all that."

"Can I study the instructions here?"

"Jeez, mate, you've got a lot of bloody questions. Take it home. Here's a spare key. Lock up properly," he said, and started to walk out.

He turned at the doorway. "Just one thing".

"Yes?" Pierre asked.

"I know where you live, old mate."

Of course he did. A note had been delivered to Pierre's mailbox. This fellow should be in the circus.

The man strode out. A car started nearby and accelerated away.

Pierre looked over the tools piled up on the bench. That one was certainly a screwdriver. The rest? He had a lot to learn.

After turning out the lights and locking up, Pierre kick-started the Honda. He put the bomb manual in the storage box under the seat and revved up. Wherever Zouzou was hiding, she'd be behind him soon.

The traffic was light—an easy run home on a warm evening. Just as he reached the toll gates on the Harbour Bridge, the motor died. Pierre wobbled into the nearside lane, just avoiding a blaring taxi. The cars behind him backed up until there was a long line of blinkers, with angry drivers craning their necks to change into the next lane. The tools were under the bomb manual. He knelt on the tarmac, groping around the hot motor to disconnect the ignition wire.

"Fuckin' wanker!" A driver yelled at him, accelerating around the bike and leaving a burst of oily smoke.

At last the plug yielded to the spanner. Pierre poked the brush into the spark gap.

He looked up. Flashing lights. A big white car pulling up in front. A uniform, gun in a holster. Torchlight. Police.

"Licence please."

Pierre blinked into the torch. The bomb manual was in the open storage box, plain as day. He put the spark plug in his pocket and found his wallet. The torch flickered from the licence to his face and back again.

"Mr O'Donnell, is it?"

"Yes, Sir."

"Can you tell me the registration number of this vehicle?"

Pierre parroted the number of the bike. Sweat ran down the back of his shirt.

"Where have you been this evening, Mr O'Donnell?" The torch found the bomb manual, lingered for a second and flicked away.

"Evening class. Motorcycle maintenance. Sydney Technical College."

The radio blared in the police car. An urgent voice cackled under the static. The policeman cocked his ear, thrust the licence back at Pierre, and ran to the car. It roared away with the siren howling. Pierre let out his breath.

The Honda coughed twice and started.

Where was Zouzou? She must have raced past him during the breakdown. He slipped into a gap in the traffic. The sign for Lavender Bay loomed ahead. Damn, three lanes to cross to get to the Mosman-Manly lane on the right. Pierre turned on the right-hand indicator and accelerated. It was a near-lethal manoeuvre. He rarely prayed, but uttered "*alhamdullilah*" as he shot out of the intersection onto Military Road. Alive! He was alive, thanks be to God, and eager to tell Zouzou about his meeting with the dangerously amateur Kerry Rich.

* * *

Zouzou wasn't home when he arrived at Rialto Close. He was not overly concerned. She'd be back soon with some new information, some surprise. He washed the engine grime from his hands, slid the bomb manual under the sofa cushions and made some tea.

There was a knock on the fly screen door.

"G'day, Pierre." It was Jed, the neighbour. Pierre got up and opened the screen a centimetre.

"Who've you got in there, mate?" Jed gave him a theatrical wink and peered around Pierre's shoulder.

"Er, nobody, just me. Excuse my inhospitality. Can I offer you a cup of tea?" Pierre opened the screen wider.

"Wouldn't touch the stuff, buddy. Anyway, I thought I'd let you know a lady was looking for you earlier."

"Did the lady have a name?"

"I didn't ask, but I tell you what, you can send her next door when you've finished with her." He made an obscene gesture with his palm and forefinger, and guffawed again.

"Thanks."

"No worries, mate. See yer later."

The Vespa pulled up. Zouzou came in, wrenched the helmet off, unzipped her jacket, fanned herself with a *Manly Daily*. She must have news, but how long would she take to divulge it without being prompted?

"Tea, Pierre, please. Ouf, I am so hot and tired. I must lie down. And is there a morsel of that *baklava* left from last night?"

"*Habibti*, might I ask you to tell me immediately where you have been, and what morsel of news you are bearing?"

She embraced him and he drank in the intoxicating warm scent of her body.

"You know me so well, Pierre *habibi*. I won't torture you this time."

So far so good. News was imminent. She released herself and looked into his eyes.

"I followed him home. It took a little while because I had to hold back when he was stopped by the police. He lives at Point Piper."

"With the millionaires! And why was he stopped by the police?" Pierre asked.

"Just a speeding ticket, I think. But there's more. I talked to his *bawwab*."

"*Bawwab*?" Pierre visualised the doorkeepers of Cairo with their turbans and sandals and sharp gossip.

"The concierge. A Chinese with loose lips dressed up like Prince Rainier of Monaco. He thought I was a prostitute visiting Mr Kerry. On the basis of—let us say a certain suggestion on my part—the foolish man spilt the beans from the bag, and even sent me up to the man's apartment."

"Dressed like that?" Pierre asked. She was wearing stretch pants and a cheap motorcycle jacket. Her hair resembled a heavy-duty feather duster.

Zouzou sniffed. "You obviously didn't see me in *Undercover Agents in Love*."

"I confess I did not. And did you enter his apartment?"

"Forget the tea, Pierre. I need a cognac."

Pierre fetched the bottle and two glasses, reflecting that Zouzou was now sitting on the sofa cushion beneath which a terrorist bomb-making manual was hidden. He'd wait for her to tell her story first.

* * *

Kerry was so distracted that he was nudging eighty when the speed cop overtook him waving his gauntlet. At least he was driving the old Datsun and wearing workshop gear. The cop would have creamed his leathers at stopping a bloke in a five-hundred-dollar suit driving a Porsche.

"Thank you, Sir," he croaked, seething at his stupidity. He crumpled the speeding ticket and pulled away, got up to 60k and held it there. What a stuff-up. The New Australian had run rings around him. Made him look like a dickhead. He ground his teeth, reached for a smoke, lit it and dropped it in his lap. Fuck!

Something was smouldering between his thighs. He glanced down, then looked up to see red traffic lights and a big Harley waiting for the green. Stamped on the brakes. The Datsun slid sideways, clipped the Harley and spun across the intersection. The Vita Wheat factory loomed, he went up the kerb, scraped the wall with the front tyre, and stopped.

The Harley throbbed towards him and stopped by the Datsun's window. The biker pointed at a scratch on his duco. Shit. The bloke was wearing colours.

Kerry had two or three hundred bucks in his wallet.

"Take this." He wound the window down and handed the rider half the money.

The bloke flicked through the notes. His knuckles were tattooed and one of his thumbs was missing. The stump had HELL tattooed on it. He looked down at Kerry, made a beckoning gesture with the stump. Kerry handed him another fifty. And another. The biker spat and remounted his bike. By way of a farewell, he kicked a dent into the door panel with a steel-capped boot.

Kerry eased the Datsun off the kerb with a bump. The old girl had been his dad's. Never a scratch until today. There was something so fucking disrespectful about what the biker had done. It was almost like—what was the word?—like he'd been violated.

He was out of ciggies. Ah, there was the one he'd dropped. It was a bit squashed and tasted plasticky, but the nicotine did the job—calmed the frazzle in his head, made him focus. He started the car and headed for home. A single headlight bobbed in the rear-view mirror. Jeez, not another Highway Patrol bike, but no— just some dickhead on a scooter.

A thread of worry nagged at him. There was something not right with the whole set-up. Nobody had given him any proper instructions. He'd assumed the book with the squiggly writing contained all the details, and that the New Australian would just get on with the job. The manual had been dropped off at reception in a plain package, along with a list of tools which he'd got his fixer to buy from ten different hardware stores as per instructions. There was no choice but to get back to The Impeccables for orders.

The remote control for underground parking at Palladian Towers wasn't where it should be in the glovebox. Bugger. He'd left it with the Porsche keys.

Nobody answered when he pressed the buzzer to be let in. Raymond having a swift cuppa probably. Lazy bastard. Ten minutes passed. At last the roller door opened. One more mistake like that and Raymond would find himself on the bloody dole. He parked the damaged Datsun next to his Porsche and stabbed at the buttons in the basement lift, ground his teeth as it rose to his floor.

The door dinged. Home. Calm.

When he got out, he saw woman peering at his door. Thick black hair, jogging pants.

"Who the fuck are you?"

She turned. Buxom, dark eyes. Not really his type but tasty anyway.

"I am looking for your neighbour."

The woman had an accent. Neighbour? There was only one other penthouse on his floor, but it was empty.

"Who let you up?"

"The concierge, Sir. But, oh dear, I see that he has sent me to the wrong floor. My apologies."

"No, no worries, I'll buzz you down."

"Thank you. But could I trouble you for a glass of water?"

He looked her up and down, stopping at her breasts. Why not?

"You're welcome. Come in."

* * *

"No, I didn't go in, Pierre." Zouzou downed the cognac and held the glass out for a refill. Her husband raised an eyebrow a millimetre or two.

"It would have been a risky move, *habibti*," he said.

"Very risky, my heart."

She took a sip of the second glass of cognac. Her cheeks warmed with an involuntary flush. Why had she lied? There was no rational explanation for going into the apartment. Just an overwhelming impulse from some hidden place in her mind, or her body, or perhaps both. Kerry Rich wasn't especially good-looking or even well-built. But he had—how could you describe it?—an aura, a force that stirred her in a way that was delicious and dangerous all at once.

"And what did you learn from the concierge?"

"Oh yes. Well, it seems that this gentleman is a businessman, and somewhat rough and unsophisticated in his dealings."

She raised the cognac to her lips to smother the memory of Kerry's man scent as she had squeezed past him in the doorway. To smother the silly thrill of knowing his eyes were on her backside.

"Rough, you say? In what way? And what kind of business is he in?"

"He has a lot of women visitors, according to the concierge. A 'regular ladies man', the concierge said. 'If you can call them ladies.'"

Rough. Yes, he was rough, this man. He'd shown her to a brown Chesterfield upholstered with iron-hard leather, and sat opposite her on an identical one. His legs splayed wide apart, his eyes appraised her with a camel dealer's eye for flesh. The water seemed to have been forgotten. She'd felt herself flush deeply, looked around the room to try to quench the flood of desire in her belly. The penthouse was furnished with expensive, vulgar items, the property of an expensive, vulgar man. She was seized with a wish to flee to the lavatory. He directed her down a long corridor into a vast black marble bathroom. She leaned against a smoked plate glass window that framed a millionaire's night-time view of the Harbour Bridge, willing her pulse to slow, looked down to see a narrow trough at the base of the window. She jumped back when a sheet of water washed down the surface of the window, so that the trough was briefly flushed.

Surely not? An expensive, vulgar *pissoir.*

She found a smoked mirror, tugged a strand of hair into place, breathed deeply, and willed her pulse to slow.

Back in the lounge room, the man waited with a crystal glass of iced water. Zouzou gulped it down and spluttered some nonsense about a friend she had to meet. Kerry Rich sat back in his Chesterfield and stared at her with amusement as she fumbled her way out of the apartment door.

"Zouzou, you look unwell," Pierre said, jogging her from her reverie. "Can I fetch you something? Perhaps you can tell me the rest in the morning?"

"Thank you, I'll just finish the cognac. Now tell me how your evening went."

Pierre wrung his hands together. He was always the same, wishing to spare her unpleasantness. She was devoted to him, but there were times—more frequent these recent months—when she screamed inwardly for this man 'turned in on himself' to rip his shirt open, to shout obscenities, to get up and dance like a Hottentot, to pin her to the floor and make love like . . . she forced the leering Kerry Rich from her febrile brain.

"I have a matter to report, my heart," Pierre said. "If you wouldn't mind moving sideways a little, there's a document under the sofa cushion I must show you."

Chapter 8: An Invitation to Dinner

Kerry had the car radio up loud, tuned in to Max McNamara's talkback show. Now there was a bloke who could argue the socks off the left-wing dopes. Talkback was Kerry's favourite, especially when you got the do-gooders phoning in about refugees. Anybody could see it wasn't right that the government handed out free houses and dole to these people when there were honest Australians going without. Max had a way of tying the callers in knots till they lost their tempers. A true genius and a true Australian, was Max McNamara. It was ridiculous that they couldn't make him Prime Minister. Look at Cabramatta! It was disgusting that you never saw a white face there. The old Aussies in the area would call Max's radio show and tell him about the filth and crime and the monkey meat they sold in the market. He never lost his cool, Max. Always polite, just asking questions that brought out the right answers.

It was early afternoon and hot as buggery, especially with the roof down on the Porsche. He always folded it down if it wasn't raining. After all, the convertible had cost a motza, so why drive it with the lid on? But he'd left his New York Yacht Club cap at home and the top of his head was almost on fire. A genuine NYYC cap it was, not a replica from Paddy's Market.

Liz'd got her spoke in before he'd had a chance to confront her. She'd called him out of the blue, all businesslike, wanted to meet in a car park at North Head, had a proposition for him.

"Come alone," she said. "If I see anyone, I'm out of there quick smart."

OK, she had the advantage by getting in touch first. But he'd better bite the bullet, find out what she was up to, get it sorted out. He hadn't had time to check out the Liz Cruickshank story at the library, what with the resort and the bomb, so he'd have to play it by ear. Better watch his step. She could be a killer.

He pulled up at the lights by the Manly ferry, eased open the glove box to check. The gun was still there— his dad's old service weapon. For show of course—the old man had taken out the firing pin.

The road wound up the steep hill, past the Hospital and through an estate of Army bungalows. It flattened out to a long plateau of thick bush. It was hot as hell up here. Not an ounce of shade. He bent sideways and sniffed his armpit. Not so good. Where was that can of deodorant? Ah, got it. He pulled over. Two quick squirts and she's apples.

There was the yellow Veedub, parked facing across the harbour. Stunning, that's all you could say about the view, stretching from the high cliffs all the way to the Eastern Suburbs a kilometre across the water. His apartment block was over to the right, the marina dead ahead.

He parked the car twenty metres from the Veedub. Slipped the gun in his pocket, got out and looked around. No sign of her. He walked slowly through a tangle of weeds to a dilapidated brick hut, peered inside the doorway. It smelt of piss. His shoe caught on a mess of broken beer bottles and used condoms. Kerry turned back into the sunlight and there she was a metre away.

"Jeez, you took me by surprise." She was wearing a long dress, shades and a wide brimmed straw hat. Had him baled up against the hut.

"Hello Kerry."

"G'day. You'd better explain yourself, Missy."

She took a long look at him.

"Do you know who I am, Kerry?"

"Course I do."

Yep, a woman who might have shot the face off some poor cow having a snooze.

Her fingers opened the flap of a shoulder bag. His eyes darted down. He grasped the gun in his pocket. She took her sunglasses off and slid them into the bag. Green eyes. Steady. Calm.

"There was a reason I led you on, Kerry."

"You never led me on."

She gave him a mocking look, tipped her head slightly to one side. "You know I did."

"Yeah, alright, so what if you did? I was just going along with it." He was getting riled with this crap. She kept on looking at him with that steady eye.

"So why do it, Liz?"

"I had to get your attention, Kerry."

Bloody oath, she'd done that on the boat, lying around in the buff.

Enough was enough. He snatched her wrist with his left hand, gripped it hard. She stiffened. The green eyes widened.

"I know something that will change your life, Kerry. And you're hurting me. I'm not partial to men hurting me."

He let go her wrist. "What the fuck are you on about, Liz? I'm not partial to being dicked around by a bloody chick. If I want my life changed, I'll fuck'n change it myself."

There were tiny beads of sweat on her brow, a delicious scent of perfume mingled with warm woman flesh. But no fear, no anxiety.

He'd done hundreds of business deals and knew the signs of someone who was rattled—licking the lips, eyes darting sideways, bad breath. This chick might be hot, but she was as cool as a frozen daiquiri at the same time. She knew something, something dangerous.

And bloody hell, it was exciting.

"There's someone you need to meet, Kerry."

His mind did cartwheels. Maybe she had a twin sister? Now that'd be exciting. But he'd better play it cool. Better look nonchalant.

"What if I don't want to meet this person, but?"

She leaned in so their faces were almost touching. He felt the faint brush of her hand below his belt.

"You will, Kerry. Believe me." His heart battered his ribs. Sweat bathed his chest. His cock strained against the tight pants.

A car appeared around the bend and parked beyond the Porsche. A man got out and lit a cigarette. Another car drove up and parked next to it, woman driver. The man ground out the cigarette and got in the second car. The couple threw themselves into a passionate clinch.

"Are they with you?" Liz asked.

"Nah. Office romance, I reckon, the way they're getting it on," he sniggered.

Liz didn't react, just kept staring at him.

"What do you think I'm inviting you to, Kerry? " she whispered.

He croaked some dry sounds.

"It's something that'll turn your life upside down."

Enough was enough. A cock tease was one thing, but this was way over the top. Bugger her. He could play the old psychological caper if that was the game.

"Tell you what, Missy," he said. "I'll think about it." He slid into the Porsche and roared off, adjusting his tackle once he was out of her sight.

* * *

Raymond handed him an envelope when he got home.

"A gentleman delivered it."

"Did he give a name?"

"No, but he said you'd know who it was from."

"What did he look like, Raymond?"

"Well built, curly hair. Like a perm, maybe."

"A perm?"

"Yes, Sir, like Kevin Keegan."

"Who?"

"The football player. He transferred to Hamburg last year."

A perm. It must be Clem. Kerry slipped the concierge a five dollar note and headed for the lift.

In the privacy of the apartment, he ripped the envelope open. The message was pasted on with letters cut out of a newspaper, just like in some dopey spy film:

DAWN. ANZAC DAY. RADIO CONTROLLED.

Bloody hell. This was un-Australian, which the whole idea obviously. But The Impeccables must know what they're up to. At any rate, he could tell the immigrant what he had to do now.

The house phone rang.

"I'm sorry, Mr Rich. There was another letter. Will I bring it up?"

Kerry was knocking the top off a Dinner Ale when the doorbell rang. Raymond offered the letter on a silver tray, made a little bow—Kerry appreciated that—and slid away.

It was an invitation on posh paper—creamy with scallopy cuts around the edges.

Sir Robert McDougall and Lady McDougall have
the pleasure to invite

Mr Kerry Rich and companion

to

A Black-Tie Dinner to celebrate twenty-five years of
fundraising by the
McDougall Family Medical Research Foundation
8pm North Wahroonga Golf Club

Master of Ceremonies—Mr Max McNamara
RSVP

He stroked the soft paper, held the invite up to the light to see if his name was printed properly like all the other words. It was. Not stamped on afterwards.

Phew! Kerry Rich was going up in the world. Black Tie? He didn't have a black tie. But hang on a sec, didn't black tie mean something special? Raymond would know. He grabbed the house phone to ring the desk but stopped. The word 'inadequate' popped up. Wouldn't do to look inadequate in front of the concierge. Dictionary. Yes, there must be one among the books the interior designer had brought in. He ran his eyes over the titles in the bookcase. Yep, got one. Hadn't looked in a dictionary since he was at school, but it wasn't so hard. And there was the answer—'black tie and tuxedo'. Perfect! He had a fabulous sharkskin tux with a frilly shirt that he wore when he went to a casino.

'Companion'. Well, that'd take some thought, but she'd have to be pretty special to take his arm at a posh charity do. And very grateful, come to think about it.

Kerry grabbed another DA and spreadeagled in the recliner. Two contacts from The Impeccables in one day. He wasn't such a dill to think they weren't related. The invite was an encouragement, a little sign that he was doing OK.

Dad peered out of his picture frame. Maybe he was up there somewhere looking down and feeling proud of his boy.

The evening was drawing in. He had a poker game with some mates down in the Cross later. The New Australian had to be told the routine. Why not pop over to Manly, get it done now, and be back in time for a shower and change before the game?

The Datsun sat in the underground car park next to the Porsche. A tan 120Y, never dripped oil in its life, no rust, not a scratch on it—at least until the bikie had kicked it. Dad had looked after it like a baby. The scuff on the tyre from his argument with the wall at the Vita Wheat factory barely showed; no damage to the wheel rim. But, oh shit, there was a little burn mark on the front seat where he'd dropped the cigarette. It wouldn't rub away. He brushed the niggle of worry aside: Grow up, man. Your dad can't see it.

Kerry started the car and drove through the exit, finding a gap in the rush hour traffic, up through William Street and right onto the Bridge approach.

The Datsun chugged through Neutral Bay and in twenty minutes he was parking in a back street in Manly. He put on a beanie, pulled it down over his face. Here it was, Rialto Close, a scruffy cul-de-sac with a strong smell of marijuana on the warm night air. Nobody was around. The house numbers were all over the place— painted on a wall, tacked to a fence, missing altogether.

Yes, there was the New Australian's front gate. Nobody around still. He stooped to push the stupid cut-out letter into the mail-box, and stood up to go when the sound of singing stopped him. In the front window of the house he recognised the woman who'd come into his apartment the other night. She was wearing a black slip and singing to a man. The song made him shiver, like no singing he'd heard, liquidy, bendy, words he didn't understand. She stopped and the man turned so that Kerry could see it was the New Australian. The man pulled her towards him and kissed her, caressed her bare shoulders.

The bastard! The New Australian had sent his bitch to spy on him.

"Oy, who are youse stickybeaking on, yer perv?" A young woman in the next front yard flashed a torch in Kerry's face. "Piss off or I'll call the cops."

* * *

"It will take months, Zouzou." They were in bed, Pierre propped up on pillows with the bomb manual, Zouzou studying a *Practical Electronics* magazine. The neighbours had finally vacated the front yard and gone to bed.

"Hush, let me finish this section, Pierre. Oh, yes, I see how that works."

The bedside tables were piled with books and magazines from the Manly Council Library. Zouzou had spent hours among the shelves, looking for anything that might help them with the skills for bomb-making. The translated manual had taken her so far, but there were critical parts missing when it came to remote detonation. The problem was in the radio control, but Zouzou was making slow progress on the theory front. She always borrowed extra books on subjects like knitting and cake decorating.

"A precaution," Pierre had advised her, "against a librarian putting two and two together".

How had it come to this, Pierre wondered? A respectable married couple planning such an outrage? The Opera House bomb was surely an act of terrorism, however the pudding-faced civil servants at Ealing might dress it up. He'd seen their handiwork in Cairo and Malta, carried out their trash on the promise of a US passport. And where had it got him? Tricked into being dumped in Australia, and now back in Ealing's foul employ, no doubt with the local spooks aiding and abetting. These damned *mukhabarat*—Mossad, MI5, CIA, ASIO—they stole your loyalty, your honour and your integrity, and when they'd taken everything you had, they stuffed you in a corner to use again one day.

The ghastly fundamentals were clear: Mr Kerry had acquired a package of gelignite and some detonators. Somehow, the bomber—Pierre shuddered at his role— was supposed to throw a switch from some distance away to fire the detonator at dawn.

But why set off a bomb on Anzac Day? Pierre knew the facts about this date: It commemorated the Australians and New Zealanders who had died in wartime. Old men paraded with their medals all over the country, and dignitaries turned out for services at dawn. He'd read about the controversies—the veterans of Vietnam who wouldn't march because of the bitterness about Australia's involvement; women who planned to disrupt the march to protest about rape in wartime. He'd even heard the homosexuals were planning something. And why this obsession with Gallipoli? Why celebrate being defeated by the Turks, of all people? Yes, Anzac Day was just another odd-shaped piece of the jigsaw of Australia. A jigsaw that a half-Armenian, half-Coptic exile would take a lifetime to put together.

The words of his old mentor Major Ahmad Fawzi came back to him. Dear Fawzi, who'd perished in the bungled Cairo operation: 'Think like an Armenian, my boy. All the angles, sideways, upside down.'

Enough! Enough bitter thoughts and sentimental memories! Feelings got you nowhere in this world. Facts, order, logic, planning: These were the indispensable foundation.

Zouzou nudged him.

"Pierre, the solution is clear. We need to visit Dick Smith."

"I do not know this person."

"Ouf, you are so unworldly, Pierre. The idea came to me when I was watching some men playing with their toy boats in Centennial Park."

"Men with toy boats? What kind of men are they?"

"Hobbyists. Enthusiasts. They sail elaborate model boats that they control by radio."

"And is Mr Dick Smith one of these men?"

"It is a shop, dear heart, where they sell kits of electronic parts."

He gazed at her in wonder, as he had two years ago when she cracked a deciphered message sent between Ealing's agents. She was his true companion, his equal, his partner in all things. He took the *Practical Electronics* magazine from her and drew her close. They made love slowly and deliciously.

Afterwards, as they smoked, an idea occurred to him. He asked her, "Zouzou, can you make this bomb fail to explode?"

"I cannot be sure, but I will try, Pierre."

"And it would look genuine if somebody checked the mechanism?"

"Let me work on it."

"Then, that's what we will try to do—to fail."

"And what will happen to us, Pierre? When we fail in our mission?"

"Trust me, Zouzou."

He turned over and listened to the waves in the distance. Zouzou fell to sleep instantly. A worm of doubt wriggled deep in his mind, or perhaps in his heart. What was Zouzou hiding, and—the idea appalled him—could he trust her?

* * *

She was up early the next morning, bustling in the bathroom. He heard her banging the door above the vanity cabinet.

"Pierre, do we have any aspirin?"

"Try the sideboard drawer, *habibti*."

More bustling and puffing.

"*Maa feesh*. We've run out."

She crawled back into bed, rolled onto her side and hugged a pillow against her belly.

Pierre got up and started to dress.

"And Pierre, I need some, you know . . . "

"I'll be back in ten minutes."

There was an early opening pharmacy nearby. He revved up the Honda.

A strange country, indeed, where a wife asked a husband to buy her sanitary items, grown men played with toy boats, and you took your own kebabs to a barbecue.

Chapter 9: The Girl from Nordia

"I've got a statuesque Nordic beauty for you," Zelda had said. It wasn't the first time Kerry had taken one of Zelda's girls to an event as an accessory.

"Wide range of conversation", Zelda had said, "fluent in four languages", as well as "poised and discreet in elite society". How was she at brain surgery, he asked, but Zelda just sniffed.

See, he said to himself in the back of the stretch limo, I can appreciate a woman for more than just the pink bits.

But there wasn't much conversation coming out of Miss Krystal right now as they whooshed across the Harbour Bridge in the lovely long white Statesman. A cargo ship hooted somewhere down below them. The big wheel at Luna Park twinkled. To the right, the top of the bone-white Opera House sails peeped above a ship's funnel.

"Champagne?" He pointed to the ice bucket and the crystal flutes. He'd had a couple of refills already.

"If you don't mind, I'll wait until we reach the venue."

"Suit yourself." It was French, not the local rubbish. Her loss.

"So Zelda said you're from Nordia."

"Nordia?"

"Yes, Nordic, that's what she said you were."

"There's nowhere called Nordia," she said. "Nordic means something from Scandinavia. I'm from Chatswood."

"So, you're not a migrant?"

"Can't we just keep things businesslike? I prefer not to discuss my life with clients. It's not very professional. I'm sure you'd understand that."

Jeez, what a world! Even the chick from the escort agency thought she could backchat him. Didn't people know their bloody place anymore?

The driver jammed on the brakes, and Miss Krystal's handbag flew onto the floor.

"Sorry, Sir. Some idiot up ahead decided to stop in a hurry."

Kerry gallantly leaned over to pick up the handbag's contents. Actually, he was curious to know what was in there: Make up, purse, keys, condoms, and a book. *Advanced Statistics for Psychology.* He flicked the pages. Tables, columns of numbers, very long words. Christ, the woman was a bloody Einstein. Never mind—she looked like a zillion bucks, and that was all that mattered.

"Thanks," she said, replacing her property in the handbag. "That was kind of you."

"Come again?"

"That was kind of you to pick up my things."

Miss Krystal's words lit a dim lamp in Kerry's head. She'd spoken to him with—what was the word?—with respect. No woman ever called him 'kind'. He'd been called 'sweet' and 'generous'—as long as his wallet was open. But 'kind'? He was lost for an answer. He topped up his champers and lit a ciggie.

"If you wouldn't mind, Sir, not smoking in the vehicle," the chauffeur said.

"Jesus fuck'n Christmas cake! The world's gone mad," he muttered.

* * *

If Kerry knew one thing about working a room, it was remembering names. The trick was to take an extra second to listen when someone introduced themselves, take a mental snapshot of the face, and then repeat the name back when you answered. A last look at the face, and the name was imprinted for ever.

There was a line-up of meeters-and-greeters in the foyer of the North Wahroonga Golf Club, half a dozen blokes in tuxedos and their women in shiny dresses. Typical posh club: Glass cases full of silver cups, lots of varnished panelling, chandeliers. Kerry glanced at the Nordic beauty. She'd switched on what must be her 'poised' act. Perfect, just the ticket.

OK, first off the rank was an old bloke he recognised from the papers.

"Warren Hardington, Minister for Financial Regulation, and this is my wife Judy."

"Very good to meet you Mr Hardington and Mrs Hardington. I'm Kerry Rich, Chairman of the Rich Group, and this is my associate Krystal . . . " Shit, he'd never asked her surname.

"Krystal Blomberg, lovely to meet you." The old boy's eye glinted, and it was on to the next, a cop in a fancy uniform, also with a wife, a frightened-looking little scrap.

"Deputy Commissioner Peter Stackwell . . . " Wifey didn't get a mention.

And so it went down the line—a bishop, a company chairman, a bloke who owned a TV station, their wives all soaked in French perfume—until Kerry was face to face with Sir Robert McDougall, the top man in The Impeccables.

"Kerry, so pleased you could come. This is my wife Lady McDougall."

"You can call me Dawn, Kerry." Bloody oath, thought Kerry, an axe murderer dressed up like a Christmas cracker.

"Very good to see you again, Sir Robert. This is my associate Krystal Blomberg."

Sir Robert turned to greet the Nordic beauty. He opened his mouth to speak, but his face went stiff and turned a deep red.

"Are you alright, Dear?" the axe murderer asked.

Miss Krystal nudged Kerry in the ankle and hissed, "Walk". Sir Robert recovered and turned to the next guest in the line-up. Krystal shoved Kerry into the banquet room.

"What's going on, Krystal? Do you know him?"

"I know a lot of people. These things happen."

"Shit's happened. That's what's happened. Grab a couple of drinks while I go to the gents."

The toilets were empty. Kerry's first instinct was to put a boot through the stall door. Stone the fuck'n crows, the humiliation! I turn up with a posh tart on my arm, and she's already done a turn round the kitchen with the bloody host!

But no, wait. That was all arse-about. Who was humiliated even worse? Who had a guilty secret? The look on Sir Robert's face! Beetroot boiled in cat piss.

Winner, winner, winner!

He trotted back into the banquet hall, where he found Krystal surrounded by half a dozen salivating old blokes in black tuxes and white dicky shirts.

"Kerry, darling, you're back. Let me introduce you to these fascinating gentlemen. Now, this is Dr Zacharia. He's a plastic surgeon . . . "

She performed like a pro. Outclassed the lot of them. All Kerry had to do was nod and grin while Krystal fed the penguins. By the time a gong went to announce dinner, they would have eaten sheep shit on crackers if she'd told them to.

Kerry drew her aside.

"We've got a situation here, Krystal," he said out of the side of his mouth.

"I'm guessing you might be in the market for information, Kerry."

"Could be. We'll talk later."

A waiter led them to a round table with six places and about two hundred different knives and forks and spoons all lined up next to the plates. Kerry swallowed hard.

"Just work your way from the outside. Your bread roll's on the left," Krystal whispered.

Their fellow diners appeared, four well put-together blokes in the kind of tuxes you didn't buy at Gowings Emporium. Lots of fruity aftershave. The men checked the name cards. A bit of giggling. Sorted out who was sitting where. Introductions, handshakes. Kevin was with George, Martin was with Kumar. A right bloody mixture—a Singaporean, a Canadian, an Irishman and an Aussie. Must be a bar joke in there somewhere. They were all over Krystal like the measles, going 'ooh ah' at her shoes.

"Where are their wives?" Kerry said into his sleeve to Krystal, who rolled her eyes.

The clanger dropped.

He didn't have a problem with poofs—each to his own—but he'd have preferred some proper company, men with women. Women drinking a lot.

"Stay there, Krystal." He headed into the crowd to find someone to complain to, but his arm was gripped by none other than Max McNamara.

"You must be Kerry Rich. Let's catch up later in the evening. Where will I find you?"

Kerry pointed weakly at his table. Max waved at the poofs. They waved back.

"Oh, aren't you the lucky one? You'll have a lot of fun sharing the table with those boys. Off you go, better get sat down . . . "

A cymbal clashed and everyone stood up for the National Anthem. Kerry scooted back to his place just as the singing began. Krystal and the benders were belting out the song like Dame Joan, but he had to just flap his lips because he couldn't remember any of the words except for 'we are young and free'.

The music stopped, and Max jumped onto the stage in a dinner jacket covered in tiny mirrors.

"Ladies and gentlemen, never have I seen such an IMPECCABLE gathering on a Saturday night in Sydney. I'm profoundly honoured to open the evening by introducing the supremely IMPECCABLE patron of the McDougall Family Medical Research Foundation Sir Robert McDougall, and his IMPECCABLY refined consort Lady McDougall. Come up on stage so we can see you."

Sir Robert climbed up the stage steps with Lady McDougall, who had a backside like the nine-twenty to

Dubbo. Hubby wasn't looking too cheery. Kerry glanced sideways at Krystal. Cool, classy, doing him proud.

Hell's bells, there were some big shots here. Top cops, politicians, actors, fashion designers, doctors. Max called out dozens of them by name, pointing at them in pretend surprise when they stood up in the spotlight. Were they all Impeccables?

Max finished the roll call with a plea for everyone to keep their wallets open all evening, and he'd be back after the main course for the big presentation. Sir Robert led Lady McDougall off the stage, searching the room till he spotted Krystal, then looked away with his nose in the air. The band struck up with a guy crooning Sinatra songs.

As it turned out, the first part of the evening went well. The Irish guy had a huge stock of jokes, the lobster and champagne kept coming, and the Singaporean fellow ordered plates of hot chips with chili sauce, which everyone shared. Every ten minutes someone came around with raffle tickets for kidney transplants or whatever, at fifty bucks a pop. Krystal was drinking mineral water but everyone else was pissed as a fart.

The Canadian bloke turned out to be some kind of shrink, who reckoned Kerry might have an anxiety complex about having a small dick, and Kerry said no fuck'n way, I'll get the bastard out and you can measure it. No, the shrink said, it's to do with the distance between the tip of your nose and the top of the lip, and Kerry said you're having a lend of me, and he thought this one's not a bad bloke for a poof.

The Singaporean guy and the Aussie were practically sharing a seat, one hand each under the tablecloth, and they definitely weren't shelling peas. At the other tables, the noise was rising as red-faced blokes in bowties laughed their tits off and their wives yelled 'daahling' and 'you never did' at each other.

There was a lull in the Irish guy's jokes, so Kerry said he'd tell his top yarn. But first he had to satisfy himself about something while he had the table's attention.

"Pretty impeccable crowd, eh?"

"Lot of dills, in my view," the shrink said.

"They're not all impeccable, then?"

"What's he on about?" Kumar asked.

"So who invited you blokes?" Kerry asked.

The shrink chipped in: "Max of course. We don't know any of these tossers. We're the token gay boys. We get invited to lots of things. What about you, Kerry? And the delicious Krystal?"

"Come on gents," Krystal said. "You know what I do for a living. Mr Rich's business is confidential. Now listen to his joke."

Kerry began the story—the guy who came out of the corner shop and found his camel was missing. He was a good joke teller, got their attention, half-smiles on their lips. Just as he got to the end the cymbal clashed and the room went quiet.

He heard himself shout, "THEN THE GUY SAYS LOOK AT THE CUNT ON THAT CAMEL".

The punchline hung like a damp fart. Four hundred eyes searched for the culprit. Kerry slid down in his chair but it was no good; he'd been spotted.

Max McNamara leapt into action.

"Hey, that was my joke, Kerry. I was saving it for after dessert." Everyone laughed except Kerry.

A TV soap actress stood up and said, "I'll give you a hundred bucks for it, Max."

"I can feel an auction coming on," Max said, looking towards his fly, and they all laughed again. The bidding started, and within two minutes he'd sold the joke back to Kerry for eight hundred bucks. Everyone applauded him, so he stood up and clapped until Krystal tugged at his jacket and sat him down again.

A bloke in a dustcoat started bringing paintings onto the stage. Max auctioned them off in short order. Kerry bid for a landscape that nobody else wanted except the TV actress, and ended up paying a fortune for it, even though he knew he'd been done like a boarding school dinner.

The presentation ended with the dustcoat fellow carrying in a giant novelty cheque. Lady McDougall handed it over to a professor, who mumbled into the microphone until Max signalled a drum roll from the band and nudged him off the stage.

The night went flat after that. The band packed up, a tape of *I Can't Get no Satisfaction* started up. A few couples got up and bobbed around the dance area. Waiters brought desserts and coffee around. The Irish bloke was talking about where he bought his suits from but nobody was interested. The Canadian shrink grabbed a dame from the next table and wrestled her around the dance floor till she twisted her ankle. Krystal was talking to the Singaporean guy about some march for gay rights that was coming up.

Kerry turned around when somebody touched his shoulder. Clem, with his stupid perm. Where had he come from?

"Alright, Kerry?"

"All good, mate."

"Sure about that?" he asked, nodding towards Krystal.

"Never better, mate."

Clem gave Kerry a long look and walked away.

"Who's he?" Krystal asked.

"Just a bloke I know. I didn't know he was here."

"He was in the foyer watching the line-up," Krystal said.

"Was he now?"

"Do you want me to find out who he is?"

"What, are you a private eye on the side?"

"I like to find out who I'm dealing with. You never know when a bit of information might come in useful," Krystal said.

"Nah, he's nothing. No worries, darl."

But he'd have to watch that Clem. For now, though, he had to get Krystal up to the penthouse, pump her for everything she knew about Sir Robert, open up the safe, and count out a decent bonus for her. He wondered for a moment about a roll on the waterbed, but truth be told she wasn't his type.

* * *

When she'd gone, he lay back in the recliner to ponder Sir Robert's sins.

Once a fortnight with Krystal at a hotel in Parramatta, a place the posh git would never bump into anyone he knew. McDougall called himself Mr Ross, said his wife didn't understand him, paid in cash, usual crap you'd expect. Not very adventurous, Krystal said. No special requests. No toys. They never entered or left at the same time. OK, so the old bugger took precautions, but one thing was for sure; Sir Robert McDougall would never be able to look Kerry in the eye again.

The words of the shrink came back to him: Token gay boys. The phrase had just flown over his head, but when he gave it some thought it became clearer: The poofs had been invited for show, to give an effect, because they were different and interesting. They made Sir Robert and his mates look—what was the word?—tolerant, that was it. Come to think of it, there'd been a table of Indians and a table of Chinese. Were they tokens too?

But what about yours truly? He was different from these silvertails and their dahling bloody wives, no question. Was he the token rough diamond? But why would that be interesting? What effect had Kerry Rich made at the dinner? Rough diamond, all bloody right: He'd turned up with an escort, made a mug of himself and emptied his wallet.

No, there was something else here. Sure, they knew he could get his hands on explosives, but there'd be other Impeccables with the right contacts.

OK, turn it upside down, try to imagine what he'd do if he was McDougall.

The answer stared him in the bloody face.

Chapter 10: The Quarry

Liz lay flat on the surfboard and paddled into the waves. This was her drug. This was how she started her day. She stopped forty metres out and waited, facing the line of brown brick houses on Manly Beach where the morning sun made the windows flash and gleam. The sea mounded up behind her, she got her knees on the board, caught the crest and stood up to sweep across, racing to beat the collapse of the wave. For half an hour, Liz Lanzoni was a sea goddess, defying the ocean beneath her feet.

Afterwards, she sat outside the Manly Surf Club, watching the ancient sunbathers bag their spots for the day in the suntrap where the seawall made an angle. The day was heating up; it would hit thirty by mid-morning.

Her university friends had given up persuading her to move to Balmain or Glebe. She'd been tempted. These inner-city suburbs were Sydney's intellectual hub, the natural destination for university lecturers, writers, artists, left-wing politicians, gay activists. The old dockworkers' cottages were being snapped up for gentrification, and there were poetry nights in the pubs. Every week a new ethnic restaurant opened up. Every night there were dinner parties where you could find yourself sat between a trade union leader and a professor of anthropology on one side of the table and a lesbian poet and a gay priest opposite.

It was tempting but for one drawback: There was no beach. And even if there had been a surf beach on Darling Street or Glebe Point Road, Liz just didn't fit the mould of inner city intellectual, or any other mould really. She preferred to live life on the very edge, and she preferred men who lived the same way. That was how Andrew Cruickshank happened. That was how a string of other thrillingly disastrous men happened. Maybe that was how Kerry Rich happened.

Her career was the same. She didn't want to be just a journalist. She wanted to be the journalist who put important noses out of joint, the one who stuck her finger into the throbbing heart of corruption and graft. The one who could pull off a surprise nobody could anticipate. Like the surprise she had for Kerry.

Right now she was aiming to break a blockbuster story for *The Australian Examiner*, a piece that would put her by-line up in lights with the best and most notorious in the business. So far she'd given the paper enough crumbs to keep her on the payroll—a car insurance scandal, and a soap actor caught with his pants down. But she needed more, and Kerry Rich was the paydirt.

She strapped the surfboard to the roof of the Beetle and drove the five minutes back to her flat on Eastern Hill. It was Saturday and she'd set aside the morning to sort through her notes on the Kerry Rich story. She rinsed off the swimsuit, put on a sarong and filled the coffee plunger.

The second bedroom was fitted out as a study with one book-lined wall and a desk laden with notebooks and folders facing the window over Manly's little harbour. Opposite the bookshelves Liz had fixed four big corkboards that covered most of the wall. At the centre of the display was a 10 x 4 glossy photo of Kerry Rich.

Her editor Jock Shields had given her the original tip that Kerry Rich was worth looking into; the paper hadn't dipped its toe into the underworld for a while, and Rich had a bit of family history with one of the far-right nutjob organisations—maybe Liz could have a crack at it?

The print was surrounded by dozens of file cards, a few newspaper clippings, and photos that told a story of dodgy real-estate deals, money laundering, escort agencies and tax evasion. Liz had spent three months researching her quarry's background—his businesses, his associates, his family. She had to admit that a lot of the evidence of his dodgy dealings was pretty thin; Kerry Rich was too smart to leave a long paper trail, and his associates didn't exactly jump out of the Yellow Pages. Would the story stand up? Did she have enough for an exposé? *Seamy Secrets of Eastern Suburbs Millionaire*? No, Sydney had plenty of Kerry Riches; the place wouldn't function without them. She needed more than a cork board of half-truths.

She was on the point of confessing to Jock and getting her final paycheck when he phoned about a new source who he reckoned had the goods on the Southern Cross League; might be worth talking to, might not. See what he had to say, see if there was something in it.

The source turned out to be gold, so Liz codenamed him 'Nugget'. There was still a lot that needed independent corroboration before Jock would give it the thumbs-up, but she sensed that 'Nugget' was the real deal. They'd never met in person, just over the phone.

When she asked Nugget what he wanted in return for the information, he just said, "Nothing. It's personal".

What fascinated her about Kerry Rich was his politics: According to Nugget, he was a life member of the Southern Cross League, no less. Apparently, there were only half a dozen life members, most of them nut jobs who collected Nazi memorabilia or spent the weekends doing paramilitary training in the Blue Mountains. Kerry, Nugget assured her, was the unseen hand who refined the League's ideology and organisational strategy, the brains of the outfit. He was the one who identified prominent immigrants and Jews for targeting by blackmail or racist attacks. And his businesses funded many of the League's activities. A clever operator, pulling the levers and pressing the buttons behind the charade of a bent, blokey business tycoon.

The cork board display expanded with more file cards. But it was still mostly unsubstantiated or hearsay. She needed something more. Something with a sting in it. Should she discuss the dilemma with Jock? No, he'd given her enough slack.

The phone rang late one night when she was slumped at her desk about to chuck it all in. It was Nugget.

"I have some new information about our friend."

"Go on."

"There's someone you need to meet."

Liz scribbled down the information with shaking hands. Nugget rang off.

It was manna from Heaven.

All the bits were in place; they might be a bit wobbly here and there, but the combined impact was explosive. Jock would buy it.

Kerry had fallen for the 'accidental' meeting in George Street. She'd played him like a mug—or had she? The day on the boat had been a close-run thing; she could barely credit that he'd believed her trick with the fainting fit. But maybe he hadn't. The more she saw of him, the surer she was that there was more to Kerry Rich than the bluff, blokey image he projected.

* * *

Liz sat back and stared at the glossy picture of her quarry. Clever bastard! He'd put on a real professional performance up on the cliffs at North Head, looking confused and defensive like a puppy that had lost its bone, pretending to flinch when she reached inside her bag. She'd thought she blown it giving him the come-on, but he'd played along, pretending to drool over the vague promise of an orgy. Or was that bit real? Underneath the play acting he was just another man, after all. Another man whose brain was ruled by his cock. Funny, if his politics weren't so repulsive, she might have been attracted to him. She had to admit there was something about him, physically at least. Maybe he was wearing that pheromone spray she'd heard about.

The surprise she had in mind for Kerry Rich was unbearably delicious. He didn't have a clue what was coming.

Did he know who she was? He must have done his homework, but she hadn't detected the typical reaction when people knew she was Liz Cruickshank—wary respect. Or perhaps he'd disguised it with his confused act.

Nobody ever asked about the night of the shooting, and that was how she preferred it. Jock had been blunt about it when he'd taken her on two years ago:

"I don't give a flying fuck whether you shot that woman or not, but I'll give you some advice. Write yourself a good elevator pitch and stick to it."

"Elevator pitch?"

"It's Yank for your life story in twenty seconds. You say what you want people to remember about you."

"You mean something like *I'm Liz Lanzoni. I'm into writing and surfing?*"

"Bloody hell, Liz. What am I paying you for? What's the thing that makes you different from every other budding journo in Sydney?"

That evening she wrote out her elevator pitch and put it in a frame on her desk next to the photo of Andrew and her in Miami, learned it word for word:

Hi, I'm Liz Lanzoni. I was married to a murderer, but that's all behind me.

I went to uni, got a degree in English, and reinvented myself as an investigative journalist. Here's my card in case you have any tips.

* * *

"It will work, Pierre, I am sure."

They opened the roller door. Zouzou changed into overalls as Pierre took occupation of the only chair. He'd given up feeling useless in the face of Zouzou's astonishing technical competence. Unlike him, she'd immersed herself in the values and customs of their new homeland. If she was a woman of the modern world, then his duty as a man was to preserve the best of the old values, the standards that kept the world's compass set to true north.

Khara! Horse shit! He was a fossil, a man turned in on himself. His own compass sent him in ever-decreasing circles, and even a fool knew where that ended.

113

"Please close the door, Pierre."

He looked around before closing the roller door. The industrial estate was deserted at midday on Sunday. The white concrete apron hummed in the roasting heat. An ugly black bird *kaarked* accusingly at him. The Blue Mountains formed a shimmering line of soft grey humps far away to the west.

He watched her bend over the manual, which was interleaved with her own jottings. She arranged the tools on one side of the bench, various components on the other. A twist of smoke from the soldering iron in her right hand made a mineral tang in the hot air. With her left hand, she manipulated a delicate piece of wire in a pair of pincers. A silver bead of sweat sparkled on her upper lip.

"A cigarette please, my heart."

Pierre lit a Winfield and placed it in a tin ashtray next to her.

"And a drink, too, please."

He twisted open a warm *SevenUp*.

"Zouzou, I . . . "

"Yes? Ah, that has joined nicely. Now I will make two holes here . . . and here." An electric drill yowled, and tiny spirals of aluminium fell away from the holes.

"Swarf," she said.

"Swarf?"

"It is the metal waste from drilling and sawing, Pierre."

A fine thing, he reflected, to be given lexicographic instruction from one's bomb-maker wife.

"You started telling me something, Pierre."

"It was nothing." He'd meant to say he loved her, but the word was too bland, too simple, to convey his swirling feelings for her.

She worked with patient determination for two hours.

"Here, Pierre, plug the wires into this lamp. You see, the lamp will represent the explosive when we perform the test."

She lifted up the little aluminium box with protruding wires that would connect to the detonator.

She was a genius.

"And when will we test it?"

"Tonight?"

"Tonight, Zouzou? Why not here and now?"

"Because, my heart, it must be tested *in-situ*."

"I see." He didn't see it at all. She evidently sensed his puzzlement, and gently explained that the device must be tested where it was to be used. The range of the radio control device, for example, was unknown. The effect of tall buildings or adjacent bodies of water could influence the efficacy of the device. Yes, of course, he saw it now. And he saw that he wasn't puzzled, but indifferent—a man who had lost control of his fate.

"We move tonight, Pierre."

* * *

Liz stood up and stretched. Her back was stiff from crouching over her papers. It was lunchtime. The desk was still a disaster zone. She scooped up a pile of notes, and slipped them into a folder marked 'filing'. Time to head down to the ferry wharf to eat a burger in a shady spot before getting back to Kerry Rich.

A new angle on her quarry had come out of the blue, and not from Nugget. She'd tailed him to a warehouse in the south-western suburbs, where he met a man on a motorbike. A woman on a scooter seemed to be acting as a lookout. By chance, his new friends lived in a tatty flat just down the road in Manly. What did the *eminence grise* of the Southern Cross League want with these two? And what was in that warehouse? The motorbike guy hadn't been home when Liz visited; she'd try again over the weekend, spin some story, see what she could deduce. Probably nothing.

As for Kerry, she'd need to plan the meeting carefully. A hired room would work, maybe in one of the hotels on the Manly Corso, maybe two rooms so she could stage things properly and get the sound recording gear in place. The lure was the big question. Sex. Yes, it had to be sex.

The phone rang. She let it ring. It stopped. She pulled out a foolscap pad and started to work on a timeline for the denouement of Kerry Rich. Was that the word? *Denouement?* Yes, it had the right ring for *The Australian Examiner*. The 'Chardonnay and film festival set', Jock called the readership. The paper was a left of centre weekly offering progressive politics, book reviews, wine writing and exposés. The exposés were Liz's speciality.

Roget's Thesaurus lay on the desk, practically begging her to look up *denouement*.

Conclusion, finale, ending, it suggested. No, she needed something with a bit of edge. *Undoing? The undoing of Kerry Rich.* No. *The unmasking of Kerry Rich.* Now that had a good ring.

The phone rang again. She snatched the receiver off the cradle.

"Yes?"

"No need to yell, Liz." It was Jock.

"Sorry, boss. I was working."

"Well, I'm not paying Saturday penalty rates. But since you're hard at it, I've got something you might want to follow up concerning your little mate Kerry."

"Go on, Jock."

"You see, an acquaintance of mine was at a charity dinner last week—keen-eyed sort of fellow—and he noticed something funny going on."

"Funny peculiar or funny hilarious?"

"Bit of both, really. Kerry had a girl on his arm at this event, and when said mademoiselle was introduced to the esteemed patron of the charity, the gentleman went almost apoplectic."

"What gentleman?"

"Sir Robert McDougall."

"Never heard of him. Who was the girl?"

"An escort, apparently. That's all I have. Oh, the venue was the North Wahroonga Golf Club."

"Any chance I can talk to your source?"

"Have a nice day, Liz."

She leant back in her chair and looked down over the bay. The ferry was chugging in towards Manly, ten minutes till it docked.

Keys, notepad, pen, a bag of 20c pieces for the photocopier. Liz threw some clothes on, ran down the hill to the ferry wharf, and pushed through the holidaymakers disembarking from the Baragoola. She grabbed a seat on the upper deck, drumming her heel on the floor while the deck hands winched up the gangplank. The boat gave a jolly hoot and churned away from the wharf into the dancing waves whipped up by a south-easterly. In forty-five minutes, she'd be at the City of Sydney Library in the Queen Victoria Building, ready to grind through an afternoon of microfiche in the hunt for Sir Robert McDougall.

* * *

At 11pm, Zouzou dressed in dark clothing and slung the backpack over her shoulders. Pierre was already outside, waiting for the street to quieten. His backpack contained the radio control device and the UBD, with a paperclip around the map of the Opera House and Circular Quay. Zouzou stepped into the front yard. Pierre kick-started the Honda and she watched him drive gently to the end of the street. She would leave in ten minutes; if one ran into trouble, the other would still be in action. They would rendezvous in The Rocks in an alley near Argyle Street.

A bunch of drunks shouted a stumbling course past the end of Rialto Close. "Fuck you, fuck this, fucking fuck," they screeched. That word, it was on every lip. She imagined each tiny Australian struggling from the womb, piping "fuuuck" at its doting parents, who would exclaim "fuuuck' in delight that their offspring had announced its entry to the world in the proper style.

When the louts turned the corner, she eased the Vespa into the street.

She encountered no difficulties despite a flashing blue light ahead of her on Military Road: A gesticulating driver leant on his car arguing with two police officers. She caught a shouted snatch of "Fuck you," as she rode past.

The Harbour Bridge was almost empty. The nodding attendant in the toll box took her twenty cents without raising his eyes from the newspaper. Zouzou turned left to enter the streets that formed The Rocks, a scruffy knot of lanes huddled around the point where the southern pylon of the Harbour Bridge was rooted in the ground. Pierre had walked her around the area pointing out the historical features, the place where the early settlers had encountered the Aboriginals. She hadn't cared for the cobbled lanes, the mean slums and smelly pubs. A union leader, Jack Mundey, had saved the area from being turned into nice blocks of flats. *Mish ma'uul*, an Egyptian would have said: *Makes no sense!*

The alley off Argyle Street stank of stale beer. Pierre's Honda was parked behind a stack of aluminium barrels.

"Ready?" He was a smudge against the dark wall. She tutted 'yes' in the Egyptian style and set off alone on foot past the line of sleeping ferries. A few late-night revellers scuffed around the Opera House podium. A cargo ship crawling towards a birth to the west of the Harbour Bridge made a block of darkness against the lights of Kirribilli.

Zouzou ducked down, pulled the hood over her face, turned left past the last wharf and onto the road leading to the Opera House a hundred metres away. It took her just a few minutes to climb the steps and skirt the huge tiled sails until she reached the glass front of the restaurant. She squatted against the window, peering across the water to the dark clump of buildings at The Rocks, where Pierre hid. A train rattled across the massive span of the Harbour Bridge. A night breeze ruffled the water's surface, cooling her damp brow.

There it was. A dot of white light flashing three times—Pierre's torch: READY. She flashed back with her own torch. The prearranged signal meant that Pierre was to press the activator button in one minute. If the device worked, the lamp fixed to the detonator wires would glow orange, just as she had demonstrated at the workshop a few hours before. Zouzou turned to the glass window, crouched over the backpack, undid the zip so the lamp was just visible, and counted off the seconds in her head.

She got to fifty, and began to whisper the last ten seconds.

wahid wa khamseen

itneen wa khamseen
talata wa khamseen
arba'a wa khamseen
khamsa wa khamseen

"Oy!" The window was splashed with brilliant white light from behind her. She zipped up the backpack, which was now in deep shadow.

"Turn around." A silhouette behind the blinding flashlight. Zouzou blinked. A uniform? Police?

"What you up to?" The flashlight now probed the areas to her left and right. She could pick out 'Acme Security' on the man's shirt. He was a big man, swarthy, long overdue for a shower. He stooped to see her better.

"What's in the bag?"

"Nothing, Sir."

"Must be something."

"It is not something you would wish to see, Sir."

"Show me."

"You are sure?"

He nodded.

"It is my husband's head."

The swarthy man's jaw dropped to his neck. His eyes opened wide enough to pop out of their sockets.

"Here, Sir, see the blood, see his eye," Zouzou said, making to unzip the bag. She braced herself to perform the trick she'd learned in Beirut as a young actress at the mercy of lechers, young and old: In his confusion, she would rake the man's eyes with her nails, and drive her knee into his manhood as his hands flew to his face.

The light caught a flash of gold around the man's neck: A tiny *Allah* on a fine chain. She looked up to see that he was smiling. She hesitated.

"Say it in Arabic," he said.

Was he mad? "I don't speak Arabic, Sir."

"You do, lady. I heard you counting. *See the blood. See his eye.* Say it in Arabic."

He was definitely *magnun*. She should humour him."*Shuf iddamm, shuf 'aynuh.*" It slipped from her lips so easily.

"I knew it," the man said, continuing in Arabic. "I saw all your movies. That line was from *My Sister the Assassin*, the scene with the head in the bag. I saw it at the Rio Cinema in Bab El-luq in June 1971, no July. It's incredible that you are here. Zouzou Paris, here in Australia."

A fanatic. She'd met plenty of them in Cairo and Beirut.

"There are stranger things under the sun, Sir."

The man's earthy Egyptian speech, the memory of the open-air Rio Cinema, its floor littered with peanut shells, the lines from the film script: They hurtled her back to her beloved Cairo—*umm iddunya*, Mother of the World.

The man was still smiling, worshipping her with his eyes.

"Your autograph, please, for my wife you see." He already had a pen and notebook in his hand.

"What should I write?"

"Please, if you permit, write 'To my greatest admirers Bashir and Layla from Zouzou Paris'".

She began to write.

"And please add my mother and father . . . ."

"*Yalla* Bashir, I'm not writing *The Thousand and One Nights*." She scribbled and handed the notebook back.

He eased it into his pocket as if it were a gold amulet. A worried frown swept his face. He began to peer about.

"Lady, I'm sorry, but I must ask why you are here. It is my job, you see. I have a mortgage and two children, and I cannot afford to lose my employment. I am qualified as an agricultural engineer from Cairo University, but I have been waiting two years for my qualifications to be recognised. You see, my boss will be here in five minutes . . . "

"Bashir, can you keep a secret?"

"I would keep a thousand secrets for Zouzou Paris."

"I am here on location for a new film. I came here tonight to absorb the atmosphere."

"To absorb the atmosphere?"

"Yes, Bashir, we actors must experience the invisible vibrations of the places where we perform."

"Invisible vibrations. Yes, of course."

"May I go?"

"Go in peace, lady."

"And don't tell a soul."

"By God no!"

Zouzou hugged the shadows as she made her way back to The Rocks. It was the first time she'd been recognised in Sydney, even though she sang at least once a week at a wedding. But who looked at a common singer in a blonde wig when a young bride was the centre of attention?

Pierre emerged from an alley.

"Did it work, Zouzou?"

"There was a technical difficulty." Who could know whether the lamp had lit in the zipped-up bag? The devil take the fanatical film buff!

Pierre said nothing. She knew he was tired of this game. She knew he yearned to remain Kevin O'Donnell of Rialto Close, a man 'turned in on himself'.

Chapter 11: Warhead

After half a day of poring over dusty stacks and fuzzy microfiches, Liz discovered that Sir Robert McDougall was conservative, rich, and totally uninteresting. She recognised a prime specimen of *Homo Mosmanicus* when she saw one. After all, her parents belonged to the same species. Or had, until Dad's unorthodox business practices landed him in jail for ten years, and Mum retreated penniless to her family's redoubt in the Southern Highlands.

She'd been eighteen when the Mosman house was sold. A month after, the furniture was auctioned off, and the receivers took the Palm Beach cottage and towed the *Andiamo* off its mooring at Pittwater. She didn't miss her parents, but she missed that glorious yacht!

Saint Ethelreda's had let her stay on for her final term when the fees couldn't be paid, but her grades collapsed, along with her dream of studying journalism at university.

Liz was saved from homelessness when the lawyers told her an investment flat in Manly was registered in her name. She was saved from having to work for a living when she met Andrew Cruickshank. She wondered if Andrew and Dad ever bumped into each other in Long Bay Jail.

Sir Robert had lived an apparently spotless life: A school where they played rugby with a view over the Harbour, Law at Sydney University, and a clear run into a business career in McDougall Industries. He held a part-time commission in the Citizen Military Forces for a while. She made a note to follow this up later. This paragon of silvertail virtue married into a pastoral family who owned cattle stations as big as European countries. At sixty, there was barely a board or commission or worthy trust he hadn't discreetly sat on. Five years ago, Her Majesty had made Mr McDougall a Sir. There was a Lady McDougall, a daughter at Saint Ethelreda's, and a brace of spotless sons at the school overlooking the harbour.

But having an Imperial handle on your name wasn't a guarantee of spotlessness. Look at Lord Lucan. OK, she didn't anticipate Sir Robert murdering the nanny and sailing to Africa, but an embarrassing connection with an escort had to point somewhere. And right now, the signs led to the North Wahroonga Golf Club.

Back at her flat, Liz grabbed the Yellow Pages and dialled the number of the golf club. A sniffy functionary with a Pommy accent tried to fob her off but eventually revealed there had been a fundraising dinner for a Medical Research Foundation last weekend. Liz laid on a dollop or two of charm and soon had the old boy chatting. He was evidently at a loose end, up for a cosy natter. Did he happen to have been at the dinner? Oh yes, he was the honorary *sommelier*, wine being a hobby of his. The club cellar was exceptionally fine . . .

He was evidently settling in for a long detour.

"If I might ask, Mr . . . ?"

"It's Squadron Leader, Squadron Leader retired Giles Cracknell."

"I see. Thank you, Sir. Now did you happen to notice anything out of place, any strange behaviour?"

"Good lord, yes. A dreadful man turned up with a— well, not exactly a North Shore lady—and made a terrible racket at a table full of nancy boys, if you'll pardon the expression. I haven't heard such language since I visited the aircraftmens mess."

"Do you happen to know who the man was?"

"Yes, I checked his name on the list to suggest to the manager he should be barred in future."

"And the name?"

"Kerry Rich."

Liz hung up the phone and poured herself a very large vodka.

* * *

"Something for you, Sir. It arrived by courier." Raymond handed Kerry a big yellow envelope. The return address of the law firm in Cairns was splashed with water spots. It must be the signed contract for the resort.

Bloody oath, that was the wettest place he'd ever seen. But the vision of slashing rain and the poor little vendor with the varicose veins dissolved, to be replaced by the endless beach, the green of the cane fields, and the layers of luminous blues where the hills merged with the sky. He wondered vaguely if he could buy a painting of it. His mind wandered to a cane chair outside the manager's residence, a cold Fourex, a nice old wooden-hulled yacht bobbing at anchor, a girl in a very small bikini barbecuing prawns.

Jeez, if only! Meanwhile he was stuck here juggling a smart alec New Australian, a psycho girl reporter, and a bunch of upper-class drongos who wanted his arse on toast. On top of all that, he was due to pick up the detonators and explosive tonight from a mate in the Shire.

He made a coffee and went out onto his balcony. That view was the best cure when things got on top of him. The Harbour, the Bridge, the Opera House, the poor buggers working like ants down below. Yes, he told himself, he'd made it. A resort owner.

Kerry finished his coffee. Better have a quick look at the contract. He'd skimmed over it in Cairns, asked the solicitor to send him a copy and another to his own lawyer in Pitt Street. There was a covering letter: Dear Mr Rich . . . blah blah . . . pleasure to do business . . . blah, blah. And the contract. Leafing through it, he saw it was mostly legal guff, a site plan, certificates. He turned back to the plan to remind himself where the residence was. The land looked a tad bigger than he remembered it. His finger traced the boundary way beyond what he recalled till he got to a bunch of buildings marked 'crocodile farm'.

He went around the boundary line again. What?

It went right round the fucking crocodile farm.

He grabbed the phone.

"Wallace, Bisley and Associates. Judy speaking."

"Gimme Russell."

"That would be Mr Rich on the line, would it?"

"Too right, darl."

"Putting you through, Mr Rich."

Some screechy violin music played. The buggers always kept you waiting, charged you for listening probably.

"Kerry, Russell Wallace here. Funny you rang now. I was looking at a contract that just came in from Cairns. I see you've got into the aquatic livestock business."

"The what?"

"Crocodiles. Good move, ticks all the boxes—tourism, gourmet food, handbags. But you should've shown me the contract before you signed it."

"It was too good a bargain to wait, Russell. Motivated vendor."

"Looks like it. You got it for a song. But even a tiny mistake can bring you a lot of pain."

" So, the contract's all good?"

"There's just, hang on a minute." There was a long silence. "No, all good. You've signed, initialled every page, paid cash. Nope, all good. Nothing else I need to know?"

"Not a worry in the world, Russell, just checking."

Yeah, just checking what a dickhead he'd been.

"Fine then. Watch your step with those crocs, Kerry. They reckon the big ones can eat a grown man in two hours and not leave a trace."

* * *

Russell's comment about the digestive capacity of crocodiles sat in a corner of Kerry's thoughts as he went about the rest of his day. Over a pre-lunch rum and cola at Toni's Surf n'Turf at Bondi Beach, he dallied with the vision of the New Australian's legs disappearing into the jaws of a monster croc. Followed by Sir Robert McDougall.

"Miles away."

He looked up. It was his lunch companion, a fellow he was meeting about a venture into selling rare varieties of wine grapes, or more accurately, selling the rights to sell grapes, or not to put too fine a point on it, selling the rights to sell the rights. The commissions flowed back down the chain. Everyone was a winner.

"Huh?"

"You were miles away, mate."

"Sit down, buddy. What's your poison?"

"Lemon squash, Kerry."

"Whaaat? You off the sauce?"

"Doctor's orders, old chum. It's me blood pressure—up and down like a bride's nightie."

"Maybe I'll just stick to the one," Kerry said, finishing off the rum and cola. It wouldn't do to be driving home later tipsy with a bootful of explosives.

"Two lemon squashes, love," he said to a passing waitress.

Kerry did a lot of work in Toni's. Today was no different. By the time they'd finished the entrée—warm pork and veal pâté in pastry with kiwifruit chutney—there were half a dozen paper napkins covered in figures. When the girl brought in two New York steaks with chargrilled oysters and banana prawns on the side, they had the deal worked out.

Kerry took a clean napkin and wrote a number on it with a dollar sign in front.

"That's what we'll clear."

"Fucking 'ell, That's a motza."

"It's a fuck'n shitload."

"See, it's all about one upmanship," his mate said, putting on his managing director tone. "When you've got a renovated terrace in Paddington, a French car, kids at a nice private school, what's left? A stake in exclusive wine, something to brag about at the squash court, that's what. They'll be gagging for it."

"So just to be clear, what happens to the actual grapes? "Kerry asked.

"Huh? Oh, the grapes. Well they're more of a concept."

"Thank Christ for that. "I thought for a minute we were supposed to grow some fruit."

"Fuck that, mate! Anyway, in six months, we'll on-sell the business and move into something else. Macadamias, exotic puppies, game meat, whatever."

"Ripper."

* * *

Kerry had two more appointments. Well, the second was more of a surprise visit than an appointment. He took a cab from Bondi back to his apartment, picked up the Porsche and took an easy afternoon cruise down to the Shire.

The southern suburbs where he'd been brought up filled him with an uneasy mix of feelings. Nostalgia wasn't something that often bothered him, but the wide roads, the dusty palm trees, the names of the suburbs—Cronulla, Menai, Sutherland—stirred up a sludge in his soul. The fish and chip restaurants on Tom Ugly's Bridge belonged in his past. The well-to-do areas had no appeal; he wasn't interested in the yachts moored outside the mansions at Sylvania Waters. If he thought about his feelings, he might have picked out sorrow, regret, resentment. But he didn't bother; his Shire days were behind him, and he had a Porsche and a swanky apartment to prove it.

The bloke with the explosive materials lived in a fibro cottage in a dead straight street of identical dwellings. The heat beat down on the cracked concrete roadway. The odd dog limped in the shade of a fence, and the aircon boxes hanging out of kitchen windows throbbed a losing battle against the westerly sun.

The screen door of the cottage opened and a skinny guy shuffled out, dressed in shorts and a check shirt with the sleeves cut off.

"G'day mate. We'll go to me lock up."

"Hop in."

The explosives guy got into the car and Kerry followed his directions through a grid of straight streets, turning off into a weed-strewn lane that led to a small pig farm bounded by a wire fence. Beyond the fence was a scruffy paddock with a rusted-out Kingswood sunk up to its wheel arches in dried mud.

"Stay here. Open yer boot so I can chuck it straight in." The man disappeared behind a shed.

He was back soon with a package the size of a shoe box, wrapped in foam and gaffer tape.

"I said the boot, not the bonnet," he said.

"It's a Porsche, mate. The motor's in the back."

"Suit yourself, Kerry."

Kerry got out and wedged the package next to the spare tyre cover with a jerry can.

"What's in that can?"

"It's petrol. Jump in. I'll run you home."

"No worries, I need the exercise."

* * *

It was evening by the time Kerry drove the Porsche into Sir Robert's driveway in Mosman. Thank God he hadn't had a prang or been stopped by the cops. The stupidity of transporting the stuff in his car hit him the moment he left the pig farm. If he was honest with himself, he'd been a bit cavalier about the gelignite, a bit arrogant, the big tough guy everyone depended on to make the bomb work. All that bullshit fell in a heap when he hit the road. He'd been practically crapping himself.

He nudged the Porsche into Sir Robert's drive and parked half-way down. The Impeccables had strict rules about contacting members: You waited until you were summoned. Turning up at the top dog's house was definitely not within the rules. But they hadn't figured on Kerry Rich, the bloke who made his own rules when he was in a jam.

Someone had seen him: A twitch of a curtain, the easing of a blind. A figure peeped out of a door at the side of the house—a woman in a maid's uniform.

Kerry lit a cigarette and flicked the ash over the door of the Porsche onto the drive.

The maid approached. Asian. Filipino maybe.

"There is nobody home, Sir."

"I'll wait."

She scuttled inside. Kerry started up the Porsche and revved the motor loud enough to wake up the statue in the middle of the lawn. A neighbour parted the bushes on the boundary to stare at the growling car. Kerry gave him the finger and pressed the horn. This brought Lady McDougall striding down the path.

"You've no business here. I will call the police if you do not leave the property immediately."

"Where is he?"

"Where is who?"

"Hubby, who else?"

"Sir Robert is not available. He is a busy man. Please telephone his office to make an appointment. Good day to you."

Kerry got out of the car. The wife stood her ground. Hell's bell's, she was a big unit.

"Cut the crap, lady, and send him out."

At this, the woman burst into tears and ran back into the house. Poor cow, Kerry thought. The bastard sends his wife out to do a man's job.

Sunlight flashed on a window in a little turret on the upper floor of the house. Peering up, Kerry saw a face behind the glass. He walked around the car, calmly opened the bonnet, and peeled the foam covering from the package. The brown tubes were clearly marked 'Dangerous—Blasting Gelignite'. The upstairs window slammed shut. Kerry stood, legs apart and arms folded, waiting for Sir Robert. Thirty seconds later, the boss of The Impeccables strode down the driveway.

"What's the meaning of this?" He was sweating buckets, his ratty grey hair slimed down on his dome.

"Don't blow a gasket, old chum," Kerry said.

"Don't tell me what not to blow, you despicable, money-grubbing, low class swine."

"Well that's got things out in the open, Sir Robert."

"What do you want? Come on, spit it out."

The next-door hedge parted, and a voice floated across. "Everything all right, Bob?"

Sir Robert waved the neighbour away. The gap in the hedge closed.

"Well, Bob. I'm here to take out a bit of insurance."

"How dare you talk about insurance?" Sir Robert spluttered. "You took an oath of loyalty."

"Like bloody boy scouts, eh? Aren't your lot a bit old for that? Did you want to have a peep at the gelignite, by the way?"

The leader of The Impeccables forced his eyes to look at the deadly package. He shuddered and turned white, thrust his face into Kerry's and hissed, "you fucking bastard," thick spittle spraying from his lips.

"Jeez, your breath stinks," Kerry said. He almost felt sorry for the old prick. There was something pathetic about a man losing control, even if he was a conniving bastard out to use you like a doormat.

"Finished your tantrum, Bob?"

"Tell me what you want and get off my property."

Kerry looked around. The house had fancy brickwork, and maroon and cream tiles in the entrance.

Graceful trees surrounded the front garden, and banks of flowering bushes lined a lawn like a pool table.

A teenage girl ran down the path holding a dog's lead.

"Daddy, will we take Prince for a walk now?"

"Get inside for Christ's sake, Rosie." The girl stood, shocked, and ran back to the house.

"Nice place, Bob. Nice family. Does Rosie know about your girlfriend?"

Sir Robert ran a hand across his sweaty scalp.

"Just tell me what you want."

"It's simple. If you or your people harm one hair of my head, I'll make sure you're ruined. That includes your bum boy Clem, the one with the perm. Got it, Bob?"

The man stood rigid and purple-faced.

"I'm disappointed, Bob, disappointed I have to do this. I thought you were different."

Sir Robert's lips moved as if he was about to say something, then shut tight. Kerry locked eyes with him while he slid the gelignite into the wrapping and closed the hood.

He eased the Porsche down the driveway, hands trembling now after the exhilaration of the confrontation.

Now for a slow drive out to the warehouse to offload the warhead in the nose of his car. Very slow.

He meant what he'd said about being disappointed. He'd have had more respect for the old bastard if Sir Robert had squared up like a man, maybe even taken a swing at him, rather than calling him names. They could have had it out like men. Why couldn't he have told Kerry to get lost, threaten to break his legs? At least there would have been some honour. At least he could have pretended to have some . . . what was the word? Some dignity, some fucking pride. They could have parted with both of them knowing Kerry had it over him, but both of them keeping their pride. But the despicable wet dick had left Kerry feeling like shit, like a low-class cunt.

A car horn blared, brake lights flared in front of him. He stabbed the brakes, gritting his teeth, easing off so the Porsche stopped a centimetre behind a taxi. Bloody oath, he was getting too old for this lark. A side road appeared up ahead—the back way, just a couple of k's to go. He turned off the Parramatta Road and released a gigantic sigh.

Chapter 12: Chemistry

The southerly buster whipped across the parade of Norfolk Island pines separating Manly Beach from the road. It had been a furnace of a day, with the beach packed on a Thursday afternoon. The school holidays still had a week to go, and Sydneysiders were enjoying the final days of vacation before the city went back to work.

The violent wind change sent beach umbrellas skittering across the sand. Black clouds chugged out of nowhere, horizontal rain splatted the sunbathers as they gathered up their belongings and ran for their cars.

Zouzou crouched over the Vespa, stopping at the crossing by the North Steyne Surf Club while a gaggle of shivering bathers hopped across the road. She'd spent the last two hours in line at the Motor Registry waiting for a registration sticker and fuming over these Australians with their 'fair go' and equality: No skipping the line here, no way to slip somebody a little *baqsheesh*, no flashing of *kohl*-lined eyes to flatter a tired clerk. In Cairo, she would have been in and out in five minutes, escorted by a couple of the broad-chested men in aviator glasses she paid to look after her safety. That's if she hadn't sent a servant to get the job done.

She turned into Rialto Close. A shower, a glass of *karkady* and a cigarette—that was the priority. She'd planned earlier to pick up a makeshift picnic at the Greek deli in the Corso and take it down to the ferry wharf in time for Pierre to return from work; stuffed vine leaves, cheese pastries, *tahina* salad, roasted red peppers. They'd eat it on a bench overlooking the little beach, letting their taste buds transport them back to the Middle East. So much for that plan.

Zouzou parked the Vespa and took off the helmet. Her hair was a sweaty mess and her make-up was itchy with dust. If her fans could see her now! The southerly blew like a demon, spinning eddies of street dust and dirty scraps of food wrapping, rattling the windows in the tatty rental cottages of Rialto Close. But it would exhaust itself in an hour, giving way to a chilly shower.

Instead of dinner at the beach she'd prepare baked beans on toast, a delicacy they'd adopted in London. 'Low class food,' they both averred when they first tried it. 'Low class perhaps,' Pierre argued. 'But were not the Pyramids raised on a diet of horse beans and onions? Does not the most sophisticated Cairo theatre afficionado enjoy a late-night street dish of lentils and macaroni?'

She scratched her gritty scalp. There was a wedding scheduled for Saturday night, and she'd need to invest half of tomorrow in washing and ironing her hair. The local hair salons hadn't a clue. How could they, these skinny girls with thin blonde fluff that looked as if it'd blow away in a strong wind? A trip to a Lebanese *coiffeuse* in distant Lakemba was too unbearable in this weather.

And in any case, Zouzou had developed a niggling neurosis since the incident with the security guard that night at the Opera House. The thought of singing at a wedding provoked a watery wriggle of anxiety in her abdomen. What if she were recognised? What if she drew unwelcome attention to herself, a bomb maker?

But the thoughts were cut short by the sight of a woman on her doorstep.

"Hello, my name is Liz Lanzoni."

"And?"

The woman turned her face into the light. Good looking, dark-haired, but of course emaciated like all of them. A strong face, resolute. Zouzou's kind of woman. She reminded her of Emma, the English girl she'd been imprisoned with in a rusty ship moored off Malta in 1975.

"I'm Liz Lanzoni," the woman said, handing Zouzou a business card.

On the front was the name and phone number. On the reverse, it said *I was married to a murderer, but that's all behind me. I went to uni, got a degree in English, and reinvented myself as an investigative journalist.*

"A journalist married to a murderer?"

"Yes."

A brash one, this, with a stare that was a whisker short of impudent.

"Well, Miss. That makes a change from the Jehovah Witnesses. I think I might know who you are. Come in and have a cold drink."

* * *

Chemistry, Liz thought, was an overworked word. But she felt an immediate emotional attraction to the translator's wife. Zouzou, she said her name was. She had a bold eye, an expression that appraised without judgement, a woman not easily intimidated. There was arresting beauty in her face, the features intense, eyes dark.

"A murderer, you say?" the woman said, and peeled off a yellow plastic wind jacket to reveal a figure struggling to contain itself in tight gym wear. "Excuse me while I change. Make yourself comfortable."

Her English was formal and correct, but the accent heavy and deliberate. 'Comfortable' seemed to be rendered with at least five syllables.

Liz sat at a Formica table while Zouzou was in the adjoining room. The little lounge was neatly furnished—mostly second-hand judging by the mismatched pieces. On the coffee table was a scatter of magazines—she recognised *Paris Match*—they'd read it in French classes at school—and newspapers: *The Guardian Weekly*, *Nation Review*, and others printed in Arabic writing. She knew that Persian and Urdu used Arabic characters as well as Arabic itself; where was Zouzou from? The corner of another magazine peeped out. Liz slid it out an inch or two with a finger: *Practical Electronics*.

The sideboard and windowsills bore a variety of oriental-looking glass ornaments on lacy doilies. The sofas sported antimacassars. An alabaster figure of an Egyptian mummy stood on the edge of a chrome ashtray with a central button. When Liz pressed the button, the ashtray spun, releasing a whiff of stale butts. On one wall was a large framed poster showing a dense city with a great dome, minarets floating on a sunlit haze. Istanbul?

"It is Cairo." Zouzou came back in, wearing an odd baggy gown. Liz's mother's cleaner had had one just like it—a brunch coat, she called it. But Zouzou's was made from a fabric printed with pyramids and camels at zany angles.

"You're from Egypt?" Liz asked.

"I am familiar with that country."

"I went there once. I hitch-hiked from Australia to London when I left school."

"Whatever for?" asked Zouzou. "Could you not afford an aeroplane ticket?"

"Actually no. My father had just gone to jail and I needed a break."

That stopped the lady in the brunch coat in her tracks. She went to the kitchen and came back with two glasses of Ribena.

"Karkady."

"I'm sorry?"

"An infusion of hibiscus leaves. You have never tried it?"

"Maybe when I visited Egypt, but to tell the truth I spent most of my time there stoned or sitting on the toilet with the runs."

"What an exciting life you have had, Miss. When was that?"

"Probably the summer of 1971. Were you there then?"

"Yes, let me think. Oh no, I spent that summer in a villa in Beirut with the owner of a fleet of oil tankers. My job was to wonk him off—is that the correct term?—while he watched two manservants pleasure his wife. He would hold a revolver to my head as the men laboured at their duties." The brunch coat lady took an emery board from her pocket and filed a thumbnail.

Touché, Liz thought. "I think you mean 'wank'."

The woman looked up, mouth open, slapped her thigh and laughed.

"I believe I like you, Miss. Now what do you want? And why have you been following me?"

"Can I have some more of this drink, please?"

"Yes, please wet your dry whistle, Miss."

"I'm sorry?"

"Oh dear, my husband always says my English is so egregiously archaic."

Liz sighed. A slippery one, this lady. She'll run rings around me if I'm not careful.

"Your English is laudably proficient, not egregiously archaic. Will we get on with it, please?"

Zouzou shrugged.

"I wanted to ask you about someone called Kerry Rich . . . "

"You *wanted* to ask me? When was that, last week, last month?"

"Oh, I'm sorry. I *want* to ask you. It's just a thing we say—*wanted*."

"Excuse me, I am a mere foreigner. But I am curious still. Why do say *wanted* when you mean *want*?"

"Well," Liz explained, "Maybe just before I asked the question, I had the idea of wanting to ask you, and since that was before I said it, it was in the past by the time I said it." Liz stopped. The woman was taking the piss. Time to rewind.

"Never mind why I said I *wanted*. Can you tell me about your relationship with a man called Kerry Rich?"

"Why do you want to know?

"I'm writing a story about him for a newspaper."

"A newspaper? Where I come from, nobody believes anything they read in a newspaper. But if you insist on knowing, he is in business with my husband."

"What kind of business?" Liz asked.

"They repair motorcycles."

"I don't think so."

"Then we agree to differ, Miss Liz. I think it is time for you to leave." The woman searched the brunch coat pockets for her nail file and resumed work on her left pinkie.

Liz was damned if she was going to leave empty-handed.

"Before I leave, perhaps you can tell me something about Mr Rich. What's he like? What does he talk about?"

Zouzou looked up.

"Ouf, he is a boring grub, and I can tell you that I have no idea why my husband has relations with him."

"Look, Zouzou, I'm having trouble understanding where this conversation is going." That was an understatement. The woman seemed not to observe any of the conventions of a normal exchange of ideas. Acting friendly, playing dumb, telling outrageous anecdotes obviously designed to shock.

"Conversation?" The woman asked. "Were we having a conversation? I don't remember agreeing to have a conversation."

"But you asked me in for a drink."

"A drink, yes. That is a common courtesy where I come from."

"But you must have had something in mind when I came in?

"Must I? Oh, I see, a discussion about the meaning of existence? A *tête à tête* about our love lives? You see, I don't recall having any such idea in mind."

"So there's nothing you can tell me?"

"No. Why should there be?"

"Thanks for nothing." Liz said, getting up to leave.

"Miss Liz, some advice before you leave. You are stepping on quicksand."

"Quicksand?"

"You see before you an ordinary woman, a foreign wedding singer, married to a lowly courtroom interpreter. But I have lived a life you could not imagine. My husband and I have cheated death, been imprisoned, tortured even. We have been pursued half-way across the world by our Nemesis. You live a life of charm and ease in this innocent country. Why interfere in matters that will only bring you doom, when you can take luncheon with friends, and sip Campari in fashionable outfits?"

"I don't take luncheon, and I don't drink bloody Campari. You've got the wrong idea about me, and I think you know it," Liz said, getting up to leave.

The woman turned a languid eye in Liz's direction.

"I meant it when I said I like you, Miss Liz. We will speak again."

The southerly had eased when Liz stepped out of the Rialto Close flat. A soggy, cool breeze blew, laden with the allergens that had half of Sydney stricken with hay fever on nights like this. She stopped to sneeze, and was mopping her nose when the court interpreter passed her. The door opened and she heard Zouzou say something in Arabic, something angry perhaps.

Chemistry! Damn the woman!

* * *

"Pierre, she is dangerous and naive all at once. But we cannot shake her off."

Her husband lay back on the couch with a cold towel over his forehead. How thin he'd become in recent weeks, how pallid. Pierre had always been the active core of their partnership, the one with the strategies, the ruses, the carefully composed plans built on tiny observations, acute calculations, calculated risks. And Zouzou's place—as befit an Egyptian woman—was as his handmaiden, his assistant, the one who moulded his plans into workable solutions. She recalled the days in London when she had walked the streets of Kilburn on the hunt for a nest of Ealing spies; and when she had helped crack an enciphered message Pierre had given up on. Now her beloved had the air of a man defeated.

The awful thought occurred to her that she had emasculated her husband. The business of the electronic bomb controller was perhaps the fulcrum; in asserting her superior skills in building the device, the balance between them had tipped beyond the point of no return. And the latest disappointment over their infertility— well, was it a surprise that Pierre had 'turned in on himself' to the point where he was fading from view?

"What can we do?" he whispered, slumping his shoulders over his chest.

Zouzou's heart ballooned with sudden anger. She slapped his face but caught the outside of one eye with a sharp fingernail. Pierre sat bolt upright, mouth open, fingers feeling for the trickle of blood.

"You strike me?"

"I strike what you have become," Zouzou shot back, horrified at what she had done, but at the same time detached from the drama. What next? Break down in tears? Stare back in defiance? Say nothing? Walk out and never return?

She lowered her eyes and waited.

Her husband stood up.

"Come here."

She approached him, head still down.

"Look at me. What do you see?"

Zouzou said nothing. She raised her eyes.

"You see the man who rescued you from certain death in Cairo, the man who married you in France when we were fugitives, the man who held you in his arms when you lay burnt and bleeding from the grenade in Malta."

She waited for a moment and whispered, "I see half that man, Pierre."

He seized her, grabbed her hand and pressed it to his chest.

"Feel it beating, feel it. Is that the beating heart of half a man?"

"I feel it, *habibi*," she said. She pulled him close and placed her tongue tip on the blood where she had raked his face. He shuddered and slid his hand over her breast. But she had to lower her eyes again, not bearing to look into the eyes of a man she knew she could betray.

He let go her hand and walked to the open front door, looking into the dark front yard as if searching for an answer to an unasked question. The waves crashed in the distance. When he turned around, she saw that he was a whole man again. He rolled up his sleeves, went to the kitchen and came back with a bottle of wine and two glasses.

"Tell me your story again, Zouzou. She's a journalist, you say? And will you make us some beans on toast? With cumin and parsley if you don't mind."

Chapter 13: A Week in the Country

"It's just a week, *habibti*."

"I shall be bereft, Pierre," Zouzou said.

"Nonsense. And in any case, what can I do?"

He'd been putting off the training course for months—a week on a college campus far beyond commuting distance from Sydney. Everyone in the State Translation Office but a handful of stragglers had done the course. Pierre had been ordered to attend on pain of acquiring an 'adverse entry' on his personnel file—open to appeal of course, but nevertheless exposing him to the risk of not being a 'team player'. Work was a never-ending football game to the hearty public servants overseeing the fractious New Australians who did the actual work in the State Translation Office.

His Iraqi colleagues, the fellows with the PhDs, had returned to the office clapping their brows when asked how the course had been.

"We discussed weighty matters in groups and wrote the conclusions on butcher's paper," they said.

"What weighty matters?"

"Curiously, they dissolved like whisps of cloud shortly after we handed in our butcher's paper," said Hamdoun.

"Or like half-formed dreams," added Jassim, a well-known poet in his homeland.

"And how was the food?"

"There are no words in English, Arabic or Kurdish that would do it justice," said Hamdoun.

"Nor in Persian," said Jassim.

The wheels of the New South Wales government apparatus moved forward several cogs overnight. On a Friday morning, Pierre's office mailbox contained a rail warrant to a country town six hours away, and a form to submit *per diem* receipts within 7 (seven) days of return.

They had a gloomy Saturday at home. On Sunday they dined in Chinatown on yum-cha, which Zouzou found too oily. By Sunday evening, Pierre had sunk into the sofa with a novel, while Zouzou irritably ironed a week's worth of shirts for her husband.

"My dear, let me do that."

"No need," she sniffed. "By the way, what about— you know—the thing?" They'd taken to referring to the bomb plot as 'the thing', even at home when the chances of being overheard were minuscule.

"We wait for instructions. We have done all we can."

It was true. The controller and the bomb mechanism were completed, except for a proper test *in-situ*, although considering they had no intention of blowing up the restaurant, it hardly mattered. It remained to unite the apparatus with the detonator and explosive, which they presumed Kerry possessed. And of course to discretely render the whole device inoperable.

As she assaulted his shirts, Pierre reflected that a few days apart might do them both good.

* * *

Pierre waited for a taxi under the portico of the remote toytown railway station with its brick chimneys and lacy ironwork. The air was different here—dry and scented with something peppery and minty. A taxi arrived after half an hour, the driver making no bones about the inconvenience at having to work at his 'teatime'. Pierre was used to this odd expression: 'Having me tea' could range from a mid-morning cuppa and a scone to a foot-long steak at dinner time.

Pierre had slept through most of the six-hour journey, lulled by the interminable vista of grey woolly-topped hills He had woken up briefly at a town called Junee to see that they were in plains country.

The taxi dropped him outside a bleak college accommodation block made of prefabricated panelling. As Pierre stepped out of the car, he remembered the need for a receipt to accompany the *per diem* form, but his words were swept away as the driver sped off for his tea.

The hostel sat desolate among silvery gum trees and tough shrubs. A gust of hot wind blew a cellophane pie wrapper against his trouser wrapper for a moment until it fluttered off to rest in a sclerotic bush of the ubiquitous greyish green.

A notice in the vestibule listed room numbers against names. He lugged the holdall to Room 6 and entered to find a narrow bed, a student desk, a sink, and a miniature table with an electric kettle and toaster. His first reaction was embarrassment at intruding. It was obvious that the occupant was a male student who had gone home for the summer vacation. His personal items were untidily piled on the desk: Underwear, records, deodorants, boxes of chocolate, tins of fish, study notes, an empty packet of Durex. The walls were covered in posters of Che Guevara, shiny motorbikes, and women so naked as to make one gasp. The tiny sink held plates and cups bearing flecks of crusted food from their hasty rinsing.

Pierre hung his ironed shirts in a dusty closet, and sat on the bed. He took a smeared glass from the sink and rinsed it thoroughly before filling it and drinking. A movement caught the corner of his eye—a huntsmen spider the size of a plate scuttled behind the headboard of the bed.

His stomach growled. There must be some variety of catering. He went into the corridor and walked past half a dozen doors identical to his. From behind one came faint music, from another coughing. A door with a round window was marked Male Bathroom. The end of the corridor led to a dining area big enough for a dozen occupants. On a serving bench stood a glass-fronted electric food warmer with four or five pies on the top shelf and a metal tray on the lower shelf. A sign said, 'Course participant's self-service. Limit 1 (one) Pie per person'. Pierre slid one (1) desiccated specimen onto a plate with the edge of a large spoon. He eased out the metal tray and spooned a clot of rice next to the pie. The rice was mixed with flaked fish and dried-up peas. He sat at a table and poked at the meal with a fork.

"Not exactly appetizing, by the look of it." A fat man in his sixties appeared in the doorway. He was wearing a crumpled linen suit. Pierre shrugged in response.

"I am Marcos Tawadros, Liverpool Office. I do not think we have met."

Pierre choked on the morsel of food he had managed to ingest. An acid surge flooded his gullet. He looked down and muttered, "How do you do?"

The fat man plumped down opposite Pierre. He mopped the back of his neck with a handkerchief and put on a pair of thick-lensed glasses.

"Perhaps there is a restaurant nearby," the newcomer said without conviction.

"Perhaps." Pierre hunched over the plate, feeling the man's attention sharpen.

"No, it can't be." He switched to Arabic. "Pierre, it surely is you, brother. My uncle's cousin's son, your father a martyr for Egypt, may God bless his soul. And your mother, the Armenian lady, her name escapes me, how is she?"

Pierre was drowned in a torrent of emotions: The words in Cairene Arabic, the dimly remembered Marcos, the shock of discovery. But he must maintain his bogus persona.

"I do not understand what you are saying, Mister. I am Kevin O'Donnell."

"Look, there's a spider on your shoulder," Marcos said, again in Arabic. Before he knew what he was doing, Pierre peeped sideways. He was undone.

"All right, Uncle. It's me," Pierre continued in Arabic, "and as for my mother, God has taken her unto Him—in America."

The fat fellow uttered the formulaic response of condolence, and arranged his face accordingly. But Pierre caught the flash of an old memory in those porcine eyes. Marcos—the uncle with roving hands and a mean heart. The uncle you'd best steer clear of in case he'd fleece you. The uncle who borrowed from everybody—permanently. How had he got to Australia? Perhaps on the coat tails of a relative, the family reunion scheme.

But for now, what was to be done?

An idea sprang forth.

"Uncle Marcos, I'm going to let you into a secret, but first I need to understand where your loyalties lie."

"My loyalties?"

Pierre switched to English. "Your devotion to our adopted land, to this wide brown country , to . . . to mateship and the fair dinkum, and you know, those kinds of matters."

"Brother, I am a true believer, a devotee of Australia," Marcos said. "Egypt? It is the dust on my shoe." He mimed brushing invisible specks from his plump knees, perhaps the nearest he could get to his shoes.

"Then, I will tell you my secret, Uncle Marcos. I am an undercover agent for an Australian intelligence organisation."

The piggy eyes almost popped out of the fat cheeks.

"I am on a mission of the utmost importance to the Australian government. Kevin O'Donnell is merely my cover. You see before me Pierre Farag, an Australian patriot."

Marcos frowned, and then burst out laughing.

"Rubbish. You must have got here on a false passport. You're probably shitting yourself. I've got a good mind to tell the police."

"No, Marcos, no. I'm telling the truth."

Pierre's distant relative sniggered. "I can keep a secret, brother."

For a price, Pierre thought. For years of blackmail and extortion.

"You've got me by the shorts and the curlies, Uncle Marcos. What do you want?"

A conveyor belt of expressions passed across Marcos's face as if he were viewing the furling pages of a golden book displaying a cornucopia of gifts, a myriad of opportunities, and Pierre Farag on a skewer.

"Want? All I want is your happiness and ease. What do they say here? *No worries, mate.* Let's say nothing more about it," and here he made an extravagant wink, "*Akhuuya* Kevin."

Ahkuuya? You're no brother of mine, Pierre thought.

An awful idea danced around the edges of his mind.

"No worries, then, Uncle Marcos. Now, look, I could do with a good meal. I saw a restaurant from the taxi, just a couple of hundred metres back from here. What say we stroll out for a bite?"

Marcos's face worked vigorously, swinging between suspicion, appetite and pure guile. His digestive juices evidently won over the scorched fare in the hot food cabinet: "*Yalla, habibi,* is this a canteen or a crematorium? Lead the way."

The fat man was surprisingly nimble on his feet. They trotted out of the access drive and turned left onto a dark road. The sun had dipped under the horizon and was but a fading orange evanescence. Marcos pointed at some distant lights ahead and chuckled. Pierre turned and looked back at the student hostel. Lights on in some of the windows, but not a soul about. No chance of there being the kind of security cameras that were appearing in city streets. They may well have been on the dark side of Mars.

The sole occasion when Pierre had resolved to kill a man was five years ago in London. It was a damp Christmas Eve at Ealing Broadway station, and he had rehearsed the murder meticulously. His prospective victim was an Egyptian intelligence officer called Dimashqi, a man who had rendered unspeakable harm to Pierre and his family. Now a double agent, Dimashqi stood among a mass of Christmas shoppers on the edge of the platform, Pierre behind him with an umbrella readied to push the cockroach under the through train to Reading. Dimashqi was spared when Zouzou tapped on Pierre's shoulder; he turned to face her smile of pure sunlight in the grim fug of the underground station. When he turned back, Dimashqi was gone.

With the Egyptian intelligence officer, it was vengeance, justified by a tissue of arguments and propositions that Pierre spun together to ennoble the act of murder.

With this pathetic Marcos, it was pure survival, a rat's instinct to kill for advantage. It was statistics, probability; Marcos's longevity *versus* Pierre's.

The rural darkness soaked up light like a black sponge. The men stubbed their toes on unseen stones and twigs. Pierre shuddered when his hand brushed a thorny bush and the sticky whisps of some horror's nest.

He picked up a chunk of rock, clueless so far on how he would kill Marcos. The rock was a starting point, a fallback perhaps.

A gravelly strip indicated the edge of the road. Vehicle lights bore down on them from nowhere—no, not from nowhere, but from the crest of a hill up ahead. Pierre felt Marcos's cushiony form bump into him as his relative drew back from the danger.

"Take care, Uncle Marcos."

The fat man tripped and fell.

"My spectacles, my spectacles." He hauled himself to his knees and scrabbled in the gravel. "Help me, *akhuuya*, they are gone."

Another vehicle whooshed past in a blinding silvery blaze. Marcos was now on his feet, stumbling in circles. Pierre watched the dark human mass meander into the centre of the road, heard the pitiable bleating. He stood inert, unwilling to save the half-blind man.

The third vehicle was a roaring cube of lights, a truck as big as a house, a twenty-tonne ballistic slab hurtling towards the capering Marcos.

It was seconds away. Seconds when Pierre could have leapt out and crash-tackled Marcos onto the gravel. Seconds when he could have saved his life.

There was a gut-sickening crunch of smashed bones and exploding flesh. The truck's wheels locked. A screaming skid. A satanic liquid glimpse of red and white and smoking tyres.

Pierre backed away into the darkness, stooping behind a shrub. The truck driver fell out of his cab, stood in silhouette with hand on head, then bent over to vomit.

The walk back took just a few minutes. The scene at the hostel was unchanged. Pierre slipped inside and took his seat in the dining area where his pie and rice still sat.

He made eating motions, forcing crumbs of the cold food between his lips, trembling and nauseous, until distant shouts and a siren indicated that Marcos's demise was now a public matter.

At two in the morning, the police had finished with the course participants. The hostel was surprisingly full, each room disgorging a grumpy State Translation Office employee in pyjamas or dressing gown. They nodded to each other, keen to get back to their Greek novels or their stores of Chinese snacks. Was anyone missing from the group? Yes, the Assyrian interpreter said, the chap from the Liverpool office, Marcos something. The police checked the list on the door and made notes in their books.

Nobody had heard anything amiss. The police were close-lipped. An accident. A deceased male. Can't comment further. Next of kin to be informed. Pierre's interview with the police officer was brief. No, he had recently arrived and was enjoying his dinner along the corridor when he heard the siren. Mr Marcos Tawadros, yes, he'd heard the name, but Tawadros is common among Copts. He'd never met anyone with that name at work.

The remaining hours of Pierre's night were filled with supersaturated visions of the gristle and smoking rubber. He fancied he remembered glimpsing a bloody chunk of forehead with a staring eye attached. The more he pushed the image away, the more it forced its attention on him. He wept and laughed into the student's stained pillow, vomited in the sink, smoked, sweated, wished himself dead. In the few moments when he drifted towards sleep, the memory of the spider behind the headboard shocked him to wakefulness.

At six in the morning he gave up trying to sleep. Funereal birds wailed outside. He lifted the window blind to face a crowd of stock-still kangaroos in the paddock glaring at him in condemnation, and the flaming disk of hell's own sun rising in the sky.

Still trembling, he went to the Male Bathroom, where the calves of men at their morning ablutions—two brown sets and one white—were visible under the economically constructed toilet stall dividers. A shower with two coy colleagues in a communal room of six spouts shocked him awake.

By eight o'clock he was sat with ten other participants in a horseshoe of chair-desks in the Workshop Room. A toothy man handed out marker pens and butcher paper.

Pierre's heart was a shrivelled nut of horror and remorse. He yearned to see Zouzou.

The toothy man was talking.

"Good morning, I am Gerald, your facilitator." The fellow held up a toy kangaroo. "And this is Horace. Why don't we start with an ice-breaker?"

* * *

With a week of buzz groups ahead, he made a stone-cold decision to bury last night's event. For Pierre, whose survival depended on information, sorted and classified in multiple cross-referencing categories within the mind of a man 'turned in on himself', the death of Marcos was—he told himself—a mere fragment of information with its associated plusses and minuses filed in close proximity for retrieval if ever required. Preferably never.

The office had put on a demonstration of a 'database' recently. The staff sat at green monitors peering at white blips. "You're now logged on to the Univac mainframe," the instructor said in awe. "It can import thousands of pieces of data, search for them on multiple parameters, and store the results for ever."

Yes, this machine was not unlike the man 'turned in on himself'—a calculating device without a soul.

He made another decision: Never to tell Zouzou what he had done. Never admit to the woman who had once saved him from committing murder that he was now—on the balance of probabilities—responsible for a death.

"Pierre, what do you think of Clothilde's group's ideas?" It was Toothy, pointing to a sheet of butcher paper sticky-taped to the whiteboard.

"Admirable. A credit to her profession." He hadn't a clue what the discussion was about.

Clothilde, a French lady just past her prime, shot him a smile that was less than chaste. He looked away.

Chapter 14: The Rendezvous

Anzac Day was a month away. Liz pulled out some notes for a story she'd been working up—women students planning to crash one of the marches. But her contact had gone cold on her, wouldn't answer the phone.

The tip on Sir Robert McDougall had gone cold too. Probably just some crossed wires. So what if Kerry Rich went to a charity dinner and the host had a funny turn? It could have been indigestion. She didn't have time to waste on useless leads.

Kerry's big night was all planned. He'd taken the bait—the veiled promise of a romp at a hotel with Liz and a special friend.

"Special in what way?"

"In a way you'll never forget," she replied, making what she hoped sounded like a purring sound over the phone. She was hopeless at purring.

She knew it was probably illegal to secretly tape record the meeting, but the cassette would be backup in case something needed verifying later. Or if things got nasty. The recorder would be in the bedside drawer with a mike taped to the back of the headboard.

The hotel was booked from check-in at 2pm. Kerry was to meet her in the bar at 8pm. Her plan was to warm him up over a drink or two, then take him up to the room. She'd been into the city to buy a skimpy dress and a pair of porn-grade shoes.

The two mystery guests were due at 7pm. They'd be installed in the adjoining room with a room service dinner and free videos. She looked at her watch—5pm. Time to head for the hotel. She'd walk down in sensible clothes—a summer dress and flatties, and get changed into her seduction outfit at the hotel once the guests were installed. A last check of the wheelie bag, and she was ready: Outfit, notebook, camera, cassette player and microphone.

It was a fine evening—a Tuesday—with the day-trippers filing back along the Corso to ride the ferry back to Sydney for their trains out to the suburbs. The pubs at the beach end of the Corso had the ground floor shutters open, the regulars leaning on the windowsills sipping early evening lagers to loosen up a for a midweek skinful.

As she approached the end of the Corso, a woman caught her eye. It was Zouzou strolling towards the beach a holding a plastic bag containing what was obviously an outdoor dinner. She was wearing a European-looking skirt and blouse. A stylish foreign woman enjoying a stroll on a balmy afternoon.

Liz put her head down and veered left to overtake her, but the Egyptian woman—as if by telepathy—turned around.

"Miss Liz, please walk with me." No preliminaries.

"Oh, it's you. Look, I'm sorry but I'm on the way to a meeting."

The bloody woman completely ignored her objections.

"Join me for a picnic. My husband is away, so I am dining alone *en plein air*. And I wanted to speak with you more."

"Look, I'm just not free right now. What about tomorrow?" This must be some stunt. Maybe Kerry had put her up to it? But why?

"Perhaps after your meeting, Miss Liz?" Zouzou asked. "I have something to tell you. about Mr Rich."

"I'm sorry, I have to go." She half-ran, turning left towards the hotel on the beachfront where the rooms were booked. Whatever the woman had to tell her could wait. Or could it? She turned back, but Zouzou had gone.

* * *

Whatever sort of show Liz was putting on, Kerry was sure it was more than just a bit of nooky. But just in case, he had a packet of rubbers in his shirt pocket— some fancy ones with knobs on that he'd bought down the Cross, supposed to drive women insane. Be Prepared, that was the way. He'd been in the Boy Scouts for two weeks before working out that saluting and following orders was for mugs, but the motto stayed with him.

He was driving the Datsun tonight, dressed casually in tan slacks, a brown shortie leather jacket, and a paisley shirt. The parking area at the Queenscliff end of the beach was empty; a ten-minute walk under the Norfolk Island pines to the hotel. It was dark now, with a cool breeze off the sea tempering the heat of the day. The walkway beside the sea wall was busy with dog walkers and joggers.

Whatever Liz Lanzoni had in mind, he'd play it by ear. One false move and he'd be out of there quick smart. His fixer was already drinking tonic waters in the hotel bar, having tipped the barman to hold the vodka and hand him the phone if someone called Kerry rang down.

There was a phone box outside the North Steyne Surf Club. Not a bad idea to check things out. The barman answered and told Kerry to wait. The fixer came on.

"All good, Kerry mate?"

"Yep. What about your end?"

"Fillin' up here. Your woman went upstairs an hour ago. Haven't seen her since."

"Anyone looking suspicious?"

"Nah, mate. There's some fuck'n talent here, but."

"You're not there to size up the talent. Just keep your eyes on the job."

"Hang on, Kerry." The fixer must have put his hand over the phone. Jeez, he wasn't paying the dickhead to tell him to hang on.

"Sorry Kerry, some chick's all over me."

"What chick?"

"Dunno, mate. Lebo or something, big tits."

"Fuck's sake, get rid of her and get on with your job. I'll be there in five."

"Right-ho mate." The phone clicked off.

Five to eight. What was is they said about being on time? Fashionably late, that was what you were supposed to be. Bugger that. Whatever Liz Lanzoni was up to, he wanted to get into it A-S fuck'n A-P. Eight o'clock in the bar, she'd said.

At exactly eight, Kerry stepped into the lobby and scanned the bar area to the right. The lighting was low, the tables close, the air thick with cigarette smoke. There was the fixer, wedged into a corner. But who was the woman with him? Lovely arse, dress up to her thighs, black hair. The idiot fixer looked he was about to blow his stupid wad. The black-haired woman turned away from the fixer for a second. Shit! It was the New Australian's tart. What the flaming fuck? Was this some kind of trap?

He turned to scan the bar, and Liz walked in. Every pair of male eyes locked onto her. His free will melted away and he glided towards her like a cock-controlled robot.

* * *

Zouzou observed Kerry and Liz in the mirror behind the oaf with the tonic water. The fellow had been ridiculously easy to spot as part of whatever was going on in the hotel. After bumping into Liz in the Corso, she'd watched the hotel entrance from behind a pine tree, drawing on the surveillance skills she'd learned from Pierre in London. After noting the characters who entered the hotel, she hurried home, changed into one of her wedding singer dresses and splashed on some *eau d'* whatever was in easy reach. Now she sat in her finery, wagging her eyelashes at Mr Tonic Water.

Liz and Kerry were sat on high bar stools, heads close together, obviously engaged in some steamy conversation. Zouzou flicked her eyes away from the mirror to prise Mr Tonic Water's fingers off her knee. The man stood up abruptly. Had he clicked that she wasn't a bar floozy? No, he'd noticed that the couple had eased off the stools and were heading slowly for the lift. Liz had an arm around Kerry's waist; his hand was on her bottom. Kerry turned back for a second to look at Mr Tonic Water, giving him a wink. Mr Tonic Water gave Kerry a surreptitious thumbs-up, sat down again, and sized up Zouzou as if she was a three-course meal he'd like to get stuck into. Perhaps it was his break time now that the boss was busy.

"Don't go away," he warned and walked towards the gents with the hopping gait of a man with a full bladder. Zouzou slid his glass off the beermat. There was a biro next to the ashtray. '304' was written on the beermat.

She slipped out of the bar and crossed the road to take up surveillance among the trees facing the hotel entrance. Two passing men gave her a leer and a whistle.

* * *

Kerry squeezed up behind Liz while she unlocked the hotel door. By the way she was wriggling her bum, this girl was gagging for it. And hopefully her friend too. They stepped out of the lift. As the hotel room door opened, he glimpsed a woman sitting on the bed with her back to him. But hang on, she was old. And who was the old bloke sitting in the armchair? He turned to Liz, who was kicking off her sexy shoes.

"Hey, what's the game?" he yelled. It didn't make sense. Was it some kind of pensioners' sex party? You never knew what people got up to these days.

"Kerry, keep calm," Liz said, then to the woman on the bed, "Mona, say hello to Kerry."

The old woman turned and smiled.

Kerry clutched his heart. His ears rang. He rubbed his eyes, looked at Liz and back to the woman. The old bloke was beaming, just like the old dear.

Kerry broke down sobbing for the first time since he was a boy.

"Mum," he whispered.

Now his mum broke into tears. But what the fuck? His mum was dead. He looked closer. The woman looked like Mum, but different. He spun around and pointed his hand at Liz.

"What's going on, you conniving . . . "

But the old mum woman had him in a bear hug. She stank of garlic. He shoved her away.

"I'm your auntie Mona, Kerry. We're you're family. Say hello to your uncle Moussa."

The old guy moved in for a hug, and Kerry took a swing at him. But he was solid, this Moussa, built like a truckie, and just walked through the flailing fists.

"Calm down, mate." Kerry squirmed to escape the bear hug, but lost, clamped immobile by muscular hairy arms.

"That's better. Yer uncle Moussa's got yer. Now what's all the fuss about? This was supposed to be a nice meetin'."

The old woman and the old bloke looked at Liz.

"What's going on, Liz?" the mum woman asked. "Doesn't he know?"

"Know what?" Kerry roared. Liz stared back at the old folks.

"I wanted it to be a surprise," Liz said. "You'd better tell him, Mona."

The old bloke relaxed his grip. Kerry was back in control of his senses. He sat on the bed, but he could feel Moussa close by, ready to grab him again.

"I'm all fuckin' ears."

The mum woman knelt in front of him and took his hands.

"Your mother was my twin sister, Kerry."

"Bullshit, you're a wog."

"We're Lebanese. We were born there, came here when we were kids."

"I've heard enough of this crap. I'm out of here."

"No, just stay a minute. Look at my face and say I'm not your mum's twin."

Kerry gulped. It didn't make sense. He seemed to have lost the ability to move his legs. Some kind of shock, he thought, or maybe he thought he thought that. Fuck it, this was weird. Yeah, she was exactly like his mum.

"Can someone tell me what's going on?" His gaze swivelled from Liz to the mum woman and to Uncle Moussa.

The uncle guy gave him a glass of water.

"When she met your dad," the woman explained, "he had to hide it from his family that she was Lebanese. Your mum had to pretend she was an Aussie. His family hated immigrants. And our dad threatened to disown her if she went with him. The shame, you see. Especially since your dad belonged to that gang, that organisation."

"So why did she go with Dad if the family hated immigrants?"

"Isn't that obvious, Kerry?"

"No."

"They were in love."

Kerry slumped forward. Love, for fuck's sake. Liz pressed a glass of whiskey into his hand. He gulped it down. He was in one of those dreams where you can't escape from a room because the doors don't lead anywhere and your feet are sucking in wet concrete.

The old sister and brother looked none too impressed with Liz. They got up. The mum woman said to Kerry, "We'll get in touch when you've got over the shock. It wasn't supposed to be like this. I'm sorry. We're both sorry."

The uncle bloke glared at Liz. "You buggered this up good and proper."

When they'd left, Liz said, "I'm sorry Kerry, but all's fair in love and war."

"What's that supposed to mean, you crazy bitch?"

"Whoops, mind the language, Kerry."

"Or you'll shoot my face off? Is that what you'll do?"

Liz slid her hand behind the headboard of the bed and retrieved a small tape recorder. She shifted towards the door.

"Better than that, I'm going to tell the whole of Australia about how Kerry Rich, the top fascist in Australia, the leader of the Southern Cross League, is half-Lebanese. And if you've got any ideas about sending any of your thugs to my place, I won't be there."

Jeez, she was nuts. Top fascist? Like Hitler, was that what she meant? Certi-fucking-fiable. Off her rocker.

But that woman, his mum's double. Who was she? It was a shitting nightmare. He'd wake up soon. He stared at Liz and began to laugh hysterically.

The hotel door slammed and she was gone.

* * *

From her vantage point under the Norfolk Island Pine, Zouzou saw an elderly man and woman exit the hotel. She was sure they were a couple she'd observed entering earlier. They stood at the taxi stand, the man running his fingers through his hair, the woman mopping her nose with a handkerchief. Who were they? The woman had heavy hips and unfashionable clothing, flat clumsy shoes. The man's complexion was swarthy. He carried himself like a working man, in cheap casual clothes, a K-Mart plastic bag in his hand. Immigrants, they were immigrants—Turkish, Lebanese perhaps.

Next, Liz came out. The three briefly argued, and Liz walked away. The couple hung around, but after five minutes gave up on a taxi, and trudged away in the direction of the ferry. A few minutes after, the Mr Tonic Water came out. Zouzou shrank behind the tree as he crossed the road. He lit a cigarette and cupped it in his hand. Pierre had pointed out this method of smoking to her. "It often means they've been in prison."

When he'd sucked the last bit of nourishment from the cigarette, the oaf got into a big station wagon and roared away.

No sign of Kerry. Zouzou could go home and forget the entire episode. What would Pierre do? He'd wait all night under the tree ruminating over the evidence, sorting the pros and cons, calculating the odds of taking action against waiting for a new opportunity.

But Zouzou wasn't Pierre.

She crossed the road, entered the hotel and walked straight to the lift.

"Are you a resident, Madam?" It was a teenage bellhop with spotty cheeks, possibly a boy or perhaps a girl.

"I am the new hotel owner of this hotel. Take me to Room 304, then go to the lavatory and wash your face."

The lift dinged. Zouzou stepped in and stared straight ahead. The bellhop cowered, pressed a button. They ascended. The lift dinged again.

"What is your name?"

"Kim, Madam. Just turn right for 304."

"Thank you, Kim. And don't forget that grubby face."

"Goodnight, Madam."

Zouzou looked up and down the empty corridor. She tiptoed to Room 304, put her ear to the door. No sound.

She knocked.

No response.

She knocked again.

Nothing.

Was he in the room unconscious, dead? Had he slipped out of some back exit? Should she phone the management? Or perhaps make an anonymous call to the police? No, she had to know whatever truth had occurred this evening. And Pierre had to know.

"Madam?" Kim was back, pushing a trolley laden with suitcases.

"Ah, there you are. Do you have a pass key? I've mislaid my handbag."

Kim frowned.

"Madam, I need to check with reception."

"Kim, this is an emergency. I have a medical condition. I must take my medication in the next ten minutes. My syringe is in the bathroom."

Kim looked up and down the corridor.

"Our secret, Kim. I will not tell the manager."

The boy-girl unlocked the door and shoved the wobbling luggage trolley away at high speed.

The lights were off. Kerry stood on the balcony watching the night seascape. He turned.

"Who's there?"

Zouzou turned on the light.

"You. I might have known you'd turn up. Where's your husband? Lurking outside, I suppose."

"Away. In the country."

The man reached for a whiskey bottle on the balcony table, looked at it and put it down. The bottle was almost full. He was steady on his feet. At least she wasn't dealing with a drunkard.

"What do you want?"

What did she want? The question was meaningless. What you wanted was seldom what you got. Fate would decide what happened this evening, not what she wanted.

"I don't know what I want. The truth perhaps."

"The truth? Ha! What a fuck'n joke. I don't know what's true and what's not." His voice was bitter as funeral coffee. He turned and looked at the sea.

"What happened here this evening?"

"I met a ghost." The words were drenched in acid.

Zouzou stepped onto the balcony and stood next to him, their shoulders touching.

"Whose ghost?"

"Forget it. I was set up by a conniving journalist and a couple of out of work actors. They took the piss, threw me off—whatever—off course, I dunno."

"A journalist, you say?"

"Yep, the bitch lives around the corner."

When Zouzou was in a jam, her first instinct was to dissimulate. *Why tell the truth when an untruth will suffice?* she often told Pierre, whose own instinct was to keep quiet. But perhaps if she told Kerry she knew Liz—the journalist had to be Liz—this uncouth fellow would open up.

"I have met her, this journalist. Liz, she calls herself. She visited me, tried to learn my secrets."

"Did you tell her anything—you know, about the thing, the you-know-what?"

He'd skirted around 'bomb'. Perhaps he suspected a bug in the room.

"I told her nothing. She's a fool."

The man let out a huge sigh. His body slumped and he leaned his elbows on the balcony. Zouzou lay an arm across his back, squeezed his shoulder gently, not knowing why. He shuddered and exhaled again.

The night wind shifted with a rustle in the trees and a waft of sea-scented breeze.

"You know," he said, "I don't really know how to say this, but did you ever feel that all that mattered was the moment you're in, sort of thing? Like right now?"

Kerry Rich an existentialist? She'd enjoyed Pierre's Camus paperbacks. Perhaps he was a kindred spirit? No, just a simple man encountering a complicated sentiment. Better play along.

"Yes. It's normal. Everybody feels like that sometimes," she said. Of course she knew how he felt, the woman who'd lived a dozen lifetimes in one, the woman who'd lived under false names for years. To live in the moment was survival.

"Like, all the rest of it—the past, the future—it's all shit," he continued. "Like whatever you've done has kinda led up to this moment and it's all sorta . . . " He fizzled out.

There was something else needling him. He wasn't the kind of man who'd be easily conned, not a man given to pondering the meaning of life.

He stood up. Zouzou let her hand slip down to his waist. They continued to look out to sea. He slid a hand down to her backside. His fingers roamed. Zouzou could barely concentrate, but she had to know what irked him.

"Mr Kerry, has something gone wrong with the you-know-what? My husband and I must know. We have put ourselves at great risk."

"I don't know. Maybe, maybe not. I can't tell you right now." The voice had changed from plaintive to sly.

"When can you tell me?"

The hand explored more freely.

So that was how it was to be. A quid pro quo. There were times you had to choose at a fork in the road.

"You will tell me in the morning, Mr Kerry." She went inside the bedroom. He followed. She undressed and lay on the bed, knowing it was wrong and it was right. An act of love for her husband, perhaps. An act of betrayal, an act of madness?

Kerry stripped and crouched over her, a carnivore about to devour its prey. Zouzou pushed him off and straddled him. He grunted in surprise and flipped her back. His eyes were wide, his body hot and rankly fragrant above her. He groped with one hand for his crumpled trousers where he'd flung them on the bed, fished in the pocket.

"Here, I've got a rubber."

Zouzou snatched the condom and flung it over her shoulder.

"No rubber."

* * *

They woke several times during the night. He made love—if you could call it love—like an excavator. Each time he'd done shovelling, he threw himself off and went into a deep sleep. Once, Zouzou satisfied herself to the sound of his snores, and once she climaxed despite his inexpert pounding. She lay stock still on her back after each episode, imagining his hot fluid seeping into her depths.

She blinked awake at six with the easterly sun blazing through the window. She closed the blind and wrapped herself in a sheet, used the bathroom, and made a cup of instant coffee.

"One for the road?" Mr Kerry was awake now, making a tent under the sheet with his *zubr*.

Should she—just to increase the odds? She faintly remembered from the fertility clinic that a spent man needed time to regenerate his sperm.

"*Kifaaya ba'a.*"

"Wassat mean, darl?"

"It means enough. Please. I am sore."

He shrugged.

"We will never talk of this. It never happened. It will never happen again."

"Dunno about that," he said. "Bit of alright though, wasn't it? Any chance of a cuppa tea? I could murder a couple of them biscuits."

His melancholy of last night had evaporated. He was, she reflected, a simple brute, quite opposite to the intense, complicated man she had married on that damp afternoon in France. This Kerry's needs were basic, concrete, animal.

They'd both done what they needed to do. Now she wanted answers.

"The things we spoke about last night," she asked. The you-know-what. Tell me what is going on."

Kerry sat up and took the mug of tea from Zouzou. He wedged a whole biscuit in his chops.

"It's time for a bit of tit-for-tat." The words came out in a shower of biscuit crumbs, the jammy buttery smell mixing with last night's sweat. He brushed the crumbs off his chest hair.

"What is this tit-for-tat? Have you not seen enough of my breasts?" She knew the silly expression, but she needed to slow the conversation down, plan her moves.

"Nah, it means you tell me something, then I tell you something."

"I see. This is being 'fair dinkum Aussie', I suppose?"

Zouzou had a choice: She could stop now or continue. And the choice was Pierre's too. Her decision was her husband's decision—to learn of and absorb when he returned. She chose.

"What do you want to know?" she asked.

"Who you are."

"My husband and I used to be spies. We live here under false names. We thought we had been forgotten, until you came along."

"Spies? Don't bullshit me. You're terrorists, you're professional bombmakers. Your hubby barely blinked when I told him what he had to do."

"We have been called many things. And you, Mr Kerry, what are you?"

"I'm a patriot. I'm an Australian".

"Do patriots let off bombs in their own country?"

"If it's for the right cause."

"What cause could be so important?"

"To make Australia white, to get rid of the wogs who are ruining the country."

"I am a wog. Am I ruining the country?"

"You? Yeah, well you're different."

"How different?"

"I dunno, just different. I mean the ones getting the dole and free houses."

"Don't white people get the dole and free houses?"

"Yeah, well, if someone's down on their luck . . . " He stopped, apparently pondering something weighty, or perhaps merely light.

"You know I said you were different just now?" he asked.

"Yes."

"Well, it's like, you can meet a woman, and you know, sometimes it's like they're different and you don't really know why . . . " He turned to look into her eyes.

She had to stop this line of talk.

"You are right, we are terrorists, but we were not always so. My husband was a private detective in Egypt and I was a famous film star. We have been deceived and manipulated, and we desire nothing else but to live quietly, to have a family, to be forgotten by the world."

It was no good. His eyes were locked on hers. Perhaps a direct question would break the spell.

"Why did you choose Pierre for this job? I must know."

He got off the bed, still naked, went into the bathroom and turned on the shower.

"C'mon then."

Zouzou swallowed hard, unwound the sheet and stepped into the shower with him.

* * *

He wouldn't stop talking afterwards. But should she be surprised? In the end, what was a man but a bundle of hot urges draped in a delicate cloak of emotion? As Kerry Rich lay naked, bathing in the afterglow of his sexual prowess and fondling his testicles, the words came easily. Was this an unburdening, a kind of epiphany?

She listened, seldom interrupting. He told her about a chance meeting a year ago with a man called Clem in a bar in Kings Cross. He'd dropped his wallet, and Clem picked it up from under the bar stool. Kerry bought him a drink, they cracked a few jokes, had some more drinks. Kerry was meeting a few mates to drop into a strip club and then head back to his apartment for a poker game. The mates arrived and Clem joined the party. He had a lot of good jokes about the Chinese and the Aboriginals. The drinks flowed and the chat turned to the wogs ruining the country.

"Then what?" Zouzou asked.

"So the party broke up. Clem asked for my number. He said he knew a guy who might have a proposition for me, you know about the wogs and all that. Well, one thing led to another, and before long I'm a member of this secret club of high-ups who want to overthrow the government. I swore an oath, hand held up, blah blah blah."

" You swore an oath of secrecy?"

"Yeah, but I had my fingers crossed behind my back. I mean, just because you say something it doesn't mean it's true."

"You mean," asked Zouzou,"why tell the truth when an untruth will suffice?"

He sat up and looked at her.

"Jeez, you could have taken the words out of my mouth. We're a bit alike, me and you." His hand started to roam. She plucked it away and pulled a sheet over herself.

"Who were the high-ups, as you call them?"

"Oh yeah. So there's Sir Robert, the boss, big shot in business. There's some general, and a high-up in the police, a bishop or something, blokes who own newspapers, bankers."

"Does this club have a name?"

"Yes, The Impeccables."

"A curious name."

"Yeah, a bit of a laugh seeing how they turned out to be a pack of dirty bastards."

"So why did they ask you to join?"

He sighed.

"They wanted a fall-guy, a patsy. Fucking cunts. All they wanted was for me to get the explosives and carry the can."

"The can of explosives?"

"Nah, it's just an expression. Jeez, you're funny sometimes." He stroked her ear.

"And what of my husband and me? Where do we fit into this menagerie?"

"You get caught blowing up the Opera House and I go down with you."

She got up, wrapped herself in the sheet and stood on the balcony. Ealing's hand was clear to see, but whose arm was it attached to?

"You still didn't tell me why you picked my husband."

"Come back to bed." The man was making frog eyes and licking his lips.

"By God, Sir. I am not your breakfast. Answer my question." She'd raised her voice. His eyes widened. She waited.

"Just for a cuddle."

His brain had gone soft. Better humour him.

"I will not take off the sheet."

"That's fine."

"I will lie with you, then."

She lay rigid next to him. His arm wound chastely around her shoulder. He bent across and kissed her gently on the cheek.

Maa shaa' allah. The dreadful man had fallen in love with her.

"Now tell me why you picked my husband."

He rolled over and gazed at her.

"You know, I've never met a woman like . . . "

Zouzou placed her forefinger on his lips.

"We will speak of this later. Just tell me why you picked Pierre."

"I didn't. He was chosen for me. By that bastard Clem. If I ever run into him, I'll tear his balls off and stuff them down his throat."

Now, Zouzou thought, we are getting somewhere.

Chapter 15: The Palace is Unhappy

It had been a disaster. Liz's ears burned as she walked back up the Corso. She gulped air, trying to clear the buzzing in her head. A drink, she needed a drink. The New Brighton was packed but she squeezed through the crowd to reach the bar.

Two straight vodkas later, her mood had shifted from panic to defiance. The dirty little criminal could go to hell. His dimwit aunt and uncle could take a walk. OK, so there was nothing she could use in her story, no tearful revelation, no long-lost hugs of joy. How stupid she'd been to imagine it would ever work. But she'd get the little shit one way or another.

Her head was a bit wobbly, and she nearly toppled off the stilettoes when a mob of drinkers surged past her.

"Yer won't get far in those, luv." It was a smelly old woman with a shopping trolley full of greasy plastic bags.

"Mind your own business." She wasn't going to be told what to do by a dero.

The pain from her twisted ankle and the agony in her cramped toes crystallised her thoughts.

Jock would fire her if he found out. Entrapment, illegal recording, no corroboration. Kerry had looked stunned when she mentioned his fascist credentials. Had Nugget spun her a fake story? The uncle and aunt had been just too pat. Were they imposters? No, Kerry broke down when he saw the woman. Or was he faking it? Had she got it all wrong? Had it all been too easy, too preposterous?

'Impulsive and hasty', that's what they'd said about her in her school reports. 'Imprudence will be her downfall.' The story of her life.

She took the shoes off for the last hundred yards of the walk home. The warm pavement under her feet and the balmy evening air revived her. She'd have a cold shower, sit down, go through her notes, figure out a strategy. Her key turned in the front door lock. The entrance was lit by the heavy alabaster lamp she'd lugged back from Bali. Two surfboards leaned against the wall in the entrance. Thongs by the front door, nice scent of patchouli in the air.

She went into the kitchen and turned the light on.

What the hell was that on the table? A parcel wrapped in birthday paper and a bouquet of flowers. Its presence didn't compute, didn't make any sense for a moment.

Ah yes, her neighbour Margie must have brought it in; they knew where each other's spare keys were hidden. But hold on—who delivered parcels and flowers in the middle of the night? Interflora, that was it. Didn't they deliver flowers 24 hours a day?

There was a card on the parcel. Liz opened it: 'Just a small gesture of appreciation for all your work, Jock.'

Phew, that made sense. You never knew what to expect with Jock—a Gorillagram on someone's birthday, six pink donuts on your desk when you arrived at work.

She tore the wrapping open to reveal a shiny metal lid, picked the thing up and tore the last bits of paper off. It didn't look right, a metal box crammed with wires and brackets and—what the fuck—something with 'Dangerous—Blasting Gelignite' printed on it.

"Don't worry, it won't go off. I've got the battery here."

Liz spun around. A big man stood in the doorway. He had a head of lush curls and a smirk on his face.

"I was just looking at the wall in your study. You've done a good job on Kerry Rich."

She knew in a flash from the voice that this was Nugget, her informant.

"You bastard." What was his game? Her heart hammered, her mind galloped.

"Get that thing out of here before I call the cops."

"That? Nothing to do with me. Your little wog mate and his wife made it. Maybe you've been looking after it for them."

"What?" The buzzing in her head was back. Her legs threatened to collapse. She lurched to the sink and threw up.

"Better now? Why don't we sit down and have a chat?"

"Fuck off and take that thing away. I said I'll call the cops and I meant it."

The man settled into a chair and put his feet on a beanbag. The creep had a self-satisfied expression, as if he knew something she didn't. Which of course was the fact,

"Y'know," he drawled, "these old houses are full of nooks and crannies."

"What are you on about?"

"That nice little stash of heroin you've hidden."

"Stash? I don't do heroin." She stopped, felt her shoulders slump. "You've got it all sewn up, haven't you? Listen, I've got connections. Do you know who I am?"

He chuckled. "My name's Clem, by the way. Yep, I know you used to be Liz Cruickshank. I know about your connections. I know your reputation—much overrated in my opinion by the way. But I've got connections that make your ex-hubby's mates look like Blinky Bill. By the way how's your dad?"

"My dad?" This was going from bloody awful to intensely bloody egregious.

"You hear terrible things about what can happen to people in jail."

She felt herself slide off the chair. Not Dad. She wasn't close to him. He was a shit if the truth be told, but no, she couldn't bear the thought of someone stabbing him in the kidneys with a sharpened toothbrush handle.

"Up we get, then." Strong hands lifted her under her armpits, plonked her back in the kitchen chair. He rummaged in her fridge and came back with a bottle of apple juice.

"Drink this. The sugar will help clear your head."

She drank the soothing juice in a single draft. He was right. Things were crystal clear. Her informant was a brute—of what variety, she wasn't sure yet. OK, time to play things cool.

"What do you want from me?"

"It's simple. I want you to write the story of your career. You're going to be famous."

* * *

It was ten-thirty at night. Clem was finishing off his bacon sandwich. He was starving, he said. It would take a while to explain, he had to eat first. The taste of vomit in Liz's mouth sat unhappily with the smell of bacon.

"Want a bit? There's another rasher in the fridge."

She waved a silent 'no' at the hefty man with the ridiculous curls, her informant Nugget, *aka* Clem. The throb of a disco party floated up from the town.

"Ever heard of Harold Wilson?" he asked, wiping his hands on a tea towel.

"Course I have." What was this? A lesson in British politics? Come to think of it, Clem did have a British edge in his voice. Or maybe he was from Adelaide; South Australians sometimes sounded a bit fruity.

"Did you know they planned a coup against him?"

"Who did?"

"Various people. Lord Mountbatten, Cecil King."

"The newspaper baron?" Liz asked. She'd never heard of any coup. And with royalty involved? Definitely not.

"I only mention it because it seems implausible, but it's true. I mean, if it happened in the UK, it could happen here." He sounded educated for a thug. Maybe she should play along with his weird game.

"Of course it could happen here. We had the Rum Rebellion," she said.

"And what about Whitlam?"

"Well, there were stories about the CIA engineering the dismissal. Where are you going with this? Is this connected with Kerry Rich? He hasn't got it in him to stage a coup."

Clem laughed. "He's junior league. No, it goes much higher up the chain than Kerry Rich."

"You're kidding me. Are you saying there's a coup being organised?"

"Go and get a notebook."

She hesitated. "Are you pissing me around?"

He took a squat torch battery from his pocket, the kind used in big flashlights.

"If I put this back into that device and cross a couple of wires, you and I will be hardly fit for dog food. I'm not pissing you around, Liz. I'm deadly serious. I'll make you a cup of tea while you get your stuff."

He placed the mug of tea next to her and splayed his fingers on the kitchen table. Liz took a lined foolscap pad and pen from a drawer.

Clem took a long swig of tea and cleared his throat.

"The story starts a year ago. Your mate Sir Robert McDougall's up in Canberra on business and he has dinner with a Liberal MP. The MP happens to bring along an old school chum of McDougall's who's now a Major General. Are you getting this all down? Ah, good girl, you can do Pitman's."

"I'm not your bloody shorthand typist and I'm not your good girl. What are the names of these luminaries?"

"All in good time. Anyway, the three get chatting about the state of the world and before long they all agree that the government's soft on almost everything."

"But it's a conservative government . . . "

"Not conservative enough for this trio—too close to Asia, big on multiculturalism, maybe some crypto-Republicans among them, that kind of thing. So while they're on the after-dinner mints, the MP drops a little bombshell about something he's heard from The Palace."

"Clem, let me stop you there. All this may be true, but there's something missing."

"Missing?" he asked.

"Yes, like who the fuck are you? You break in, put a bomb in my house, make yourself a bacon sarnie, and start telling me about the Queen. If you were me, wouldn't you be a bit curious?"

"Me? I'm like you, Liz. A seeker after the truth."

"Bullshit."

He sighed. "We're both grownups, Liz. Let's just say that I take my orders from a big office block in Canberra. We're on the same side."

"Some sort of spook, then?"

"I couldn't comment on that. Can I go on?"

She nodded. What the hell? She was in a room with a bomb. But something was off-key with this guy. He wasn't a public servant type, and he wasn't a criminal. She'd never met an intelligence officer before, if that was what he was.

"OK, tell me more."

"Righto. Now, the MP says certain individuals in the Palace are unhappy with what's going on in their old colony and have hinted that a change of direction would be welcome."

"You mean a change of government? What about the next election?"

"They're interested in something slightly sooner than the election. Meantime, our MP has been busy sounding out others—an archbishop, a newspaper owner, several police officers with scrambled egg on their peaked caps, a top military figure, businessmen . . . "

"You can't be serious. We don't do that sort of coup in Australia."

"Don't we? You already mentioned Whitlam. And what about Harold Wilson in the mother country? If it's good enough for the Poms, it's good enough for us, wouldn't you say?"

"I need a drink." Liz took two glasses and splashed vodka in each. She topped them up with cola. "OK, keep going."

"I'm not supposed to drink on duty, but thanks. So where was I? Oh yes, over the last year, this crew have formed themselves into a clandestine organisation called The Impeccables, and they've decided to stage an event that'll shock the nation. They'll then remove the PM, the cabinet, the Governor General and the head of the armed forces, and replace them with an emergency administration."

"And your people in Canberra have been watching them . . . "

"Exactly."

"And you've infiltrated them . . . "

"You're getting the hang of it."

"And what's the shocking event?"

Clem nodded in the direction of the bomb.

"Two Arabs are going to blow up the Opera House," he said.

"What the fuck are you on about?"

"What I said. Two Arabs are going to blow up the Opera House."

Liz sat back. She sloshed another shot of vodka into the glass.

"What Arabs?"

"You know them, Liz. They live down the hill."

"Those two? And where does Kerry Rich fit in?"

"He's the Arabs' controller."

Liz leaned back in the chair and looked at the ceiling. A border of plaster moulding—ornate flower shapes—ran around the edges. She focussed on the fluid design as her mind solved the equation Clem had set. She sat up straight and looked him directly in the eye.

"Let me get this straight, then, and no bullshit. You're telling me Kerry's Arabs will blow up the Opera House and The Impeccables will blame it on his Southern Cross League?"

Clem nodded.

"And Kerry's a member of The Impeccables?"

"Yep."

"But wait on, you're not actually going to let them blow up the Opera House?"

"Of course not. We'll arrest the Arabs at the last moment . . . "

"*We* being your friends in the big building in Canberra . . . "

"Yes. And then we'll arrest The Impeccables and put them on trial for treason."

She downed the vodka.

"And what happens to Kerry?"

"He'll get arrested too."

"This is crap."

"Suit yourself, Liz. I'll be out of your hair." He started to get up.

"Wait, take that thing with you if you're going."

Clem sat back in the chair.

"Liz, it's not crap. Everything I've said is true. Can we just rewind?"

She was in too far to back out. And the bomb still sat on her kitchen table.

"OK, so why am I writing the story? Why me?"

"Liz, we've been watching you. We've been feeding you the stuff on Kerry. We've seen how you can dig into a story. The North Wahroonga Golf Club, for instance. We'll have you behind the one-way mirror while the

Australian Federal Police are interrogating Kerry and the Arabs. You'll write the story and it'll be broken in the *Australian Examiner* the morning after the bomb attempt."

"Why not break it in *The Sydney Morning Herald?* And what about my editor Jock?"

"The *Herald* won't touch it. And Jock's on board with the plan. Why do you think he referred me to you in the first place?"

"And when is all this happening?"

"Anzac Day, Liz."

The One Day of the Year. It was crazy.

"And what about the names of The Impeccables?"

Clem unfolded a typewritten list. She scanned the names. The cream of the bloody Australian cream. Her skin went cold. He snatched back the list.

"Are you in, Liz?"

"Do I have a choice?"

"Not really." He looked at his watch. "I'll be off then. Thanks for the sarnie."

"Don't forget your bomb."

Clem put on a pair of plastic gloves on, picked up the box—covered in Liz's fingerprints of course—and slid it into a plastic bag.

"And the heroin you hid?" Liz asked.

"Like I said, these old houses . . . " He slipped out of the front door.

Chapter 16: Loose Ends

Pierre stepped down from the train at Central on Friday evening, sticky and exhausted from the journey. The countryside had seemed interminable, the suburban sprawl infinite. As on the outward journey, the hotbox carriage spent more time marooned between stations than in motion.

He hauled his suitcase down the steps to the City Circle Line and stood in the hot fug of the underground station. When the train came, his eyes were drawn to a spinning eye at the centre of the front wheel, and he forced himself to look away. The train rattled its way through Museum and St James to Circular Quay. The Manly ferry chugged away just as he reached the wharf; time to sit quietly for half an hour and prepare himself for Zouzou.

Would she detect the change in him? He'd left an innocent man, returned an assassin. The picture of the slaughtered body of Marcos Tawadros filled the spaces between conscious thoughts. He'd barely eaten all week, living on cigarettes and International Roast at the training facility. The mirror in the Male Bathroom showed a face that became greyer and gaunter each day. The glances of the French lady Clothilde had changed from interest to distaste.

He sat on the outside seats of the ferry among the office boys with their drip-dry shirts, swigging from beer bottles hidden in brown paper bags. Their chat was from an alien planet—Rabbitohs, Sea Eagles, Kingswoods, Little River Bands. Pierre ached to sink without trace into their free-wheeling affability, the comfort within the innocent skins they'd been born with. But he was doomed to be the lost remnant of some cosmic accident: Half-Armenian, half-Coptic, an outcast of uncertain name and shaky nationality. And now, a killer.

But he had learned one thing in his adopted city: The ferry ride from Circular Quay had a peculiarly restorative effect. Within ten minutes, his heart began to sing, the blood ran fast in his veins. The crossing at the Heads was heavy, and the captain steered the ferry directly into the waves. The office girls shrieked, the outside passengers were soaked with spray. At the last moment, the captain chose a gap in the rollers and gunned the boat hard to port so that it lurched inshore atop a huge wave. Pierre clapped and cheered with everybody else.

Zouzou was waiting at the wharf. They embraced.

"*Habibi*, you're so thin," she said.

"Ugh, the food was dreadful. I existed on coffee alone."

"But you survived."

"I did, but one of the course members was not so lucky. He was killed by a truck." The memory of the event made his stomach lurch, but it seemed prudent to mention it in case his wife had seen a news report.

"How upsetting. Did you know this person?"

"No. But let us put it out of our minds. I am home."

"And what about the course, Pierre. Was it as awful as you expected?"

"Even worse, but by Friday I was developing Stockholm Syndrome and weeping as I farewelled my captors. And you, let me look. You are positively sparkling. My absence has done wonders."

He could keep up this banter all night.

"Now what has been happening with our friend Kerry Rich?"

"Let us buy some fish and chips, Pierre. We'll take them home and speak about it after we've eaten."

* * *

Zouzou cleared the plates in the kitchen at Rialto Close. Pierre lit a cigarette.

"There has been a development," Zouzou said.

"A development. Shall we have a nip of something while you tell the story?" It would be a long night. Zouzou seldom recounted her news with alacrity.

She fetched him a glass of Armenian cognac. He sat back to listen.

"Two nights ago, I happened to bump into the journalist woman in the Corso."

"You mean Liz?"

"Yes. She was in a hurry and brushed me off. I followed her to a hotel on the seafront, where she entered, followed by Kerry Rich a little later. I hid under the trees opposite, suspecting some foul play. After a few hours . . . "

"You spent a few hours under the tree?"

"Yes, but if you don't stop interrupting this will take all night. Where was I? Yes, after a few hours the journalist woman came out in different clothes— dressed like a prostitute. She had an argument with an elderly couple—possibly Egyptians or Lebanese, or perhaps on the other hand Greek."

"Dressed like a prostitute? Then what?" Pierre sipped the cognac. The story was positively galloping along. Presumably this was merely the prologue. Zouzou continued.

"Well, if not Greek, from somewhere in the region. At any rate, the three dispersed, and within five minutes Mr Kerry came out looking worse for wear."

"Drunk?"

"Drunk as a Chinese chicken. And very unhappy."

"Did you speak to him?"

"Yes, my heart. Well, when I saw him so glum I thought there must be a story worth learning about. But a drunken man needs special attention and so I acted in a sympathetic and cautious manner—just like in *Mad for his Love* when I played a psychiatrist in a prison for psychopaths—and escorted him to a bench on the seafront where he began singing like a starling."

"And what were the words to this song?"

"He confessed that he had joined a terrorist group who want to overthrow the government."

"And the bomb is to be the catalyst for the overthrow?" Pierre said. "We could have guessed that."

"Exactly. But they have double-crossed him. Liz is involved but I don't know how."

"Who double crossed him, Zouzou?"

"I'm coming to that."

"And who were the immigrant couple?"

"He didn't say. But the name of the person who double-crossed him is Clem."

"Clem? And what did you find out about this Clem?"

"Nothing. The songbird clapped its beak shut and left."

She'd found out nothing about Ealing's man in Australia? For that must be who Clem was.

Zouzou, yawned, stretched.

"Is that it *habibti*?" Pierre asked.

"Yes, that's all. Oh dear, it's getting late."

Pierre had a long shower to wash away the grit and sweat of his long day. When he came to bed, Zouzou rolled away from him. He came closer but she tensed under his touch. Had she sensed the ghastly thing he had done on that God-forsaken country road? Had she seen the horror in his eyes?

Or was she hiding something?

* * *

The next morning—a Saturday—found Pierre in a lively mood. As he smoked his first cigarette of the day in the front yard, a clear plan laid itself out before his inner eye. It was as if his brain had magically reordered its jumbled contents overnight. Come to think about it, last night's sleep had been deep and dreamless. Had his brain cells been silently studying the contorted maze and discovering an escape route? Had Zouzou's 'development' flushed away the sense of defeatism that had dogged him in recent weeks?

The *overarching* (this was currently his favourite English word) *issue* (he loathed this pauper of a word), yes, the overarching issue was Ealing. As he had said to Zouzou at the beginning of his entanglement with Kerry Rich, he would 'stick the paddle up their arse'. He intended to remain Kevin O'Donnell of Rialto Close, not be shunted to some new exile—or even worse, to be imprisoned as a terrorist. Damn their British arrogance.

With Mr Clem now part of the drama, Kerry Rich ranked as a minor character—a character who had befallen a crisis of his own, if Zouzou's sketchy tale could be relied on. The two priorities were crystal clear: To sabotage the bombing, implicate or even eliminate Clem and Kerry, and return to Rialto Close unnoticed.

Of course, there were loose ends: The problem of Liz needed to be eliminated.

"Coffee, *habibi*." It was Zouzou. She put the coffee cup down, squeezed his arm and went back inside.

He raised the cup to his lips and shuddered as Marcos's spinning remains flashed inside his mind. The Marcos he had assassinated at sunset.

He checked himself: Had he just considered eliminating those who stood in his way? Had murderous intentions formed themselves unbidden? Had the man 'turned in on himself' morphed into an automaton capable of unsentimental killing?

No, his moral core might be tarnished, but he was not a murderer. Not quite.

"Zouzou."

"Yes, *habibi*?" His wife stepped into the front yard.

"The object, the you-know-what—have you worked out how to sabotage it?" He spoke quietly in Arabic.

"Not yet. I've tried various means but I can't find a solution that wouldn't be noticed."

"Is there an art supplies shop in the area?"

"You are taking up painting, my heart? Or calligraphy perhaps?"

Pierre dashed inside and came out flicking through the Yellow Pages.

"Here, in The Rocks. It's Saturday. They'll be open until midday. Where's my crash helmet?"

* * *

Zouzou parked the Vespa behind Kerry's warehouse and waited for Pierre to wobble into the yard on the

Honda out of sight. The industrial estate was empty but for a van parked outside a concrete block building in a side alley. The door barely took the edge off the rock band practising inside.

The wailing of electric guitars was reduced to a muffled background in the warehouse. Zouzou caught a memory of a dance floor in Soho three years before, when she coaxed the 'man turned in on himself' to jerk and shimmy with a crowd of late-night dancers as a rock band bashed out songs quite alien to his eastern sensibilities.

And now, they were sneaking around a grubby warehouse, concealing their secrets from one another, staring at a padlocked steel box.

The box contained the bomb and its remote control, the bomb Zouzou had constructed.

"Wait," Pierre said. He examined the padlock closely. "Someone has opened it, I'm sure. When I locked it last, the padlock was the other way around."

"What do you mean?"

"The lettering on the padlock was facing outwards. Now it is facing inwards."

"And the tools, Pierre, they have been moved slightly."

They looked around. No other clues were evident. Pierre shrugged and emptied the contents of his backpack on the bench: Plastic moulding clay, sheets of art paper, acrylic paints, glue.

He opened the padlock and peered in the box.

"Look closely, Zouzou. Is it all in order?"

"Stand back, *habibti*. If someone has tampered with it, it might be booby trapped."

"Then we will meet our maker together," she said. He stayed put while she played a torch over the device.

"It looks intact as far as I can see." She gently lifted the bomb from the box and placed it on the bench, then unscrewed the base of the casing and gently prised out a stick of explosive. Pierre scrutinised it minutely: The cylindrical bulk of the material, the wrapping paper, the lettering.

"Light please." He rolled up his sleeves. Zouzou switched on the inspection lamp in its plastic holder, hooked to a girder.

"Cigarette please."

"Perhaps later, Pierre."

"Good thinking."

Zouzou watched her husband at the intricate work. He'd told her how as a private investigator in Cairo, he had become skilled in creating—not exactly forging—all kinds of documents to 'advance' one case or another. After two hours' work, the components were ready. Pierre assembled the fake gelignite, gently pressed the glued seam of the paper wrapping, and laid the creation next to the real stick.

"The paper wrapping. It is not quite right," Zouzou said, bringing the inspection lamp close. "You, see, the real one looks slightly greasy."

"Hmm. Give me a minute." Pierre eased the roller door open and ducked outside. He returned with a small can of two-stroke oil from the Honda's storage box.

"Rub gently, just a smear on your fingertips, Pierre."

He tested the remedy on a scrap of discarded paper, making four daubs of increasing oiliness.

"If I am not mistaken, this one is *optimally oleaginous*," he said, switching momentarily into English to deliver the verdict.

They crouched down to inspect the finished article.

"You are a genius."

"So I have been accused."

"One more, then, my genius."

By midnight, Pierre's shoulders ached and his eyes stung. Scraps of smudged art paper were evidence of failed attempts to match the colour or accurately mimic the lettering. Two sticks of fake gelignite sat smugly on the bench.

"Now to replace the real explosives. Will you do the honours, Zouzou? But first, what do you think will happen when we trigger the fake bomb?"

"The detonator will explode and splatter the moulding clay everywhere, I suppose. Now let me concentrate on this."

She removed the remaining gelignite stick with utmost care and slid in the counterfeits.

Two lethal sticks now sat on the bench.

"What will we do with them?"

"Take them home. We may find a use for them. We'll take this too." Zouzou placed a cardboard-wrapped tube next to the explosives.

"A detonator?"

"A spare," Zouzou said. "Gelignite is no use unless you can blow it up."

"Of course."

* * *

Zouzou followed Pierre's tail-light through the back streets as he avoided the cops patrolling the main roads for drunk drivers. The storage box under his seat held the explosives. Zouzou had the detonator hidden inside a glove. If he were to be stopped, Zouzou would divert and make her own way home.

She was exhausted by subterfuge and duplicity. The account of the meeting with Kerry hung sourly in her memory. She knew as she rattled off the events that

Pierre suspected her of something. The night in the hotel with Kerry played over and over in her mind in its appalling reality.

A kerb loomed dangerously close to the Vespa's front wheel. Her heart jumped as she straightened the teetering scooter and focussed on the road. Pierre was still ahead, signalling a right turn that would take them into Chatswood and the long route home via the back roads of French's Forest and Freshwater to avoid the danger spots.

The deserted suburban streets of Sydney were as alien as ever. Broad bungalows stood in darkness, front gardens sinister with dense shrubs and trees. Her headlight picked out the eyes of a startled possum scuttling along the top of a fence. A silvery whisp strung between trees indicated the fresh web of a spider hanging at eye level, ready to tickle the face of a blundering human. The very air was alien with its blend of night aromas, some minty, some sour, some bearing an enigmatically savoury tang. A dog barked, and another replied from six gardens away—'Yes, I'm scared and lonesome like you!'

Zouzou was stricken by a sudden jolt of longing for the packed streets of Cairo, for the honest stench of donkey shit and fried beans, the cacophony of horns, the call to prayer, watermelon sellers, cops directing traffic with pea whistles.

The wide, dark streets stared back at her, telling her nothing, meaning nothing. As she turned onto the long, deep swoop of the Roseville Bridge, the black river in the gorge below added its dank odour to that of the hostile, woolly bush stretching to the north.

At the bottom of the bridge span, the Vespa's engine coughed. She realised that Pierre's light had disappeared.

The bridge was entirely empty of vehicles. She pulled over to the left just as the engine died, and took off her helmet. A wall of animal sounds washed over her from the dark bush—clicks, squeals, squeaks, shrieks, along with the slosh of water in the river below. Her pulse raced, her stomach churned, her legs went to liquid. She was stricken with senseless terror.

A huge truck roared out of nowhere, blowing her sideways with its slipstream and deafening her with its blaring horn. Her panic flicked to anger, and she shook her fist at the sixteen-wheeled monster that was now forging up the hill with a guttering roar.

The scooter started with one jab of the kick-start. It must have been low on fuel, the remaining petrol tipped forward to the front of the tank by the downhill run. She'd need to freewheel down the long decline from Beacon Hill to Dee Why to get home without running dry. Helmet jammed back on, Zouzou twisted the accelerator and pulled away, her mind now clear. Perhaps the panic attack had flushed out the demons. The open road ahead suited her fresh resolve: It led back to Pierre and Pierre only.

She pulled into Rialto Close. He was at the door, worried as an ant. Inside, she stripped and led him to the tiny shower where they washed away each other's sweat and grit and insect wings. As she made love to him into the early morning hours, the memory of Kerry Rich faded to dust and blew away on the night breeze.

Chapter 17: Coffee at Point Piper

The house phone rang in the Point Piper apartment. It was a Saturday.

"There's a gentleman here to see you, Sir."

"What sort of a gentleman?"

"Foreign gentleman, Sir."

"Did he give a name, Raymond?"

Stone the bloody crows, what did you pay these people for? He'd be giving the building management some curry about the concierge service. There was some muttering on the line, and then Raymond said, "It's a Mr Moussa, Sir."

The fake relative from the hotel two nights ago. How did he find the address? Ah—bloody Liz of course. And at eight-thirty in the morning. He'd hardly had time to get out of his jammies. At any rate, the fake uncle had saved him the trouble of tracking the bugger down.

"Tell him I'll see him in the lobby in ten minutes."

Kerry sat on the toilet smoking a Kool. Uncle bloody Moussa could wait till he was ready. He'd hardly been out of the building since the night with Zouzou, just pacing the rooms doing his head in. The memory of her was driving him insane—a weird kind of mix-up of lust and something else, little flashbacks of her eyes, her voice, the slinky way she moved her shoulders. It brought back a distant recollection from his schooldays, when he was maybe fourteen: There was a girl called Bronwyn—no Briony or Bronte—whatever, but for a week he mooned around with his mind overflowing with her, trying to catch a glimpse of her in the schoolyard, giving a shy wave when she looked his way. Dad had asked why he was acting like a poodle with a candy cane up its clacker.

"I'm counting to three," Dad said, piercing him with those cold-storage eyes. Kerry mumbled that he was in love with a girl. The eyes froze hard. Dad slowly shook his head and walked away. After that, Kerry ignored Bronwyn or Briony or whoever she was. It just didn't feel the same.

And now he had the same gooey feeling. He was in love with the New Australian's wife. Kerry Rich, acting like a poodle with a candy cane up his bum. What should he do? Maybe tell her they could go away together, get on a yacht and disappear? Come to think of it, it could be a solution to his present problems: Ditch The Impeccables, hang out in Fiji for a year or so and let Clem find some other poor bastard to blow things up. He could call in his share of *The Gull* moored up in Cairns, put his business affairs into mothballs, and sail away into the proverbial sunset.

Would Zouzou be up for it? It'd sure beat hanging around with that dill of a husband with his smart remarks and put-downs. Why was she interested in a soft dick like that? His mind was made up: He'd talk to her today, one way or another.

The internal phone rang again on the toilet extension. "What?"

"Terribly sorry, Sir, but Mr Moussa says it is urgent that he sees you."

"Get his address and tell him to fuck off."

"Certainly, Sir."

Kerry lit another Kool. While Zouzou occupied most of his waking thoughts, the remaining moments were filled with deep rage at the way The Impeccables had screwed him over. They'd pay, for sure, especially that bastard Clem. As for Liz, he still couldn't figure out her game. Bugger the lot of them. Once he'd got rid of Uncle Moussa, he'd take a spin over to Manly on the off chance of seeing Zouzou.

Freshly shaved and turned out in Levis, a blue-striped shirt and a white leather shortie jacket, Kerry grabbed his keys and opened the apartment front door. Moussa stood blocking his way.

"How did you get up here?"

"Told your bloke downstairs I was an electrician. Look, we need to talk."

"Get off the premises right now."

"Let's go for a coffee and a chat. I didn't come here to make trouble."

Jeez, what a situation. This Moussa didn't look like a bad bloke. He'd just got the wrong end of the bloody stick. If it was a quick chat and a cup of coffee, that'd be OK. Put him straight and send him on his way. Maybe with a few bucks in his pocket for his time and trouble.

"OK, let's go."

They took the lift to the lobby. Raymond jerked to his feet when he saw Moussa with Kerry.

"I'll have a word with you later," Kerry grunted.

They walked down to Rushcutters Bay past the park where the bloke had accused Kerry of playing with his tackle.

"Beautiful morning, Mr Kerry."

"Hmm?"

"You're lucky to live here," Moussa said.

"You make your own luck, pal."

The café was almost empty—just a couple of women in tennis gear. Kerry gave them the once over—the older one looked like a good sort—and pointed to a table on the pavement. The owner came out and Moussa asked for a short black.

"Flat white, Judy, and one of those custard slices."

"All good, Kerry." She went inside and busied herself behind the counter.

"OK, Moussa, how much did Liz pay you for that little performance at the hotel?"

"Performance? You've got it all wrong, my boy. We're your family. Liz was the one who tracked us down."

"What do you mean, tracked you down?" The big fellow didn't look as if he was bullshitting. Kerry would hear him out.

"So a while ago, I get a phone call at night from a young lady asking me if I know anything about a gentleman by the name of Kerry Rich, so I said well I might know someone called Rich, and who might you be anyway . . . "

"Stop. Who was the woman? Liz?"

"Yeah."

"And what did she say then?"

"She asked if we had my sister-in-law's birth certificate. Well, I got a bit suspicious. I mean I don't want any funny business, you know us being Muslims and all."

"Muslims? You're Muslims?"

"My word, Kerry."

"Jesus Christ. It gets worse. Alright, get on with it. What happened next?"

"She says she's from the Australian Women's Weekly and she's writing a story on people who get separated from their family and she's got some news about someone called Maryam and could she come round to check the certificate in the evening. Anyway, I say yes because my wife's sister's called Maryam, and she turns up at the house."

"Did you ask for ID?"

"No, I didn't think of that because she's holding a copy of the magazine with her and she says that's who I work for. Anyway I give her the certificate and she says she has to get a photocopy and she'll return it. Sure enough she drops it off in the mailbox the next day fair dinkum."

"And where is it right now?"

"Right here." Moussa unfolded a paper and laid it flat.

"It's all in fuck'n foreign writing, mate."

"Here, I got it translated." He pulled out another sheet with *State Translation Office—Authorised Translation* printed across the top. Kerry studied it. Sure enough, it said a woman called Maryam had been born in Lebanon on his mother's birthday.

"And here's the one for Mona." Out came an almost identical document for the sister.

"Twins, see, Kerry?"

"This is bollocks. I'm out of here."

"No Sir, wait. I need to tell you about what happened next.

"Go on, and make it quick."

"So a week later, nothing's going on when we get a call from Liz. She says her magazine has done some investigating and she has some sad news and can we meet her at the Rookwood Cemetery. Me and Mona go up there and Liz takes us to a grave in the Christian part and tells us it's Mona's sister Maryam and she died five years ago. Well, Mona's ready to slap her, but I say we haven't seen Maryam for thirty years and didn't know if she was dead or alive, so maybe she's right."

"Hang on, mate. I need another coffee." Kerry signalled the café owner and lit a cigarette. The tennis woman gave him a smile and leant in to whisper to her friend. Kerry turned to Moussa, who continued the story.

"So Liz takes out a photo from a newspaper and says, is that Maryam? There's this woman cooking chips and the headline says CHIPPIE WIDOW VOWS TO KEEP FRYING. I remember the words exactly. Anyway, she's the spitting image of Mona, and Mona starts crying, says *alhamdulillah* we've found her. Sorry, we still speak a bit of Arabic sometimes, you know, weddings and funerals and . . . "

"Never mind about that. Didn't you know she was dead?"

"No. See, when your mum married your dad she didn't want to know us and the feeling was mutual thank you very much. We lost touch. But Mona, you know, she always wondered what had happened to Maryam."

Bloody oath. It could all be true. His mum a Muslim. He didn't even know what a Muslim was—the ones with turbans maybe—but he didn't like the sound of it. If he came across that Liz, he'd bloody kill her. No, it was a scam, a bloody prank. Someone had it in for him. But that face on the mum woman. He shuddered at the memory.

Moussa kept rambling on. "Yeah, so then Liz says do we want to meet our nephew, he's a lovely young man, very respectable, he's heard all about you, he's called Kerry Rich, and I say to Mona *maa shaa' Allah* that's the surname of the fellow Marian married—Rich, she must have had a baby. Anyway, Liz says we're gonna have a reunion at Manly and the magazine's gonna write it all up in a really nice story. And then we went to the hotel that night . . . "

A red rage surged through Kerry. He grabbed the certificates and jumped up, tipping the table over. Coffee splashed on the tennis woman's white skirt. Moussa stepped back, tripped on the woman's tennis bag and crashed into the owner. The pot of tea the owner was carrying sprayed all over the bag.

"That's a Louis Vuitton, you oaf. What's your name? Hey, you in the cheap leather jacket. You don't walk away. You don't walk away from me."

Kerry turned and looked back. The tennis woman's ugly mouth yelling at him like he was a Lebo; Moussa on the ground grimacing and massaging his hip; Judy the owner dapping the Vuitton bag.

Losers. They could go to hell. He lived in a penthouse in Point Piper. He owned a resort. He was Kerry Rich. But something squirming under his ribs asked, "Who's the loser?"

He strode back to his apartment. Cheap jacket! Snobby cow. He needed to get into the Porsche and hit the open road, put his foot down and hear the growl, get the shit out of his head.

Roof down, the Porsche shoved and harried a path through the Saturday traffic and in no time Kerry had left the Shire behind and was flying down the Princes Highway towards Wollongong. He weaved between the thundering coal trucks, swooping past them on the inside lane, playing cat and dog, eyes peeled for the next one. With his foot down and the car in top gear, he was king of the highway, King Bloody Kerry, hitting 120, 140, 160 as the knots of coal trucks receded in the rear mirror. He relaxed his grip on the wheel, let his taut shoulders slump, took his foot off the gas and changed down to glide around the long bend and pull over at the Panorama lookout. He got out and lit a ciggy, arms on the guardrail of the lookout. The ribbon of silvery beaches sparkled far below at the bottom of the forested escarpment. The ocean was a block of dense blue. Distant ships stood in line to enter Port Kembla. Tiny cars tootled along the coast road to Bulli and Coalcliff.

The vista calmed his grinding thoughts. He knew suddenly that his present life had to end, had to change into something else. The old Kerry Rich was a country he couldn't go back to. Maybe Moussa was right about his mum, maybe he was wrong. It didn't matter; he could never know the truth, but he'd always know his mum just might be Mona's sister. He'd always know that his old man might have pretended Kerry was a proper Australian. And now he was driving himself insane over Zouzou. Kerry Rich—the boss of the Southern Cross League according to Liz—in love with an immigrant.

There was a pattern to all this if only he could see it: The way the toffs from The Impeccable had made a tosser of him; that bastard Clem popping up everywhere like last weekend's prawn shells; Liz digging up this Muslim baloney; him falling in love with a terrorist.

It was time to split.

But he had to get a couple of things squared up first.

He shivered despite the hot wind blowing from the dry inland. Down the coast beyond Wollongong, a bank of cloud warned of a southerly buster heading up to Sydney. Kerry climbed into the Porsche, pulled onto the highway, did a screaming U-turn two k's down the road, and barrelled it back towards Sydney. He'd hit Manly by teatime.

* * *

Pierre was reading the Sydney Morning Herald in the front yard with a glass of mint tea at his side. He looked at his watch. Zouzou would be home around five from her singing job. He awaited her return with apprehension. Their predicament was dire, their future unknown. The fake gelignite was one thing; the implementation of their sabotage plan was another. A gulf separated the means from the action. But things had taken a worse turn during Zouzou's absence. The phone had rung after lunch. The man on the other end of the line announced himself as Clem. The voice was deep and muffled.

"And what can I do for you, Mr Clem?" Pierre said with his heart pounding. Was this Ealing's man?

"I understand you're doing some technical work for my colleague Mr Rich." Pierre strained to comprehend; the speaker was undoubtedly disguising his voice with some means—perhaps an electronic device or some physical prop. He remembered experimenting in Cairo with wrapping a scarf around the receiver and placing a cardboard box over his head.

"Before I reply, may I ask what your connection is with Mr Rich?'

There was a long silence.

"Mr Farag, you're an intelligent man. You have a very interesting past. I'm sure you've guessed what my connection with Mr Rich is. And with your friend Mark Bellamy."

"Indeed. Then I presume that I am actually doing technical work for your good self. What is the exact nature of your call?"

"I'm interested in a progress report. Is the technical work finished?"

"Yes, it is."

"Then I would like to bring the date forward."

"To when?"

"Two nights from now."

"But we need to test the . . . equipment."

"I believe you have already trialled it. Isn't that the case?"

"Yes." How did he know about the trial? And where did Mr Kerry figure in this plan?

"Then, it's all settled. Half past midnight, the day after tomorrow."

"Will there be instructions?"

The phone clicked.

Pierre's mint tea had gone cold. Where was Zouzou? He needed to sit with her, talk over Clem's demand, come up with a plan. Whatever the differences between them, they worked together best in a crisis.

An engine growled in the street. Not a Vespa. As he stood up, the front gate opened to reveal Kerry Rich. The man was red-faced and twitchy, clearly suffering a variety of mental perturbation.

"Mr Kerry, to what do I owe . . . "

"Where's Zouzou? Is she here?" The fellow was wringing his hands. His crumpled shirt tail hung down the back of his pants.

"No, she's not here."

"There's something I need to tell you," Kerry blurted.

Dear God, no. She'd been harmed, she'd got into some dangerous business with this fool. Pierre grabbed Kerry by the shirt front.

"What is it? What's happened to her?"

The door banged open again. Zouzou marched in, wearing her crash helmet.

"What's happened to who? And why are you fighting with my husband, Mr Kerry?"

The sweating man drew back. His face took on a wary look, eyes flicking between Pierre and Zouzou as if calculating the next move in the drama.

"Well, have you two gentlemen finished with your nonsense? Ouf, men! I need a cold drink."

She went inside. She was playing a part, Pierre knew, too brash, too nonchalant. Kerry was now bouncing on his heels, rubbing his hands and plastering a fake grin on his dial.

"Got a cold one in the fridge, old mate?"

What in God's name was going on? You could power a fan with the electricity in the air.

Zouzou came out wearing the baggy pyramid-and-camel print gown she wore around the house. Guaranteed to eliminate all traces of passion, Pierre had told her. It had become a joke between them. Had she put the garment on to damp down whatever invisible energy was crackling between Kerry and his wife? He thrust the thought back into the dirty hole it had come from.

"Mate," Kerry began. Pierre knew this tactic that Australian men used to broach a sensitive topic.

"Mate, it's like this. Your wife, well me and her, well . . ."

No, no, he had to be stopped.

"Mr Kerry. Think carefully before you make your next statement." Pierre turned to look at Zouzou. Whatever had happened—he dared not speculate—must remain sealed until the present danger had passed.

"Kerry," Zouzou said. "Listen to my husband. Please."

"Aw, c'mon . . . " Kerry said, then shrugged. "Fair enough."

"And now," Pierre said, "Zouzou will make us some coffee and we will discuss our predicament."

The crackling electricity faded. The two men smoked in silence until Zouzou brought Turkish coffee from the kitchen. She carefully poured from the *kanaka* until the three tiny cups were filled to the brim and topped with a ring of foam.

"Mr Kerry, I wonder if Mr Clem has been in contact with you in the last day or so?"

"No, he hasn't. He can get fucked anyway." Kerry threw up his chin.

"I beg your pardon?"

"I'm quitting, getting out. I've had enough of being shat on from all directions. But first I'm gonna make sure those bastards pay."

"What bastards?" Zouzou asked.

"The Impeccables, who else?"

"Who?" Pierre looked at Zouzou, who shook her head.

The front gate banged open. Pierre looked up. The journalist woman Liz poked her head into the front yard.

"Bloody oath," muttered Kerry.

"You!" Zouzou hissed.

"Come in, Miss Liz, and join the party."

Chapter 18: The Dust on Her Shoe

Just as Liz entered Pierre's front gate, the neighbour arrived home with half a dozen drinking mates. Jed hoisted himself up to peep over the fence.

"G'day Pierre. We've got a slab if you and your mates wanna drop over."

"Regrettably, we must decline your hospitality on this occasion, my friend."

Jed's face went blank for a moment while he processed the response.

"No worries, Pierre. Have a good one." He bobbed down and Pierre gestured to Kerry, Liz and Zouzou to go inside the house.

There were times, Pierre thought, when somebody had to take control, when somebody had to conduct the orchestra, so to speak. Watching the three file inside, he knew that 'somebody' was Pierre Farag, the man 'turned in on himself', the man whose stock in trade was facts, arranged, sorted, measured, analysed. And if this were an orchestra, then his task was not just to conduct it but to discover the tune it was trying to play.

The tiny lounge room was airless and hot. A two-seater sofa and two dining chairs offered the total seating. Pierre gestured to Zouzou to take the sofa. She sat impassive as the Sphinx, pulling the hideous gown down to cover her legs. Pierre moved the dining chairs to opposite corners of the room. Liz and Kerry glared at one another and took a seat each, while Pierre remained standing.

"Let's get on with it, then," Kerry growled.

"Whatever 'it' is," Liz replied. "What's going on here?"

"Surely you have some idea, Liz. You asked yourself into our house uninvited . . . "

"I saw Kerry's car. I wanted to know how he was."

"I see. To return to your question," Pierre said calmly, "*it* is the peculiar set of circumstances that have brought us here today. Circumstances that relate to a certain individual . . . "

"You mean that fuck'n Clem?" Kerry muttered.

"Please, Mr Kerry. Let us remain civil."

"Civil? Have you got any idea what that bastard is up to?"

Liz started to speak but Kerry shouted her down. "I haven't even got round to you, you bloody cock-tease."

"Cock-tease? If you kept your brains in your skull instead of your pants, you might not be in the spot you're in," Liz spat back.

"And what spot's that, then?"

"Fascist patriot bomb-maker who turns out to be Lebanese, that's what."

The pair sprang from their seats, yelling in one another's faces. Pierre realised that Zouzou had slipped out of the room.

"You shit. I knew you were up to . . . "

"Go to hell. I hope they lock you up for . . . "

"Lebanese my arse, you stupid . . . "

"Don't call me stupid. I've got all the proof I . . . "

Zouzou reappeared in the doorway.

"Enough!" she shrieked. The ranting pair turned to see her hold an object aloft.

"What the fuck's that?" Kerry yelled.

"Get down on the floor," Liz screamed.

"Perhaps you might just sit down and listen to my husband," Zouzou said, settling back on the sofa with the stick of gelignite in her lap. "It is perfectly safe."

"Perfectly safe if we don't make too many vibrations—loud shouting and so on," Pierre added.

Kerry crept gingerly back to his chair and reached for a cigarette.

"Put it away, you idiot. Do you want to kill us?" Liz said.

"Bloody oath." He slid the packet back into his pocket, all the time staring warily at Zouzou.

"That's better," said Pierre. "I am obliged to inform you that we are in imminent jeopardy."

"Whassat mean?" Kerry asked.

"It means, Mr Kerry, that if we don't act quickly, we will be killed. Now, let us all share what we know."

But, Pierre reflected, he would not be sharing Clem's demand for a change of date. Not for now, and not until he'd had time to work out the potential courses of action that flowed from this new information.

* * *

Back in her apartment, Liz opened a bottle of Riesling and poured herself a big glass. She sat at her desk and gazed out at the bobbing sailboats and cabin cruisers moored under the moon by the ferry wharf. She had to hand it to this Pierre character for style. The guy was all class with his quaint accent, insightful questioning, ornate vocabulary, and his unsettling way of being constantly a step ahead.

He'd turned to Liz first. She had a compelling sense that Pierre's warning of 'imminent jeopardy' was genuine. There was a trustworthy quality about him she couldn't put her finger on. When he asked her if she knew a man called Clem, she immediately told him about her informant Nugget. But she wasn't certain she was going to reveal everything.

"And how did you come to know Mr Nugget?"

"My editor suggested I contacted him about getting information about Kerry."

At this, Kerry nearly blew a fuse, but Pierre waved him down and forged on. Liz explained how Nugget *aka* Clem gave her the run-down on Kerry's leadership of the Southern Cross League, and how she had worked for months to build up a profile. More recently, he had told her that Kerry's mother was Lebanese.

Kerry had given up fuming. He groaned, held his head in hands, elbows on knees, muttering an occasional profanity.

Liz had been used by Clem, it was clear. Used like a toilet brush.

"So you were writing an article. What was the topic if you don't mind me asking?'

"It was an exposé. The paper I write for hunts down hypocrisy and corruption."

"An admirable purpose," Pierre said acidly. "But you use the name 'Nugget'. When did you first know him as Clem?"

"When he brought the bomb to my flat last week."

"And why did he do that?"

"To scare the shit out of me, what else?"

At the mention of the bomb, Liz saw Zouzou shoot a glance towards Pierre. The bloody woman sat stony-faced with the gelignite on her lap, but there were vibes emanating from her like a nuclear reactor. Kerry kept glancing up at her from his elbows; she repelled him with her force field. Pierre must have felt it too, but he was on cross-examination auto pilot.

"And what did Clem tell you, Miss Liz?"

"Nothing really."

"Nothing really or nothing actually? Or perhaps nothing possibly?"

"He told me about a plot to pretend to blow up the Opera House."

"Pretend? How do you pretend to blow something up?"

"He said you and Zouzou would be arrested just before it was supposed to go off."

Kerry sat straight up in his chair at that, said that wasn't what Clem had told him.

"Of course is wasn't, you dill," Liz said.

"Did Clem mention what would happen to Kerry, Miss Liz?"

"No, not really."

"What's that supposed to mean?' Kerry asked.

"That's all you get from me. Someone else can have a go now. I'm not saying anything else till I know where this is going."

Well, that was half the truth. She knew where this was going—a once in a lifetime chance to write a story that would blow the socks off Sydney. After tonight's meeting she wasn't sure how the players fell into place, and she didn't have a clue how the story would end. What was that about a malign foreign power? The US? Russia? China? As for Jock, he could take a jump. The old hypocrite must be part of the plan; otherwise, why would he have conveniently stumbled across Clem? Clem had groomed her to set up Kerry Rich, and now she was going to expose him along with the coup leaders.

"So, no more to add, Miss Liz?"

"No."

Pierre pursed his lips and turned to Kerry.

* * *

Kerry had a long, slow pee over the Harbour from his glass-fronted *pissoir*. The lights on the Bridge twinkled in the hot night; a North Shore train rattled out of the tunnel and headed across the steel span towards Milsons Point. As he let his bladder empty, he visualised Clem getting a wet head.

He was majorly shat off, absolutely filthy. Liz's story had filled in the empty spaces in the events of the last few months. That bag of slime Clem had played him like a schoolgirl. He'd been chosen right from the start. Liz said he worked for the government. Kerry had spent his life keeping away from the government and their nosey public servants in fucking safari suits and knee socks. The accountant gave the tax office a few crumbs to keep them sweet, and every couple of years he went to the polling station and put X in the first box on the voting paper. No point in calling attention to yourself by getting a fine for not voting. 'Under the radar', that's where he told his lawyer and accountant he wanted to be.

So that was how his mum's birth certificate had come to light—Clem and the government. He was sure now it was true about his mum. Too many things added up. But there hadn't been time for it to properly sink in yet.

What really got up his arse was why he'd been chosen? Did Clem or his bosses just decide one day, oh yeah, let's find some guy with a secret Lebanese mum and make up a load of crap about him and talk him into thinking he's a big shot? Or maybe they had a file on him for years? He'd read about it once in the paper—how the special police or ASIO or whatever collected stuff on troublemakers and pooftahs and communists so they could blackmail them. But why him? He was just a bloke running cash businesses and keeping out of trouble. No drugs, no violence. All sweet.

Pierre had kept pecking away about what he knew, so Kerry had spilled his guts about The Impeccables and how they were going to overthrow the government and the pricks had tricked him into thinking he was one of them. Liz snorted and called him pathetic, but he was too bloody fed up to go back at her.

His right leg was going numb. He realised he'd been standing at the pisser for twenty minutes and he still had his old man in his hand. Which brought him to Zouzou. He zipped up, went into the lounge and poured a big Jack Daniels. Dad peered at him from the picture frame.

Watching her in the house in Rialto Close, Kerry knew he was out of Zouzou's league. He'd been conned by Clem, and by her. Why, he didn't know. You could see how they operated, Pierre and his wife, like two creepy aliens, like they could read each other's minds. Zouzou didn't give a shit about Kerry Rich. He'd made a dick of himself with all that falling in love caper. Liz had been screwed over too, making up all that garbage about the League at Clem's beck and bloody call. He had to feel sorry for her really. An amateur being played by a pro. Ha! Join the club.

But what to do? The New Australian was dead right about his intimate jeopardy stuff. Look at it: A bomb floating round Sydney, a bunch of Mosman pricks wanting him in jail, the cops probably snooping round soon. One of The Impeccables was a top cop; Clem worked for the government. And what was all that about a pretend explosion?

He was fucked.

And when you're fucked, what do you do?

Leave town.

But where to? An idea flashed before his eyes.

He had to talk to Liz. Get things straight with her.

* * *

Pierre was asleep. Zouzou fidgeted alongside him, hoping he'd wake so they could talk. It was past midnight and the only sound was the surf crashing onto the beach four streets away.

Before Kerry and Liz had left, Pierre made a solemn speech: They were all at the mercy of a foreign power, whose intentions towards Australia were malign, he said. He and Zouzou had suffered at their hands for five years. The foe they faced was relentless in pursuit of its enemies.

Poor Kerry was obviously confused by her husband's ornate vocabulary, but judging by his furrowed brow, the general message had sunk in. Liz reacted with something between a sneer and a frown; but Pierre's words had hit their mark. He ended the meeting by telling the pair to return to the house the next evening at 11pm.

"Approach quietly. Make sure you are not followed. I will have instructions for you."

When they had gone, her husband fussed around the apartment, whistling a tuneless tune, self-satisfied as a cat with a sparrow. At one point, he stopped, held up one finger, said, "The Impeccables—very clever", and resumed the irritating whistling. Zouzou gave up trying to get his attention and went to bed, eyes shut fast and stomach churning with irritation. He joined her and within minutes the whistling turned to heavy breathing.

It was hopeless. She slipped out of bed, aimed a flick of her hand at his backside but changed her mind; it was too late for talk even if he did wake.

A glass of karkady in the front yard—that would settle her.

Kerry and Liz were exposed as amateurs—not that she'd thought otherwise. But this Clem, she'd met his type before, these hardened Ealing agents who knew no boundaries; men who'd sell their children to the devil—if they ever summoned up the humanity to acknowledge fatherhood. She recalled Donald Waters with a shiver, Ealing's man in Cairo, who had ended his days like a cornered rat in Malta, blown up with a grenade by his own hand. And the sadistic Brian Mills who'd arranged to have her transported incognito to Malta as a hostage while Pierre was smuggled into Libya to safeguard an arms deal for the IRA. If, as she was sure, Clem was running an operation in Australia for Ealing, then Pierre's warning of 'imminent jeopardy' was in no doubt.

Kerry and Liz were the dust on her shoe. Pierre hadn't revealed his plan to her yet. The 'man turned in on himself' was probably deliberating the details in his sleep. But she was sure that Kerry and Liz would be the extras in the drama, not the principal players, whatever they might be led to believe. Nothing would stand in the way of her and her husband surviving this ordeal.

The memory of the night with Kerry was now stored alongside the scores of parts she had played in her movie star days. It had been no more than a performance—she'd played a spy's wife who slept with a foe to find out a crucial clue to save her husband's life—an act of love. It meant nothing in itself. Kerry meant nothing, this humiliated creature whose very identity had been torn from him by Clem and Liz.

In the tranquil night, she heard Pierre speak in his sleep, but the words were meaningless—Armenian perhaps, the language of his mother's people, a race Arabs like herself held in deep respect for their dignity and quiet industry. Her meandering thoughts transported her to Cairo, to a particular street near the city centre where you'd smoke a Boston and wave the flies from a plate of *bastourma* at a pavement table, watching the men at the *makwagi* shop spraying water from their lips to dampen the shirts under the charcoal-heated flatirons.

She would never see Cairo again, she knew with certainty. Cairo *mon amour.*

Sleep came quickly when she returned to bed, but her last waking thought was that another secret—alongside the night with Kerry—stood between them. Something dreadful had happened to Pierre during his week away, she was sure.

* * *

It had come to him as the first light of dawn nudged him awake. He would pay his old friend Mark Bellamy a visit in the converted garage in Wahroonga. Zouzou wandered into the front yard as he was finishing a cup of tea and strapping on his crash helmet.

"Go back to bed, *habibti.* We will talk when I return later this morning."

A few holidaymakers were setting up on the beach as he rode along the seafront. In a few hours, the ferries would start to disgorge the multicultural crowds who flocked to Manly from the inland suburbs for a Sunday of swimming and fast food.

A yellow VW caught his eye. It pulled into a parking spot and Liz got out wearing a bathing suit. She unhooked a surfboard from the roof rack. Pierre stopped.

"Good morning, Miss Liz."

"Can you pack up that Miss Liz business? I can see you're polishing your eccentric foreigner persona, and it doesn't wash with me. Anyway, I'm busy. If you've got something to say, get on with it."

"Nothing for now. See you tonight."

"Maybe."

She turned, walked across the sand, glided into the surf, and paddled out to join a group of surfers bobbing in the water. Pierre watched as she caught a wave, dancing atop the curling column of water before disappearing into the churning foam.

A fine way to spend a Sunday morning. Perhaps when this business was over . . .

The traffic out to Wahroonga was thin. The day warmed rapidly. By the time Pierre parked his bike behind a stately tree, his head was fit to boil inside the sweaty helmet. The smell of burning gum leaves drifted in the air; the old man in khaki shorts was prodding his tiny bonfire in the stormwater drain.

He knocked on the garage door marked 24A. No reply. Pierre lit a cigarette and walked across to the front door of the house. All the windows had close-fitting blinds. Who lived here? A faint noise came from inside the house—a door closing perhaps.

A final knock on the garage door. But this time, Bellamy called from behind the metal roller door, "Hang on for God's sake."

The door clattered up a metre and a half.

"Get inside, quick. I'd rather you weren't seen coming in."

Mark Bellamy closed the door and sat on a chair in front of a primus stove on a wooden crate. He dropped two slices of pink luncheon meat into a frying pan. Pierre noticed that he was dressed in a grubby singlet and grubbier underpants.

"I was expecting you sooner or later. Have a seat."

The dwelling was as squalid as on the last visit. At least, Pierre reflected, it was authentic; he had toyed with the notion that Bellamy was feigning alcoholism and that the garage was an elaborate fake. Ealing, he knew, went to extraordinary lengths to entrap or confound its foes. The smeared glass of white wine at Bellamy's elbow put aside any doubts.

"How do you live, Mark my friend? Do you have work?"

"Ha! My work is to sit on my backside waiting for whatever job they want doing. The bastards pay me a pathetic allowance, cash in hand—or rather cash in a marmalade can under the bins at the back of the bottle shop."

"Can't you leave, get on a plane?"

"Not without a passport. And where would I go? French Riviera, skiing in Zermatt? Anyway, what do you want? I assume you're up to your arse in some caper that Ealing's dragged you into."

"You could say that. I want to find your colleague Clem."

"Clem, is that what the bastard calls himself?"

"What's his real name?"

"I doubt if he's got one," Bellamy spat. "How many names have you had, Pierre?"

"More than a few. What do you know of this Clem?"

"I'd offer you a bit of Devon but the jolly old cupboard's bare until I get out to the shops."

Bellamy turned the repulsive meat from the pan onto a plate, and began to eat, sipping white wine between mouthfuls. The Mark Bellamy Pierre had known in Cairo was barely recognisable. He seemed to forget Pierre's presence while he ate.

"Mark, what do you know of him?"

Bellamy pushed his plate aside and laughed bitterly.

"Almost nothing. I've met him about four times and they weren't exactly deep and meaningful encounters."

"Did he say anything about the job he wanted me to do?"

"No, just that password nonsense."

"Do you know where I can find him?"

At this, Bellamy looked up at Pierre with a lopsided smile.

"I might."

So here it was—the bargain. There was a price on Bellamy's knowledge.

"You might know where I can find him, or you might tell me?"

"Same thing as far as you're concerned, Pierre. Either way, I need a favour."

"Name your favour."

"When you get out, take me with you, wherever, I don't care."

"Why do you think I'm going anywhere, Mark?"

"T'was ever thus. I'd take a guess you've been moving since Cairo. Can I trust you to take me along when the time comes?"

Pierre hesitated. Bellamy was right. The days of Kevin O'Donnell of Rialto Close were coming to an end. Wherever he and Zouzou might flee to, must they be encumbered by a fellow in such a pitiful condition? There was only one answer.

"You know you can rely on me."

Bellamy rose and squared up to an old fridge in the corner of the garage. He hefted it sideways with a grunt.

"Here." He handed Pierre a stained envelope that had been taped to the back of the fridge.

"He's very careful, this man you call Clem, meticulous, doesn't give anything away. But he made a mistake."

Pierre read the address on the empty envelope.

C. Lyons
16/6 Harbour View Lane
Elizabeth Bay

"How did you get it?"

"It was wet the last time he came here, late at night. When he left, he fumbled with his umbrella in the driveway and dropped a folder he'd been carrying—like a satchel with a flap. Some papers spilled out. He picked them up but as he walked away, I noticed an envelope stuck to his shoe. He must have trodden on it. It fell off after a few steps."

"How do we know it's him?" Pierre asked.

"Why would he be carrying somebody else's letter around?"

"Fair point. I don't suppose he ever gave you a phone number?"

Mark took a pen from the pockets of his shorts. "You're in luck. I memorized it. I'll write it on the envelope."

Pierre tucked the envelope into his pocket.

"I'll be in touch, Mark."

"Just before you go, Pierre. How's the lady— Zouzou, I think her name was? I just met her the once that night in Cairo when I walked in covered in blood."

"We married in France. She is with me here in Sydney. She is expecting a baby."

Pierre stopped short. Why had he said that? Why say Zouzou was pregnant? The words had jumped into his speech unwilled. What unseen combination of events and sentiments and signs had conspired to bring forth that notion?

Bellamy grasped his hand and pulled Pierre into a clumsy embrace.

Did he sob, just once? Did this broken man in Y-fronts and singlet stifle a tear for the wife and child abandoned in Moscow in an 'act of love'? Bellamy's grip relaxed and he straightened up, reached for his wine.

"Jolly good, then. We'll be in touch soon, I expect."

The Honda coughed into life. The man with the bonfire turned to watch Pierre pass.

* * *

There was no 6 Harbour View Lane in Elizabeth Bay. In fact, there was no Harbour View Lane in Elizabeth Bay. Pierre fumed over the UBD in the late morning heat. He checked and rechecked the street index, drops of sweat dripping from his forehead onto the pages. Why hadn't he confirmed the street before he left Wahroonga?

There was a phone booth further down the street. Pointless, he knew, but what choice was there? The booth stank like a urinal and the phone book hung shredded from its bracket. At least the coin mechanism worked. Two twenty-cent pieces dropped into the box. Pierre held the sticky receiver between two fingers and dialled with a key to avoid what looked like curry on the dial.

It was on the tip of his tongue to ask, 'Can I please speak to C. Lyons?' when the operator's answer struck him like a slap around the head:

"Taronga Park Zoo. How can I help you?"

Betrayed! The receiver swung on its cable, the voice squawking, "How can I help you?", then the dial tone.

Not just betrayed, but mocked, fooled, humiliated; the man whose stock in trade was facts and their proper arrangement. Mocked by a puerile joke that must have been played on thousands of unwitting nincompoops—but a joke that had never come across Pierre Farag's horizon, never been filed away for future use.

How had he ignored the evidence staring directly at him? Mark Bellamy's elaborately staged accident on the day of the barbecue; the simple task he had set Pierre to track him down; the delay in answering the knock on the garage door as, no doubt, Bellamy had dressed in his role and slipped into the garage through an internal door. Not once, but twice!

A ghastly suspicion pushed its way into his galloping thoughts. No, surely not! He needed facts, not suspicions. But how to garner the facts to confirm what he hoped was not true?

Pierre wiped the sweat from the sticky strip of forehead under the bike helmet, and turned the Honda back towards Wahroonga. He clenched his parched lips, bent low over the handlebars.

The man with the bonfire seemed to be packing up for lunch. He was dribbling the smouldering ashes with a small watering can, loudly whistling *Nessun Dorma* with exquisite concentration. Pierre parked the Honda behind a tree.

"Sir, may I ask you a question?"

The man turned querying eyes on Pierre. A beatific smile wreathed the old fellow's face.

"Daddy, have you brought me something nice?"

"Sir, can you tell me who lives in the house at the end of the street? No.24?"

"Is it Iced VoVo's you've brought me, Daddy?"

A woman strode out of the front garden opposite to the tiny bonfire.

"You, stop bothering my husband. If you're selling time shares, just clear off." She grasped the arm of the old man, who took on a mutinous look. Dear God, the poor fellow had dementia. Pierre recalled an ancient aunt in Cairo who would escape the apartment building and wander the streets looking for King Farouq.

"My apologies, Madam. I was merely asking for a smidgeon of information."

"A smidgeon? What do you mean by that? Is it a fish?"

"Perhaps you could tell me who lives at no. 24?"

"Who wants to know?"

"I am, Madam, an Egyptian immigrant searching for a relative who I believe resides in this locality."

"Daddy, is Mummy coming today?"

"Mummy's not coming, Graham. An Egyptian, you say? My father served in Egypt, filthy country he always said. Have you had your bath this morning? You look very sweaty, Peter."

"Peter?" Pierre said. Oh, dear, the poor wife was almost as batty as the husband.

"Well, it's a coincidence you mention it, there is a fellow living there. Renting of course. I mean, just look at the house, no pride in presentation". These last remarks were accompanied by a home-owner's eye roll.

"What sort of fellow. And has he been there long?"

"A single gentleman. He's lived there—let me think. Graham, how long has the curly-haired fellow been at no. 24? I never forget a date, do I Ralph? Yes, it was three years ago just after I had my knee operation."

"Madam, I thank you from the bottom of my heart. You mentioned a coincidence."

"Oh yes. I saw him getting into a taxi with his suitcases about half an hour ago."

Pierre watched the woman lead her husband into the garden. He thought for a moment of Zouzou, wondered with a deep pang of grief whether he would ever lead her through a shaded garden into a comfortable home they had shared for years.

There was a single conclusion: 'Clem' was Mark Bellamy, Mark Bellamy in a wig. Three years under deep cover. The man who said he'd left the USSR a year ago. A man Pierre had trusted like a brother.

But what would motivate Bellamy to mock him with the zoo nonsense? Why plead with Pierre to help him leave, sob on his shoulder, and then send him on a wild sealion chase?

The answer was to be found in the theatre of deception that Ealing had elevated to high art; an arena of contradictions and guile, of betrayed trust and trashed loyalties. Bellamy must have known that it was only a question of time before Pierre would connect him with 'Clem'; why not pre-empt the moment by knocking Pierre off balance, sending him spinning? Why not send a clear message that Pierre was totally in his control?

He crumpled over the handlebars of the clapped-out Honda with its worn rubber grips and rusted headlamp. A wave of despair swamped his heart and his spirit.

His watch said twelve-thirty. It was hot as a furnace. He had eleven hours until Kerry and Liz arrived at his house; he was—as the Australians so neatly expressed it— up shit creek without a paddle.

Chapter 19: Scorpions

Kerry was about to hang up when Liz answered the phone on the ninth or tenth ring. She sounded out of breath.

"Who is it?"

"Me, Kerry. Did I interrupt something?"

"Oh, you. No, I just came back from having a surf and I ran up the stairs to get the phone. What the hell do you want, anyway?"

"Look, we need to talk about that stuff Pierre was on about last night."

There was a long sigh on the other end of the line.

"What's there to talk about, Kerry?"

"I suppose what happens next. It was all left hanging in the air."

"Yes, OK. I'm feeling a bit angsty about the whole thing to be honest. That Clem knows how to get into my house."

So far, so good. Kerry was thinking clearly now, all the rage gone. When life chucked a bucket of shit on your head, you had to clean up and keep going.

"And hey, I just wanted to say no hard feelings."

"About what?" Liz asked.

"The night of the great reunion with my so-called family."

"Oh God, I feel terrible. I completely screwed up. If you don't mind me asking, what happened afterwards?"

"I had a coffee with my uncle yesterday. It was all true. My mum was Lebanese for sure."

"You don't mind being half-Lebanese? Oh, God, what a stupid question. Sorry."

"No worries, Liz. You've got to be something. But listen here, that bastard Clem, he knows a hell of a lot."

"Yes, he's a walking encyclopedia. What about you being the leader of the Southern Cross League? Was that true?"

"It's bullshit, fair dinkum."

"Why would he set me up like that? Yes, we need to talk, Kerry, but not on the phone."

"Why not?" Kerry asked, and then the penny dropped. "Ah, yeah, I get it. How about I pick you up where I dropped you after the boat trip?"

* * *

"Where's the Porsche?" Liz asked.

"Too conspicuous," Kerry replied, manoeuvring the Datsun out of the carpark at Little Manly. "I thought we'd run up Collaroy way, find somewhere to eat."

She was wearing a summer dress, looked nice. With the windows down, the hot westerly blew her hair in crazy directions.

They chatted as they followed the coast route up through the string of beach suburbs—Queenscliff, Freshwater, Curl Curl, Dee Why. Funny really, just like they were mates. She told him a bit about her job, how she needed a huge story to break into the big time. He heard how her family were wealthy—well, used to be till her old man went to jail, how they sold the house in Mosman and the yacht, and she had to leave private school.

"You know how to sail a yacht?"

"Sure do. I won races."

"Tell you what, let's keep going to Pittwater. It'll be a bit quieter than round here."

They slowed for the Sunday traffic around Collaroy, panel vans and Kingswoods laden with surf boards and bleached teenagers, sweating mums and dads prising kids and beach umbrellas from station wagons.

"So you used to be married, then?"

"You know I was, Kerry. I'm sure you've done your homework."

"Is it right that Andrew Cruickshank's doing time for you?"

"If I told you the truth, Kerry, I'd have to kill you."

"Bloody oath, Liz. Remind me to wear my bullet proof vest next time we meet."

She laughed. "Maybe I'll plant a stick of Zouzou's gelignite in your car."

"Been there, done that. You'll have to try harder."

The Datsun swept around the big curve in the road high above Bilgola Beach. Turquoise ocean filled the gaps between the cabbage tree palms.

"So, what's gonna be in your newspaper story, Liz?"

"Well that's the funny thing. A few weeks ago I thought I knew. I was writing an exposé about a colourful Sydney businessman who was secretly running a fascist organisation—that was you of course. Then it changed to a story about the leader of a fascist organisation who turns out to be half-Lebanese—that was still you. Now it's Liz's Big Story Mark III about a conspiracy to blow up the Opera House and take over the government. Quite frankly it's all over the place. The only thing I know for sure is that this Clem scares the shit out of me."

"Why don't you just walk into the cop shop and tell them what you know? Leave me out of it, but."

"No way. The cops are probably involved," Liz said. "Anyway, I'm not going to lose this story, however it turns out."

Kerry told her about the senior cop at the golf club night.

"Well, there you go. The way I see it, there's a lot more to happen yet. If I can be there when the shit hits the fan—sort of on the sidelines—I'll get the whole story. Then I'll disappear somewhere for a few months, write it all up as a book, take it to a publisher. I can't go to my newspaper with it now."

"Why not?"

"Because I'm pretty sure my boss is in on it. He's one of them. Anyway, what's your plan, Kerry?"

He didn't answer straight away. A lot of ideas had been bubbling away in his skull, but nothing was properly sorted.

They were approaching Avalon. Kerry pulled over and parked in the little shopping village.

"I'm starving. Let me get a couple of pies at the milk bar and we'll take them down to the marina. Then I'll tell you."

"Sauce with mine."

"Got it."

They found a bench under a shade tree opposite the bobbing yachts and cabin cruisers in Careel Bay, and ate the meat pies smothered in tomato ketchup. Kerry flipped the caps off a couple of soft drinks.

"So spill the beans, Kerry."

He didn't know why, but the words came easily. Maybe it was the girl, the way she listened as if she was interested. Maybe it was because he never had anyone to have a decent yarn with.

He told her how he'd slept with Zouzou and, like an idiot, thought he was in love with her, like he was under some kind of spell.

"So Zouzou was hanging around that night at the hotel, then? She's dangerous, Kerry. You're lucky the spell broke."

When he told her about meeting Moussa, he turned it into a joke—the tennis woman's ruined bag, Moussa on his arse. Liz laughed, but he said it wasn't that funny, more like he could see the whole thing sort of from the outside . . .

"Objectively, you mean?"

"Yeah, that's the word. And what I saw was that it didn't matter where my mum came from. I suppose she did what she had to do. My old man was always going on about how the immigrants were ruining the country and I just went along with it. Then, fuck me, turns out he married one. I mean, what's a bloke supposed to believe?"

"So you still haven't told me what you're going to do."

"I'm gonna settle a few things then disappear for a while."

"Settle what?"

"Clem and that bunch of Impeccable wankers."

"And disappear where?"

"I dunno, Fiji maybe. I've got some Kiwi mates there. Coupla business interests."

"How would you get there?"

Kerry nodded towards the moored yachts.

"You own a yacht, Kerry?"

"Yeah, up in Cairns. Well, I sort of own it. It's a beaut chunk of boat—a Swan 65. Reckon you could sail it from Cairns to Fiji?"

"You serious?"

Kerry nodded.

"It'd be touch and go up north. The cyclone season's still got a month of two to go."

"I'll take that as a yes, then. Do you fancy a couple of months at an exclusive private resort near the Daintree River? Wait out the cyclones and get your book written? Then we nip over to Fiji and keep our heads down for the rest of the year."

"I suppose you sort of own the resort too? So what'll you be doing while I'm writing the book?"

"Knocking around the place, doing a bit of handyman work. Keeping my head down."

"I'm not sleeping with you up there."

"Thought hadn't passed my mind."

"OK, Kerry, I'm in, but you keep your handyman work in your pants."

"Deal," Kerry said. "But we forgot something."

"What?

"Pierre. He told us to come back tonight. Will we go?"

"We've got nothing to lose, Kerry. Let's go. Find out what those two weirdos have got planned."

* * *

Kerry dropped Liz off on the Corso in Manly and headed home. He had the rest of the afternoon to call his lawyer Russell, his accountant, the fixer and various other associates; if he was going to disappear for a few months, his business would need to tick over quietly on its own. By late afternoon, most of the loose ends in Sydney were tied up. Time to get things organised in

Queensland. There was a bloke in Cairns who owed him a favour or two; useful kind of guy with his fingers in all sorts of business.

"G'day Tiny. It's Kerry Rich."

"Bloody hell, I knew it was my lucky morning."

"How's that?"

"A fuckin' parrot shat on me hat."

"Didn't I always bring you good luck, Tiny?"

"Fair to middlin', mate. Anyway, what can I do you for?"

"I'm coming up your way for a bit, might need a bit of help."

Kerry described what he needed fixed.

"Consider it done, son. Call me when you get here."

His last job was to open the safe and make up some bundles of cash.

* * *

At 11.20 pm, Zouzou turned out the lights in Rialto Close and left the front door unlatched. There was no noise from the neighbours; she assumed they had smoked themselves into oblivion and gone to bed to recharge themselves for another day of surfing, drugs and petty crime. She lay on the sofa in the darkness while Pierre sat before a large sheet of paper covered in pencilled boxes, circles, arrows and tiny notations in neat Arabic handwriting. He had spent the last three hours slowly plotting this filigree of facts, inferences, probabilities, connections and conclusions. Just ten minutes before, he put down his pencil and eraser, and said, "Yes, it is now all clear."

A whispered "Hi" announced Liz's arrival. She slipped inside and sat on the floor. Moments later, Kerry entered and sat next to Liz. What a difference a day could make, Zouzou reflected. Look at them—two scorpions in a huddle. What game were they playing?

Pierre rolled up the sheet of paper, securing it with a rubber band.

"Zouzou, let us sit on the floor with our companions."

She was about to protest that she had not sat on a floor since she was a child, when she caught Pierre's slight headshake in the gloom. These two may be scorpions, but for now her husband needed their stings where he could see them.

"Thank you for coming. There have been developments. I have been in touch with Clem and I can tell you that he is known to us from a previous operation. He is a dangerous individual. Clem has told me that the current assignment is to be moved forward. We are to carry out the task tomorrow night, and not on Anzac Day."

"Fuck's sake," Kerry gasped.

"Why change it, and who says you just do as he says?" Liz hissed.

"On the first question, I suspect that Clem is worried about leaks. Anzac Day is more than two months away. Tongues may wag, secrets may not remain secrets. I also suspect that those who planned this operation never intended it to occur on Anzac Day. It may be that The Impeccables do not even know the date has been changed."

"Hang on," Liz said. "So Clem wants to take everyone by surprise?"

Pierre had their attention. Zouzou heard the quickening of Kerry's breath.

"So what are we gonna do?"

"You're going to carry out the mission?" Liz asked.

"Yes."

"And we're not going to stop them?"

"No, Liz"

"Why not?"

"Because Clem fully intends the Opera House to be blown up."

"And you two are just going ahead with it?"

"Yes, but the device will not work," Pierre explained.

Liz snorted in exasperation. "This isn't making any sense at all."

Zouzou broke in. "We replaced the gelignite with fake explosive. When we press the switch, the detonator will go off like a firecracker and spray a little modelling clay and paper around."

"So where do we fit into all this?" Liz asked. Zouzou stared hard at her. Ha! Now she and Kerry were *we*.

"You tell me where you fit in," Pierre said. "You have been less than frank."

Kerry was fidgeting hotly in the gloom. Zouzou caught the pungent tang of his cologne and sweat. She forced down the memory of that night.

"Ok," Liz said, "I might as well tell you because it's irrelevant now. You three were supposed to be arrested before you had a chance to set the bomb off. Clem was going to let me observe you being interrogated, and I'd write the whole thing up for the newspaper."

Pierre tapped the paper tube. "I imagined something along those lines."

"Now you break the news," Kerry spluttered. "When were you going to tell me I was going to be arrested, Liz?" Liz made no reply.

Pierre waited until Kerry had settled. He rose from the floor and sat on a chair with his audience at his feet.

"Please listen carefully. I am convinced that Clem wants the bomb to explode and The Impeccables to overthrow the government. He and his associates probably planned to arrest Zouzou and me after the explosion—assuming there was an explosion. We would be blamed—two hired terrorists operating under instruction from the Southern Cross League. As for you, Kerry, you would be eliminated."

"Eliminated? As in 'killed'? Why?"

"Calm yourself. Because if you are dead, then nobody can deny that you are—if I may be blunt—a nobody."

"Hey, buddy, watch yourself. Who's a friggin' nobody?"

"I merely meant that you are not the head of the Southern Cross League."

"It's brilliant," Liz added. "The Opera House has got a big hole in it, there's a front-page story the next day blaming the thing on Australia's home-grown Nazi organisation, and a couple of bad Arabs thrown in for good measure. The government's caught flat-footed. Sir Robert McDougall's press barons call for the PM to resign, The Impeccables move their people into key posts to prevent a collapse into anarchy . . . but hang on, where do I stand in all this?"

"Also eliminated, Liz. A day or two after your article is published."

Liz gasped. "But Clem said . . . Oh, God. what an idiot I've been. Don't tell me—if I'm dead, nobody can know how I was set up."

"You are getting the hang of it," Zouzou murmured.

The dark mass of Kerry's body shifted slightly towards Liz in the faint light from the street. Now Zouzou was sure; the scorpions had made a truce. They would scuttle away, stings sheathed.

"So, it is each to his own fate. Zouzou and I will make our escape after the device has been triggered. I advise you two to disappear."

There were a few moment of silence. A police car roared past the end of Rialto Close, its siren wailing, and faded into the distance.

Kerry lit a cigarette. The flare of a match briefly showed deep concern on his face.

"Jeez, Pierre. Why don't we all just bugger off tonight? Forget the operation? Leave 'em to it?"

Zouzou watched her husband consider the question. He made a steeple of his fingers.

"I am no gambler, Mr Kerry. I deal in calculated risks based on facts. I judge that if any of us try to flee before the operation, we will be captured and permanently disposed of. Indeed, I am sure that this house is being watched at this very moment. However, if we go ahead with the bombing and it fails as we anticipate, Clem's plan will be thrown into chaos. In that brief moment of confusion, we will flee."

Zouzou knew Pierre had no getaway plan as yet, despite his enigmatic comments to her earlier in the day about 'an idea forming'. Would they trundle off on their old motor bikes in the early morning, their belongings in haversacks? Would the bikes conk out on the scorching highway the next day? Would they die in a roadside ditch of thirst and despair? Or be shot in the head by men in black overalls and baseball caps? There was still thinking to do on that point.

"The bastards," Kerry spat. "Hey, is the real gelignite around?"

"Yes. What do you have in mind, Mr Kerry?"

"A stick hidden in a certain house in Mosman, an anonymous phone call."

"Zouzou, please give Mr Kerry what he needs before he leaves. So it is farewell, I suppose, Miss Liz and Mr Kerry."

Liz jumped up. "Farewell? You've got to be kidding. I'm coming with you on the operation. I'm a journalist, remember. I wouldn't miss it for the world. But one more thing."

"Yes?"

"You seem so sure of all this. How can we trust you?"

Zouzou stepped back into the room and turned to Liz: "My husband has never betrayed a living soul. You may trust him without doubts. Or perhaps you have a better solution to the puzzle?"

"Forget it. I'm in."

"And I've got a little job to do at Mosman," Kerry said. "Where's that bloody gelignite, Zouzou?"

After they had left, Zouzou went to the bedroom to prepare her face for sleep. When she returned, Pierre was sitting on the sofa, pushing the ashtray button and staring at the spinning chrome ring. What was it that so fascinated him in that vortex?

"*Habibi*, come to bed."

He looked up. She caught a glimpse of suppressed horror before he stilled the ashtray, stood up, and led her to the bedroom with a tender arm around her shoulder.

Chapter 20: The Operation

You could sense them. Watchers. The streets were empty at one in the morning, but she knew they were there.

Liz watched Zouzou thirty metres ahead of her on Argyle Street. The Egyptian woman disappeared with her rucksack into the stone tunnel below the Harbour Bridge rampart and then emerged into the dim street lighting beyond. Pierre was further ahead, probably nearing the ferry terminal. Kerry had parked the Datsun outside the Garrison Church a little way behind, the keys in the exhaust pipe.

Liz loved The Rocks. She cherished the memories of the protests against the destruction of the twisting Georgian alleys and sandstone staircases. She'd been arrested in 1973 along with members of the Builders Labourers Federation and the local residents, and sculled celebration beers in the Glenmore Hotel when the developers caved in.

Keep split up, that was the plan. If Clem's crew intended to snatch any of them, they'd be better separated. Pierre would work his way around to the Opera House to plant the bomb, flash the torch signal and then take the longer route via Harrington Street to the garden of the Garrison Church, where he would hide in view of the Datsun. Zouzou would conceal herself among the old Georgian warehouses to trigger the device. She wasn't sure whether she would see or hear the detonator explode across the water from her hiding place, so Liz was to post herself further north at Dawes Point with binoculars.

Pierre had predicted that when Clem and his associates realised the device had failed, they would be thrown into confusion. Had it been sabotaged? Did it need to be triggered again? Should they attempt to clear away the remnants of bomb scattered around the window of the Bennelong Restaurant? Zouzou would be at the greatest risk. She needed a diversion; that was Kerry's job.

There was a watcher somewhere to Liz's right, she was sure. She doubled back through the Garrison Church garden, crouched in the gloom. There he was, a figure pressed against the massive sandstone wall below the Observatory Park, straining to catch a view of her. She flitted across Lower Fort Street, down a rank path between two crumbling terraced houses and popped out by the old pissoir under the bridge stanchion. A quick scramble down a twisting cascade of stone steps brought her back to the Argyle Cut.

She stopped in horror to see a man remonstrating with Zouzou. Should she approach, find out what the argument was about? She edged towards the stone tunnel, back flat against the walls until she reached the shadows. Zouzou and the figure were now just twenty metres away. The figure was a man, and he seemed to be protesting that he had been cheated out of a promise.

"He said he'd take me with him."

"Pierre never mentioned this to me, Mark."

"Where is he? I have to see him."

"Not now. I am busy, can't you see?" Zouzou strode away, but the man—who the hell was Mark?—ran after her. Liz caught half a sentence.

" . . . or I'll make a bloody racket."

Zouzou appeared to relent. The man Mark trotted after her as she made her way to the dark alley to obtain line of sight to the device that Pierre was supposed to be placing outside the restaurant on the northern buttress of the Sydney Opera House. Liz continued the last two hundred metres to Dawes Point, where she knelt in shadow with her eyes scanning the finger of land on which the spectacular building sat.

She seemed to have eluded the watchers, but the sound of feet on gravel somewhere behind told her she might be wrong. But there was no opportunity to watch the dark knoll behind her; she needed eyes ahead.

There it was: Pierre's torch flashing "B-I-N-G-O" in Morse, halfway between the southern steps of the Opera House and the Circular Quay ferry wharf. The device was in place! The scrape of gravel came again. Had the watcher seen the signal? Zouzou would have her finger on the button now. Kerry would be stationed in a stolen car containing a ten-litre can of petrol with a rag stuffed in the bunghole, ready to release the handbrake, light the rag and shove it down Hickson Road to burst into flames against the railings.

Liz was to run to Zouzou's position if the device didn't go off in one minute. But there it was—a faint spark of light; the detonator in the device had exploded; there followed a *pop* as the sound travelled across the water.

Liz held her breath. Yes, as Pierre had predicted there was silence as the watchers waited. She sprinted up the knoll to where Kerry was waiting.

"Kerry, good to go now."

Kerry nodded, got out his lighter. The petrol drum sat in the front footwell, the wet rag stinking.

Just as Kerry leaned over to release the handbrake, a boom shook the night air. Kerry sprang away from the car and rushed to the top of the knoll.

"It's fuck'n gone off."

They stared across the water. The Opera House stood serene and undamaged.

"It hasn't. Look, there's nothing gone off."

"Something blew up. It was up there." Kerry pointed towards the central business district. Half a dozen dark shapes materialised from behind cars and the corners of buildings. Nearby, they heard the crackle of a hand-held radio.

"Say again? George Street? The QVB? The bastards. OK, on way."

"Did he say George Street?" Kerry hissed. "Did those crazy Arabs just blow up the Queen Victoria building? What the fuck's happening?"

Sirens started to blare. A black car slewed around Hickson Road, stopping to pick up watchers bolting towards the city centre.

Liz grabbed Kerry's arm. "Let's get out of here."

In a few minutes they were at the Garrison Church, diving into the bushes to get a vantage point of the Datsun.

"What happened?" It was Zouzou, crouched a few metres away in the dark.

"You tell me," Kerry growled. "You said the bomb was a fake."

Fast running steps announced Pierre. He was out of breath.

243

"There are police everywhere. It looks as if we had competition."

Liz was focussing on the Datsun.

"There's nobody around. I'll go first and grab the keys from the exhaust. I'll drive slowly back here and you all jump in."

The keys were where they were supposed to be. She squatted by the passenger door, peering at the empty streets. Just as she was about to get in, a man ran past yelling into a radio, and disappeared down the Argyle Cut in the direction of the sirens. Quiet again. The motor fired, she eased the gear stick into first and crawled the forty metres to the church with headlights unlit. Kerry jumped into the front seat, Pierre into the back seat behind her, then Zouzou.

"Hang on," Kerry yelled. "Who's that prick?" A fifth person—a man—was squeezing in after Zouzou. The stranger pulled the door shut.

"More the merrier," Liz said. What a cock-up. What a story. What a buzz. She pulled away, hit the turning into Kent Street and in minutes they were across the Harbour Bridge and heading up the Pacific Highway. Kerry and Pierre were yelling across the back seat. The stranger had his head between his knees and was mumbling something about needing a drink.

"Enough!" Zouzou quelled the yelling. "He begged me. He is a pathetic wreck. My husband made him a promise. Pierre, tell them who he is."

"Yeah, tell us who he is and we'll chuck the fucker out at the Crows Nest traffic lights."

"Don't you know? He is Clem," Pierre wailed.

Liz turned around. The poor sap in the back seat had straightened up. She got a good look at him. Clem? Bloody hell, that Pierre had got his Egyptian knickers in a knot. A laugh welled up in her. Kerry caught it and the car wobbled across the lanes as they guffawed fit to burst.

"What is it?" Pierre asked.

"That's not Clem," Liz said. They stopped laughing.

"Will we chuck him out?" Kerry asked.

"You've got to be joking," Liz said. There had to be a whole side story attached to this one.

"Look here, Liz. We've gotta ditch the car. Have you lot in the back got anywhere you need to be?"

Pierre and Zouzou shook their heads.

"No plan, then?"

"Not exactly," Pierre confessed.

"Fancy Queensland?"

Pierre and Zouzou shrugged.

"What about the other fella?"

"He is with is," Zouzou said.

* * *

Liz took a detour back to Military Road and down the hill to Balmoral Beach. It was nearly two in the morning. She drove gently down the steep hill to the exclusive Harbour enclave of Federation period houses with gorgeous tilework and late model Mercedes Benz's.

Yes, it was still there in the carpark. She'd noticed it a few days before—an orange VW Kombi with a crude map painted on the side showing a journey from England to Australia. A little Union Jack hung from a radio aerial. A line of underwear hung between the wing mirror and a tree.

Kerry beckoned Liz to stop a little way from the vehicle, got out and strode up to the side door. He knocked, knocked again. Liz got out of the car to watch.

245

"Wot?" A skinny man in a baggy vest slid the door open. "You the old bill? I ain't done nuffink wrong." He was joined by a plump girl in a tight vest.

"Wossup, Jeff? Woss 'e want?"

Kerry peeled off some bank notes from a roll concealed in his fist.

"Just give us the keys, chum."

"Woffor?" Jeff protested.

"Ow much you got there?" The plump girl was evidently smarter than Jeff.

"Two grand and keep yer Pommie mouth shut."

"Three." The girl tipped up her chin.

"Two and a half," Kerry said.

"Give 'im the keys, Jeff."

* * *

Liz followed the Kombi up the hill, across Military Road and through Mosman's pretty village. She reversed the Datsun into a space in a long row of parked cars next to a cricket pitch, locked it, tossed the keys into a storm water drain and slipped into the front seat of the Kombi. The Datsun wouldn't be noticed for days. Kerry got out and walked around the old car, patting it here and there.

"What is he doing?" Zouzou asked.

"He seems to be saying goodbye," Pierre suggested.

Kerry got back in.

"Everyone comfortable?"

Pierre and Zouzou, along with the mystery man, were perched on the side bench seats in the back. Liz watched them all nodding in the mirror.

"We'll be off, then."

* * *

The Kombi puttered manfully through the night. Liz half-dozed, trying to follow the route Kerry was taking through the back streets of the North Shore.

"Better keep off the Pacific Highway till we clear Sydney," Kerry said, lighting his tenth cigarette since they'd left Balmoral Beach. As they drove through a leafy street in Wahroonga, the stranger in the back seat said, "Home sweet home."

Kerry turned to ask him, "Come again, mate?"

"Forget it."

"You a Pom?"

"Yeah, so what?"

"Just asking."

At the Brooklyn Bridge, with Sydney an hour behind them, Kerry took the winding road down to the mighty Hawkesbury River, glistening under the moon among the hills that marched away for ever into the night. The cool river air smelled of sulphur and honey and mint. A million night creatures squeaked and whistled and snapped. It was 4.30am.

Kerry turned off the motor and instantly fell to sleep. The three in the back shuffled and fidgeted. Liz turned to see them draped across the rancid sleeping bags Jeff and his girlfriend had bequeathed them. Her eyes fluttered as she saw a hint of pink dawn on the horizon, and then she was gone.

* * *

Pierre woke at the sound of somebody retching. He looked around. He was in a van of some kind. The van was filled with bright morning sun. A man's arm was across his chest. The memory of the night flooded back. He shoved Mark Bellamy off, and tumbled out of the sliding door. The van was parked twenty metres from some little houses of a nautical bent—dinghies and cannisters and cables strewn across the verandahs and front yards.

Zouzou was kneeling at the water's edge spluttering. He rushed to her side.

"No, leave me, *habibi*. I am fine now."

"Do you need a doctor?"

"Just food. When did we last eat?" He helped her limp back to the van. It wasn't like Zouzou to vomit.

Kerry and Liz were awake now, Kerry smoking like a blast furnace while Liz studied an Esso road map she'd found among the foil pie dishes, drink cans and cigarette packets on the floor of the van.

"Morning," Mark Bellamy groaned before flopping back down and falling asleep.

"Is there a plan?" Pierre asked.

Kerry pointed at Liz's map. "We'll find a servo at Gosford, fill up and get some grub. Then we'll put a coupla hundred k's on the clock, maybe get to Port Macquarie by tonight, maybe Yamba. Depends on this old pile of shit."

Pierre gazed at the woolly hills as they wound their way to their destination. Last night's events held no surprise in retrospect. With Ealing, every plan was the facade of another plan. Who could divine why they had caused an explosion in George Street? A diversion? But from what? A warning? But of what?

Liz spoke up, echoing his thoughts. "What the hell was that blast last night? Did Clem cause that?"

Pierre shook Mark's shoulder. "What do you know of it, Mark?"

Kerry broke in, "So why would your mate Mark know anything about it?"

"Because he works—or worked—for Clem."

"We all bloody worked for Clem, mate. So whadya got to say, Mark?"

"I need a drink."

"You and me both, mate."

An Ampol gas station appeared on the left. Kerry slid the van next to the pump. Pierre went into the shop where a sleepy kid was drinking a cola and eating a chocolate bar behind the counter. A mangy German Shepherd blinked at Pierre and went back to sleep.

"Is there a toilet?"

"Customers only."

Pierre looked around the sparse shelves. He grabbed a bottle of milk, some Iced Vovos and three of yesterday's meat pies from a warmer. The smell of the pies catapulted him back momentarily to the training course at the rural campus.

"Oh, and a *Herald*, thanks." Pierre used the folded newspaper to cradle the groceries, and paid.

The boy handed him his change and a boomerang with a key attached.

While Zouzou was freshening up in the washroom, Pierre tipped the breakfast items onto the back seat of the Kombi. He unfolded the *Sydney Morning Herald*. The headline sent a jolt of ice through his gut. He reached out to steady himself against the van, dropped the newspaper.

Liz picked it up and scanned the front page.

"Oh shit. Oh no!"

A car pulled up at the opposite pump. A man in a Hawaiian shirt got out and signalled to the boy in the shop. Pierre saw Zouzou coming back from the washroom carrying the boomerang.

"It smelt like a zoo," she muttered.

"Get in the van, now, *habibiti*."

Liz was crouched on the ground, rocking on her heels. Pierre pulled her to her feet and eased her into the front seat. He took the newspaper from her. Perhaps he'd misread it. No. Two deaths early that morning outside the Sydney Hilton. A bomb. Commonwealth leaders staying at the hotel. The army called in.

The Hawaiian shirt man had given up trying to get the boy in the shop to come outside to pump his petrol.

"No bloody service anywhere these days. Might as well do it meself."

"It would be for the best," Pierre said, fretting as Kerry took his time to pay the boy inside. Kerry stopped to glance at the newspaper rack. He raised his head, looked directly at Pierre, and walked briskly out of the garage shop with the gait of a man on the verge of breaking into a sprint.

They were all in the Kombi now. Hawaiian shirt man was frowning at them.

"Kerry," Pierre said. "Please start the van and drive very slowly onto the highway. Liz, act as if you are enjoying a day out with your husband. Mark, please remain on the floor."

"I need a drink for Christ sake."

"All in good time, Mark. Zouzou and I will lie on the benches out of sight." Pierre knew that their survival depended on somebody taking command, even if they had not a clue of the proper course of action.

"You see, we will be less conspicuous with you and Liz as a loving couple on a nice day out, rather than five adult misfits with worried expressions."

"All good, chum," Kerry said, but the quaver in his voice echoed Pierre's horror at what had happened.

"What do I do with this?" Zouzou held the boomerang aloft.

"Fuck's sake," Kerry hissed. He grabbed the thing, and tossed it to the Hawaiian shirt man.

"Dunny key, mate."

"Thanks chum, just the ticket."

* * *

The Kombi chugged steadily north, the passengers silent. From the bench, Pierre's view was a moving slice of hot blue sky punctuated by the occasional canopy of grey trees or a wall of red rock. The heat in the van was diabolical.

But the afternoon sun, the engine noise and the syncopated view lulled Pierre into a meditative state in which his mind roamed systematically through the events surrounding the bombing. Three hypotheses emerged from this process.

The prime hypothesis was that Zouzou's bomb trigger had somehow been connected to the device at the Hilton. The logic was as clear as day: Trigger + bomb = explosion. But so often in his career, Pierre had observed cold logic being confounded by human perversity. Two questions must be answered: Why bomb the Hilton Hotel rather than the Opera House? And could the bomb have actually been triggered from so far away?

The second hypothesis was that the Opera House bomb was a decoy for a more evil act of terror at the Hilton, an attempt to murder international leaders. Perhaps the authorities had been persuaded to concentrate their efforts on catching the Opera House bombers in the act, ignorant of the Hilton plot.

A third hypothesis was that the two plots were entirely unrelated.

Pierre had given up believing in coincidences long ago.

His reverie was broken by the crackle of the car radio. The triumphant fanfare of the Australian Broadcasting

Commission heralded the news. The passengers listened in silence to the shocking details of the bombing.

"What have you done?" Liz asked. "What the hell have you people done?"

"We haven't done anything," Kerry hissed. "They've screwed us over."

"You can't say that." Liz was shouting now. "You and them in the back, you all helped to build that thing."

"But we put in fake explosives."

"So you say . . . "

"Are you accusing me of . . . "

"Shuddup, shuddup, I'm trying to drive . . . "

Zouzou yelled at them in Arabic to behave like adults.

Pierre heard a siren coming up from behind.

"Cop car, cop car, cop car," Kerry intoned.

Pierre raised his head to see Liz's holiday smile clamped to her face.

"Overtaking now," Kerry muttered through ventriloquist lips. "Ahead now, he'll wave us down any second . . . what do we say?"

The car whooshed past.

"No, it wasn't us. He's after a motorbike up ahead. Phew."

The van carried on for a little while and then slowed.

"Traffic up ahead. It's gonna be a crawl. We're coming into Coffs Harbour."

"Is there a place we can camp for the night?" Pierre asked.

"There's a string of little beaches beyond Coffs," Liz said. "I know a couple of places where we can stop. But we need some supplies, food, maybe some beach clothes so we look like holidaymakers."

They agreed to drop Liz off in the town and pick her up in an hour. Pierre watched Kerry peel off some big dollar bills for her. He was wearing a green sleeveless garment—perhaps fishing garb—with multiple pockets. The roll of dollars disappeared into one such pocket. Liz walked away. Would she return? Would she head straight for a police station?

Kerry took a side road leading to the town's fishing port. They passed a knot of local shops—a milk bar, a real estate agent and a bottle shop. Pierre got out and bought a box of cheap white wine.

"What now, then?" Kerry asked when they'd parked in a quiet spot. A strong breeze off the sea cooled the air in the van. Huge seabirds whirled and dived. The sun had passed its zenith. A fishing boat puttered into the tiny harbour.

Mark Bellamy stirred and sat up in the Kombi's floor.

"Time for some questions. Mark, sit up. Kerry, pass me the wine box."

Pierre found a plastic cup in the milk crate that served as the Kombi's pantry, and filled it with wine. Mark guzzled half a cupful and got off the floor and onto the bench. He knocked off the other half.

"That's cleared my head." He held out the cup for a refill.

"You must earn it, my friend. We have half an hour before we collect Liz. Let us use it profitably. Convince me, please, that we should not drive to the top of that cliff and throw you off."

"You wouldn't, Pierre. You're not a killer. It's not in your nature."

Pierre glanced at Zouzou, but she looked away.

"So let us begin. Who is Clem, and what is your relationship to him?"

Mark Bellamy let out a vast sigh. He began to unburden himself.

The story came out in lumps and tangled threads as he backtracked and filled gaps he'd missed. Was he acting a role? No, this was a man addled by drink, a man ruined by betrayal and duplicity. He spoke of arriving in Sydney on false papers, of being collected from the airport by the man called Clem, who installed him in the garage to wait for instructions. Clem brought him occasional news about his wife in Moscow—how her swap wouldn't be long, how she'd be brought to Sydney when the Soviets let her leave. He'd done a few odd tasks—delivered packages to a dead drop, stood lookout, bought train tickets. Then Clem told him to contact Pierre.

"Did he tell you why?"

"No. Not really. No, not at all."

Pierre insisted on a clear answer, but it seemed that Mark Bellamy was utterly in the dark about the bomb plot.

"Who does Clem work for?" Kerry asked.

"Ealing of course."

"On the Underground, y'mean? Where all the Aussies live?" Kerry asked.

"Yes, well no, not exactly. Pierre, you explain it to him."

"Later. I have one more question. Why did you give me that address and phone number? The zoo, I mean."

"Clem told me if you ever came asking about anything, I had to do it. What do you mean by the zoo?" Mark clapped hand to brow. "Oh, bloody hell, not the old sealion trick?"

Kerry tapped his watch.

"We will go in a moment. Zouzou, now a question for you. Is it possible that your bomb trigger could have detonated a device a mile away out of direct sight?"

Zouzou rolled her eyes. "What a foolish question. I may have learned the rudiments of bomb making, but I cannot perform miracles."

Liz was waiting by the roadside with a clutch of supermarket bags and a bundle of bright T-shirts and shorts.

"I've got thongs and hats too."

Kerry pulled onto the Pacific Highway and followed Liz's directions to the small beach she had in mind. The radio news came on. They listened to the latest information on the bombing in gloomy silence.

"Just turn down here, Kerry."

"OK, Liz. Alright if I turn the radio off?'

"No, listen . . . "

In news to hand, New South Wales police have issued this urgent alert. Following a serious incident in Sydney, police are searching for businessman Kerry Rich and journalist Liz Lanzoni. They were last seen in the Manly area. Mr Rich is forty years old, 180cm in height with a black mullet hairstyle. Ms Lanzoni is in her early thirties, slim build, with long blonde hair. The pair are considered dangerous and should not be approached by the public.

Chapter 21: On the Road

Pierre woke to the crash of rollers. They had dined last night on the cold food Liz bought in the town. Kerry worked out how to erect a tent and groundsheet that attached itself to the side of the Kombi. The police alert for Kerry and Liz was left unmentioned; perhaps the news was beyond the capacity of the gang—Pierre could find no other word to describe their party—to process. After the scrappy meal, they had all flopped onto the ground or the floor of the Kombi and fallen asleep.

But the morning rose magnificent: An eggshell sky, crisp salt-laden air, the Kombi sitting on a cosy carpet of sandy grass amid a glade of contorted palm trees of prehistoric appearance. A concrete picnic table stood conveniently nearby, a crude toilet block just beyond. Two kangaroos stared at Pierre from deep in the trees. A track led to a majestic golden beach littered with jagged red and grey boulders as big as buses.

Zouzou tottered from the Kombi and knelt behind a bush retching.

"Still poorly, *habibti*? Perhaps we should find a doctor." A medical emergency perhaps loomed. He knelt beside her, rubbing her shoulders.

"I want to die." His wife spewed copiously.

"Bit of a coincidence, isn't it?" It was Liz, running her hand through tangled hair. "Nausea two mornings running?"

Zouzou got up, flapped a hand in Liz's direction, and tottered to the toilet block.

Kerry emerged. "Wassup?"

"It's Zouzou. Looks like she's in a delicate condition. How does fatherhood appeal to you, Pierre?"

Liz had her head on one side, an ironic smile on her face. Pierre was getting her measure now; the kind of woman who considered life a joke made for her personal amusement.

There was time for detailed character analysis later. The immediate task was to consider Liz's remark. Could Zouzou really be pregnant? He shuffled his mental calendar, refreshed his memory of the books and pamphlets they had read on fertility. Yes, the facts fit. That night they made the fake gelignite; she would have been at the peak of her cycle. He stood in stationary panic beside the Kombi, constructing a scenario that included a pregnant Zouzou as member of a runaway gang.

Then without warning, his eyes flooded with tears and he fell to his knees honking and snuffling. A hand caressed his shoulder, slipped down to his elbow. Zouzou helped him to his feet. When he looked up, Liz was beaming and Kerry was fidgeting with a cigarette lighter. Pierre wiped his eyes.

"Is it true *habibti*?"

"I am no expert, Pierre, but it looks likely." She had freshened her face in the toilet block.

"What do we do now?" Pierre looked around the gang. Mark had crawled out of the Kombi and was sitting in the doorway rubbing his eyes.

"She has to get to a doctor," Liz suggested.

"Right now?" Pierre asked. "While we have two police fugitives in our midst?"

"I do beg your pardon. I'll try my best to avoid being on the wanted list in future. Anyway, she'll have to see a doctor in a few days, you know, to get a test."

"Maybe we can all hang around in a park or something while Zouzou sees the doc?" Mark proposed.

"What's it got to do with you, you Pommy prick?" Kerry flung the words over his shoulder, walking off down the beach path.

"May I join the conversation?" Zouzou asked. Pierre nodded.

"Thank you *habibi*. It is time to be practical. Here are the facts." She began to enumerate her points starting with her index finger.

"Point one: I am most likely pregnant. Point two: Pregnancy is not an illness. I will find a doctor when I feel I need to. Point three: Kerry and Liz must now remain out of sight. Somebody else must drive the van."

Kerry came back from the beach and stood shuffling and avoiding the eyes of the rest of the gang. What was he hiding, Pierre wondered? Was he to be trusted? With Zouzou's drastic change of condition, he was desperately worried for her safety.

"Point four: Look at us. We resemble the downs and the outs. Liz, please hand out our holiday clothes."

She was right. They were still in the clothes they wore on the night of the bombing, crumpled and sweaty after two nights sleeping rough. Pierre scratched an armpit. They all needed a good wash.

"So who's gonna drive now me and Liz are in the frame?" Kerry asked, sullen and irritable.

Pierre looked around the circle. Mark held his head between his knees. Zouzou was doing a fair impersonation of the Great Sphinx of Giza's inscrutable gaze.

"How about you, Pierre?"

"I cannot. I never learned."

"What the fuck? I never heard of a bloke who couldn't drive."

What was the point of explaining? In Egypt he never owned a car. One travelled by taxi or rode a motorbike. Car driving was performed by car drivers.

"Well, that leaves him." Kerry pointed at Mark. "And that boozer's not getting behind the wheel with me in the vehicle. So what are we gonna do?"

The Sphinx turned her languid eyes on Kerry.

"I will drive."

Pierre spluttered, "But you don't know how to . . . "

She threw her head back. "You obviously never saw me in *Race for Romance*. I played a female stunt driver who fell in love with a mechanic from a poor family. I was trained on the set by the great Lebanese Formula 1 driver Roger Mansour."

They all waited. Was there more of this story? Zouzou stared into the distance.

"Well, say no more," Liz laughed.

Pierre chivvied the gang to prepare their departure. They took turns to shower in the toilet block, each emerging in jolly shorts and T-shirts, with Kerry's outfit topped by the fishing vest. Mark lay down in the floor pan of the Kombi, and Liz and Kerry stretched out on the side benches. They closed the side curtains.

Pierre sat in the passenger seat next to Zouzou, who slid the Kombi into gear and drove smoothly towards the highway.

"You're amazing, Zouzou," Liz said from the back. Pierre sat up straighter, glanced at his wife, his true partner. Yes, she constantly amazed him.

But what lay ahead? The gang had barely discussed where they were going. Cairns, Kerry had said. He had a yacht there which Liz would sail to Fiji. Pierre and Zouzou had looked anxiously at one another at the mention of the yacht; they'd had enough of boats to last them this life and the hereafter: Their escape from Alexandria in 1973 on the *Syria,* a stinking passenger ferry, as the Soviets unloaded missiles on the dock; Pierre's enforced voyage to Libya in 1975 on the putrid coastal freighter *Warda.*

Kerry had also mentioned a holiday resort where they'd stay first. That sounded more acceptable, but he had added that there was a crocodile farm next door. A proper discussion was overdue. Perhaps now was the time to raise the matter.

"Kerry, what will we do when we reach Cairns?"

"I dunno, mate. Let me think about it. I'm leaning towards us jumping on that yacht and getting the fuck out of Australia."

No more was said. They crossed into Queensland late in the morning.

"God's own country," Kerry muttered from the back.

"Back to the dark ages," Liz replied.

What did they mean? Pierre despaired at the gulf in his understanding of these Australians. He so often reflected that he was an observer on the sidelines of a game whose rules would take decades to decipher. His one sure anchor was Zouzou, who sat unwavering, navigating the clattering Kombi along the endless grey asphalt strip. What was she thinking? Was she mulling over her future as a mother? Was she wondering how he—Pierre, the man 'turned in on himself'—anticipated fatherhood? The questions were hypothetical; they were two sides of one coin, joined for infinity but unable to gaze into one another's souls.

An immense articulated truck overtook them, sucking the Kombi into its slipstream and sending it into a fishtail. As the throbbing mountain of metal and rubber tucked itself in front of the Kombi, a chrome hubcap spun the smashed face of Marcos Tawadros into a crimson vortex.

The van forged on under Zouzou's imperturbable command. The road passed through sparkling green hinterland, between ancient, forested mountain ranges and past calm blue seas inside the Great Barrier Reef. Pierre had seen photographs of the fabulous creatures that lived in the coral gardens; how he yearned to find a tiny corner along this spangled coast where he and Zouzou could finally disappear, learn to snorkel, catch flapping silver fishes . . .

Zouzou chose their stops carefully—gas stations that were not too busy, not too quiet, where the Kombi could refill and park itself in an obscure spot while its occupants sidled to the toilets. She topped up the air in the front left tyre at each stop. Pierre was of a mind to ask her where she had learned such things, but was reluctant to provoke a recounting of her vast filmography.

"Maryborough," she declared as dark fell. Murmurs came from the passengers, who sounded anaesthetised from hours in their horizontal oven.

"I mean we will stop there for gas in about half an hour, and find a place to park for the night on the road to the coast."

"Zouzou, *habibti*, are you able? Should you not take a short break?"

His wife set her jaw. "No breaks."

They found a suitable service station with a handy general store next door. While the attendant pumped the gas, the gang stretched their legs around the side of the building. Pierre remained by the Kombi.

"Local?" the attendant asked through a tiny aperture in the side of his mouth, gazing through slitted eyes into the far distance.

"Wodonga. Far from home." Pierre had found this charmingly named town on the map in the middle of nowhere.

"On yer holidays?"

"We are cousins *en route* for a wedding in Rockhampton."

"Fair dinkum?"

Pierre paid the man inside the office and stepped outside into a fracas.

Kerry was frogmarching Mark Bellamy away from a telephone kiosk outside the general store.

"Get in the vehicle, you mongrel."

"What happened?" Pierre asked. The gang were now onboard, with Zouzou about to release the handbrake.

"He was making a phone call, that's what happened. Who were you calling?"

"Nobody."

"You often call nobody, yer fuck'n moron? Zouzou, let's get out of here. We'll deal with him when we get to the beach. I knew we couldn't trust the bastard."

A police car cruised onto the forecourt, its front bonnet weaving like a shark stalking its prey. Its headlights blinked twice and it stopped. Two cops got out of the car, stretched their backs and rubbed their bellies.

"Get movin'," Kerry barked.

"Wait," Liz said. She slipped out of the Kombi, walked slowly to the pay phone and put the receiver to her ear, dialled, listened, and strolled back.

One of the police called to her. Pierre watched her, stomach churning, as she listened to the cop. She threw back her head, laughed and walked back to the Kombi. The attendant came out with cans of soft drink and the sweaty police quenched their thirsts.

"What did the copper say?" Kerry asked.

"Huh, I dunno. Some crap." She turned to Bellamy. "Double-one six-one—last number called, works every time. North Shore Office Supplies. They answered and rang off quick smart when I said hello. What was it, Mark? You needed some paper clips sent up?"

Kerry growled, "I knew I didn't trust the bastard." He grasped Bellamy's arm. "Sit tight, you drongo."

Zouzou turned off the highway, following the road into Maryborough. The little town of tin-roofed cottages slumbered in the hot dusk. She took three or four turns, guiding the Kombi through a stretch of flatlands, peering ahead for a landmark and glancing at the Esso map. The Kombi swung off the lane and stopped by a deserted stretch of water with a concrete shower block identical to the one at their last stop. Night fell abruptly. Zouzou turned off the motor.

"He hasn't had a drink today," Liz said, holding up the wine box.

"That's because he's been bullshitting us. He's not an alkie." Kerry shook Bellamy's shoulder. "What's the game?"

Pierre watched the drama playing out in the tiny theatre of the Kombi. Outside in the dark, a squadron of bugs and beetles clamoured, their varnished carapaces and sticky legs clicking and clattering against the window. Someone turned on the dim interior light: Zouzou, rigid and expressionless behind the wheel; sullen Mark Bellamy wriggling in Kerry's grip; Liz, bright-eyed and eager for the plot to move on. The trashy holiday clothes rendered the group pathetically ridiculous. The situation called—no, begged—for a resolution. Pierre made up his mind; he would tell Kerry and Liz the truth. The solidarity of the gang depended on honesty, not lies and obfuscation

"Release him please, Kerry," Pierre said with quiet deliberation. Kerry grunted and let go.

"Friends, I'm going to tell you what the 'game' is, as Kerry has requested. Mark, contradict me if I am wrong. The rest of you, listen but do not speak. Liz, this will be especially interesting to you."

Bellamy shrugged.

"Mark Bellamy and his girlfriend Lucy were on a diplomatic mission in Cairo in 1973. They were abducted to Moscow from Cairo with the connivance of a man called Donald Waters. Waters worked for a British intelligence agency we know as 'Ealing', but he was also a Soviet agent."

"Slow down, Pierre. I need to make some notes." Pierre waited while Liz angled her notebook under the dim interior light.

"Waters and his friends dressed up the abduction as a defection. Mark and Lucy were portrayed as traitors who had gone over to the other side. But they were merely stock, so to speak."

"Whadya mean by stock, Pierre?" Kerry asked.

Bellamy replied: "We were sitting on the shelf waiting to be swapped for someone the Russians wanted to bring home. Like stock in a bloody warehouse."

"Fair dinkum, you wouldn't read about it."

Pierre continued. "Ealing has a nasty habit of setting its agents up as sleepers. The trick is to blackmail or otherwise compromise the agent so that he or she can be activated to perform some task for them."

"Wow, I get it," Liz said. "The agent does the dirty deed and Ealing denies any involvement."

"Exactly. Now may I continue without interruption? Thank you. Now, Mark and Lucy had a child in Moscow. The family lived a normal life, as far as one could live in such circumstances. I assume you and Lucy had jobs, Mark? Translators perhaps?"

"Spot on, Pierre. Lucy took Russian seriously. Fitted in well. I was pretty mediocre. Couldn't find my feet."

"And after about two years, your handler asked to visit for a cosy chat—was it anyone we know, by the way?"

"No, a shit from Yorkshire called Derek. One of Philby's cronies. He'd been there for decades."

"Ah yes. So Derek made you an offer. You could return to the West alone—a spy swap of course—to perform one more mission. If you were successful, Lucy and the child would join you. The cream on the pie ..."

"On the cake," Zouzou said.

"Yes, the cream on the cake was that you were going to Australia, no less. New identities, a new life, barbecues at the beach, et cetera, et cetera. How am I doing, Mark? *Ittafa'na*?"

"*Bi-zubt*. Exactly."

"You still remember your Arabic. You spoke it well in our Cairo days. Where was I? So you were extracted from Moscow and sent here with instructions to lie low until contacted. Your cover story was—let me see—you were born in Australia but lived all your life overseas. You came back here to recover from some malady. Is that about right?"

Bellamy nodded.

Liz leaned forward. "How do you know all this, Pierre? And what's all this stuff about Ealing and Moscow?"

Pierre ignored her.

"Once you were settled in your squalid garage, the man we call Clem contacted you. He was your controller from Britain. He arranged small jobs for you on the promise of the reunion—delivering messages, identifying premises, and so on. Was it you who found the warehouse where we made the bomb?"

Bellamy nodded.

"And then you ensnared me to become the bombmaker. Did you tell Clem anything about me?"

"He knew everything, Pierre."

"Fuck me," Kerry spat. "So who is this prick Clem I've been working for?"

"Hush, Kerry. Now, Mark, when you asked to come with me after the operation, was that on Clem's instructions?

"Of course it was. I was to keep track of you."

"But do you trust Clem? Do you believe Ealing will reunite you with your family?"

"I wouldn't trust those bastards for a moment. Surely you don't think I'm naive, Pierre? They've screwed us both. But what could I do? I went for the main chance."

Kerry and Liz stared at the miserable Bellamy. Zouzou had turned to watch what must be the climax of the bizarre interrogation.

"Mark, in Cairo I trusted you without reserve."

"And I you, Pierre."

Kerry exploded: "What the fuck? You guys going in for a kiss and a cuddle?"

"Shut up, Kerry," Zouzou hissed.

"Mark, when you telephoned Clem, did you get through?"

"Yes."

"And what did you say?"

"Nothing. Kerry grabbed me and I whacked the phone down."

"So, what were you about to say?"

"That we were almost in Melbourne and heading south. A thousand kilometres away from here. I wanted to give us the best chance to get away from that bastard."

The gang sat in tense silence, each evidently weighing Bellamy's account.

Zouzou spoke first. "The choice is simple. We believe him or we kill him. I say we kill him."

Liz inhaled sharply. Bellamy slumped.

"Anyone here killed a man?" Kerry asked. "Zouzou, are you up for it?"

"Killing is not in my repertoire. But one of us may be capable. Have you taken a man's life, Kerry?"

"Never. Liz—what about you?"

"Mind your own business."

"Pierre?"

Pierre considered the question and found that he could not answer with certainty.

"Kerry, your questions are irrelevant. My wife was mistaken. There is a third choice."

"Thank Christ," Bellamy muttered.

"Very well. We will give Mark the opportunity to convince us."

"You mean get him to call Clem and tell him what he said he was going to say?" Liz asked. "What does everyone say? Will we give him a chance? Anyone think it's a crap idea?"

Suddenly, a light played on the trees near the water's edge.

"Everyone down!" Pierre pulled Zouzou towards him on the front bench and enveloped her in a clinch. He watched the light approach the Kombi through a slitted eyelid. Two voices floated through the sultry darkness, muffled by the van's closed windows—a man and a woman. A fist rapped on the van door.

"Give her one for me, mate," said the man. The woman giggled, and the couple passed along the path into the darkness.

The gang breathed out in unison.

"Now," Pierre said. How far is it to walk to that phone box? Fifteen minutes? Liz, you come with me and Mark."

He wanted to judge Liz's trustworthiness; what better way than to place her in the centre of a tight situation? Who knew how long the gang would need to remain united? He must know more of Liz's capability.

"We should tell him exactly what to say," Pierre said to Liz as they stumbled up the dark lane.

"Absolutely. We don't know what surprise he might pull when he opens his mouth."

Bellamy snorted.

They stopped in a bus shelter on the main road. Liz pulled out her notebook and scribbled some lines in the light of Pierre's Zippo.

"Here, say this."

Bellamy peered at the notebook.

"But I have to use a code name to identify myself. I have to say, 'this is Lord Mountbatten'."

"What if you're bullshitting us? Maybe Lord Mountbatten means 'what I'm about to say is under duress'?"

"You've been reading too many spy novels, Liz."

"Ditch the code name. Clem knows your voice. Here, I'll add a line: 'Look, I've only got a few seconds, so let's get straight to it'. Will he buy that?"

Bellamy shrugged. "I'll give it a try."

* * *

There was a poisonous atmosphere in the Kombi when they returned. Kerry was in the back seat, Zouzou in the front, both glaring into the night.

"Something wrong?" Liz asked. "I'd say a lovers' tiff if I didn't know better."

"Shut it, Liz. Anyway, how did it go?"

"It's settled, Kerry. Mark told Clem we're heading south towards Batemans Bay in a white 1969 Valiant station wagon with false licence plates PFR 310. Our destination is Eden, where we're to meet a colleague of Kerry's, but Mark doesn't know what plan the colleague has in mind."

"Will he swallow it?" Kerry asked.

"No," Pierre said. "But it might buy us just a little time."

"So we don't have to kill the bugger?"

"Not yet, Kerry," Zouzou murmured. "But I have something to say."

The gang waited.

Zouzou sat for a full minute, breathing deeply. At last, she twisted around in the bench seat to face the gang.

"An act of love," she spat. "Pierre. You told me Mark said Lucy and the child would be better off without a broken-down drunkard, and that she should meet somebody new, one of her Russian friends. She didn't want to leave Russia. Mark left her as an act of love."

Bellamy turned on Zouzou. "That was part of my cover story. I was to act a drunkard. Do you think I like drinking that filthy cheap wine when I'm in character?"

Zouzou leaned down, reaching under the Kombi bench seat. Suddenly there was a tyre wrench in her fist. The gang members threw themselves to the floor as the wrench swung at each of the three men. She screamed something in Arabic. The wrench missed Mark's head but struck a blow to his shoulder. It continued in an arc to sideswipe Pierre's jaw, and ended its flight somewhere in the front of Kerry's shorts. Liz leapt over the bench seat, pinned Zouzou down and flung the wrench out of the window.

"Anyone hurt? I mean properly hurt?"

"Nothing broken," Mark said.

"Nor here." Pierre rubbed his jaw. "But what about you, Kerry?"

"Mate, she fuck'n missed the family jewels by a whisker. What the hell was that, Zouzou? An inch closer and I'd have been a bloody gelding."

"The world would have been a better place," Zouzou gasped, wriggling under Liz's grip.

"Let my wife go, Liz. She will take a walk to cool off."

Zouzou climbed out of the Kombi. She turned to the gang.

"Forgive me. I lost my head for a moment."

She walked towards the water. There was the flare of a match, her face lit for a second, and then the darting tracery of the cigarette tip.

"*Al-hamdulillah*," Pierre muttered.

"*Wallahi*," Mark responded.

"Translation please."

"I thanked God, Liz, that the incident was not more serious. Mark affirmed my sentiment."

But what Pierre omitted to tell the gang was what Zouzou had screamed in Arabic as she swung the wheel brace. *God forgive me. What have I done?*

Chapter 22: A Train Trip

Pierre woke sweaty and blinded by the easterly sun. The gang shuffled and groaned in the heat. Zouzou was tottering back from the toilet block, grey-faced.

"Where is he?" Kerry sat up and lit a cigarette.

Mark Bellamy was gone.

"I heard him getting out in the night. I thought he was going for a leak," Liz said. "Christ, Kerry, can you smoke that outside? It stinks like a dog kennel in here."

Pierre and Kerry climbed out of the van. There was no sign of Mark Bellamy. They'd made a grave error in not dealing with him last night. A grave error in not killing him. Now the remains of the gang were exposed like dung beetles stranded on a rock, with hawks circling above.

"I saw a sign for the railway station last night. Let me check." Zouzou's colour had returned. She ran her finger over the Esso map.

"Why do we need a railway station?" Kerry asked.

"Use your brains, Kerry," Liz snapped. "If Mark's been on the phone to his boss, we've got to get shot of this Kombi quick smart."

"Yeah, well, I was testing you. Anyway, can you get a train to Cairns from here?"

"Sure can. I've been on the North Coast Line from Brisbane to Cairns. I remember going through Maryborough. Takes for ever."

Liz turned to Pierre. "How much does he know? Did we talk about going to Cairns in front of him?"

"There was talk. We spoke of the yacht. We have let the cat out of the sack, I fear."

* * *

The gang members left on foot fifteen minutes apart, each with fifty dollars to cover their train tickets, courtesy of yet another roll of Kerry's banknotes. He was, Pierre observed, a walking bank. Pierre left last, but not before patting the headlight of the Kombi. It hadn't been much of a home, but he felt an odd tenderness for the snub-nosed battler.

As he plodded through the lanes, abuzz with insects under the morning sun, he wondered what his employers might be thinking of his absence. Would he have been reported missing? Would the police have enquired after Kevin O'Donnell at Rialto Close? Who cared? He'd never again be the voice of hapless Arabs in those neon-lit courtrooms. He was, for the time being at least, Pierre Farag. O'Donnell was dead.

Late in the afternoon, the diesel train wheezed into the station. For the last fifteen minutes the gang members had been skulking separately along the platform in their grubby holiday garb. Where had they spent the day? Like him presumably, wandering the streets and riverbanks, sheltering under trees, avoiding passers-by. The gang climbed aboard and found separate seats for the long hours of travel to Cairns.

Pierre fell asleep immediately. He woke in the early hours of the morning to find a newspaper on the seat next to him. A fat man in elastic sided boots snored and snuffled in the seat opposite. A teenaged girl was curled up, fast asleep, on the other side of the carriage. The train swayed and murmured its progress through the tropical blackness.

The *Courier-Mail* was a Brisbane paper, mostly about politics and cricket, the news bookended by full-page display advertisements for checked shirts, discounted jewellery, and pet food. He scanned the pages to relieve the boredom. A five-line news item caught his eye: Sir Robert McDougall had been released from police custody following his arrest two days ago. No charges had been laid. Sir Robert was stepping down from his major business and charity commitments to spend more time with his family.

Kerry would be delighted. But what did it mean? Had The Impeccables' plot been rumbled? Was Clem cleaning up the mess? And was Mark Bellamy at this very moment rustling up a search party?

* * *

The gang reformed on Cairns railway station. Kerry shoved them into a waiting room where they nodded in the late afternoon heat.

"Just gonna call Tiny."

Pierre watched Kerry at the public call phone, patting his waistcoat pockets as he engaged in an intense discussion with the tiny person, whoever they might be. He put the phone down and bounced on his heels, lit a cigarette, and craned to examine each of the vehicles that swung into the station forecourt.

After ten minutes, a low-slung station wagon pulled up. Kerry beckoned to Pierre. The gang scuttled out of the waiting room and squashed into the station wagon.

"Keep yer heads down," the driver growled.

Pierre watched the sky and the crowns of passing palm trees from his vantage point among the knees and heads of the gang members in the back seat. They passed through a gateway onto what must be a wharf or a marina, judging by the sideways masts he could see. The vehicle stopped.

"OK," Kerry said. "There's the boat. Make it snappy."

Liz got out and hopped onto the deck of a small, handsome yacht tied up at the wharfside. She jumped up and down, ran around the boat evidently checking it for seaworthiness. Kerry was next. He looked back to the station wagon.

"C'mon, let's get moving."

Zouzou looked on, wordless. Pierre trembled at the very idea of sailing to Fiji in a tub no more than fifteen metres long.

"I thought it would be bigger, *habibti*."

"Tell him we cannot go."

Pierre got out of the station wagon and climbed onto the deck, wobbling to get his balance as the boat bore his wait.

"Not your cup of tea, Pierre?"

Pierre looked down, ashamed of his cowardice.

"I had me doubts, mate." Kerry squeezed his shoulder. "Don't wet your knickers over it. I've got a plan B. To be honest, it might work out better, you know, just me and . . . " He winked and cocked his head towards Liz.

"You spoke of a holiday resort, Kerry."

"Got it in one, chum. I thought maybe you and the lady could look after the place while I'm away."

Kerry led Pierre back to the station wagon. He leant in and spoke a few words to the driver, whose face was almost entirely obscured by a cap and wrap-around shades. The man nodded in reply.

"All set, then?"

"All set."

"Whoops, I nearly forgot." Kerry handed him a slip of paper.

"Tiny's number. Give him a bell if there's anything you need—maybe some ID."

He fished in an inner pocket of the waistcoat and gave Pierre a solid roll of banknotes wrapped in clear plastic.

"And here's something for the baby."

Zouzou glanced at the money and looked away. Kerry tapped the car roof twice.

"Keep your heads down till we're outa town," the driver said as he pulled away.

Chapter 23: All the Water in the World

The morning skies were charged with vast pillows of clouds that trapped the heat beneath them and coloured the ocean grey. Pierre had run the clattering air-conditioner all night, powered by its clattering cousin in the generator shed. In the daytime they were cooled by whatever wind might limply rise, or by a crashing shower of tropical rain.

At least Zouzou's morning sickness had vanished. Soon she would book herself into the Cairns Base Hospital, but first there was the matter of identity. Pierre had called Tiny in Cairns yesterday to learn if the 'items' were ready for collection.

Joseph wandered across from the crocodile farm and sat on the front step of the residence looking out to sea. Pierre had worked out the routine now. You didn't hurry things with these people. Especially, as he had learned, the resort and crocodile farm were on Aboriginal land.

The matter had arisen on their first day at the resort. Pierre and Zouzou woke up in the residence wondering what to do with their new life, two aliens on the far edge of civilisation with nothing between them except the clothes they wore and a thick wad of fifty-dollar notes.

When Pierre got out of bed and opened the door to the verandah, he saw a dark-skinned man in singlet and shorts standing perfectly still, looking into the house.

"Good morning, Sir," he assayed. The man looked at Pierre's feet, diverted his eyes sideways for a second when Zouzou came out wrapped in a sheet.

"G'day."

"Can I help you, Sir?"

"You'd be the new manager, then?" the expressionless man asked.

"I suppose I am," Pierre replied, for the lack of anything else to say. Who knew what this man was, whether he was hostile or friendly, whether Zouzou was at risk of being violated by him and his fellows.

"I'll show yer the ropes, then," he said, walking away. Pierre shrugged and followed him through a jungle pathway with a signpost saying 'crocodile farm'.

"Your name, Sir?"

"Joseph."

"G'day Joseph. I'm Pierre." Now he was getting into the swing of things.

But Joseph turned and stood half-square on to him, eyes averted. The jungle floor ticked with unseen insects. A peculiar turkey excavated a dirt mound with frenzy.

"Watch that plant there." He pointed at a scraggy tree. "Stings like buggery."

"Thank you."

Joseph stood still for a minute and said, "This is our land, mate. Aboriginal land." The man in the singlet might well have said the land belonged to Martians.

"Take it," Pierre said. "I make no claim."

They had become friends of a kind over the last two months, Pierre and Joseph, even if they spoke with economy and Joseph had only gradually begun to make eye contact. This aspect of his behaviour rattled Pierre, who was from a culture where the direct gaze was obligatory and replete with meaning and connotation.

The matter of whose land they were on was never mentioned again. They'd never enquired after one another's surnames.

"*Habibti*, will you please make Joseph a coffee?"

Pierre sat next to Joseph and offered him a cigarette. They lit up, taking their time to proceed. Where was the hurry? There'd been only a straggle of tourists, and the wet still had a month to run. When it started to dry up, Joseph had said, they'd get on with maintenance tasks—servicing the flat-bottomed boat and painting the teahouse shed. As for animal husbandry, the crocodile farm only existed on the entrance sign. The beasts wallowed on the banks of the creek that flowed through the so-called farm, achieving reproduction without human assistance.

Pierre's role as manager amounted to making tea, putting biscuits on paper plates, and writing up the primitive accounts. Who he kept the accounts for he knew not, because the business seemed to have no connection whatsoever with any institution, governmental or commercial. Cash in, cash out. Occasionally, Pierre gave the guided tour commentary at the back of the boat. He learned the patter from Joseph's cousin William, pointing out tree snakes and stinging bushes when the resident crocs Eyebrows, Slim and Pluto were not to be seen in the slime.

Zouzou handed Joseph his coffee. She sat next to Pierre and they all looked out to sea with their separate dreams in the wet heat.

"We're nearly out of diesel and gas," Joseph said. "I'd better take a drive into town."

"I need to go to Cairns anyway, Joseph."

The gas and diesel could be bought in nearby Mossman, but Pierre knew Joseph had family in Cairns he liked to visit.

"Make a day of it, then." Joseph finished his coffee and went for the truck.

When they were alone, Zouzou asked, "Did he mention the strangers?"

"What strangers, Zouzou?"

"Joseph told me yesterday that two men had been hanging around, asking odd questions. Enquiring after the new people."

"What kind of men?"

"He didn't say much, but he did mention one was a white man with curly hair like a woman. Oh, and a green and red T-shirt with a white rabbit on it."

"I think, dear heart, that you'd better come with us to Cairns." Strangers meant trouble, a commodity he was loath to deal in. Especially a stranger with a perm.

* * *

They drove down the access track, past the car bonnet that claimed Aboriginal ownership of the property. The hippy colony had grown, with two more pregnant women. It now sported a stall selling bead necklaces and shapeless clay pots to nobody.

Joseph wrenched the wheel of the truck onto the Captain Cook Highway, stamped on the throttle and crashed up through the gears until they reached cruising speed. It was too noisy to speak, too hot to open the windows. Pierre held Zouzou's hand and watched the drama of the roiling clouds in a sky as big as the world, and the endless green cane swirling in the fretful winds and the storm-charged atmosphere.

After two hours they ground into Cairns. The clouds had gone. The city lay flat and passive, its sun-bleached suburbs stretching to the foothills. The sun grilled the very particles of air, burning the lungs. No humans were to be seen on the shuttered streets of single-storey shops in the city centre.

"It is here, Joseph." They stopped outside a shopping arcade. Pierre instructed Joseph to pick them up at 6pm at the Barrier Reef Hotel, where he and Zouzou would spend the afternoon bathing and snoozing before returning to the wilderness.

The little shopping arcade was deserted. In one or two of the shops, a proprietor sat up from her slumber and raised a hopeful eyebrow as Pierre and Zouzou passed. One shop sold maps and globes, another oils and essences.

Here it was, shop 7B. *T&F Business Services*, the sign on the door announced.

"Come in."

The air conditioning inside was ferocious. A bald man got up from his desk. He wore braces over a swelling business shirt, elephantine trousers, and white leather slip-on shoes. This must be Tiny.

"G'day." He extended a hand to Pierre, and an appreciative glance towards Zouzou's breasts.

"Hope yer didn't make yerselves too obvious coming here."

"We were dropped off outside."

The man separated the slats of the venetian blind, peeped out.

"Strangers round here, yer see, on a quiet day. Stick out like dog's bollocks."

Pierre pondered the simile while the man unlocked a filing cabinet.

"Here," he said, handing over two Queensland driving licences and two Medicare cards. What were their new names to be? Pierre scrutinised the cards.

They were reborn as John and Mary Smith.

"Are they genuine?" Pierre asked. "I mean, are they likely to give us any trouble?"

"They're good as gold, son. I run a top-class service here. This is Queensland, not down south."

"I'm sorry. I didn't mean to be rude."

"You didn't come close, son."

"And . . . " Pierre summoned up a fragment of vernacular, "What's the damage, chum?"

"It's taken care of. I'll call a cab. It'll be round the back." He picked up the phone. "Bluey? Yeah, mate. Two of 'em. Usual place, by the bins."

A taxi with burning plastic seats took them to the hospital, where Zouzou was efficiently processed by the maternity department. Their new identities passed muster.

The Barrier Reef Hotel turned out to be hopelessly dilapidated. The bath, however, was deep, the water cold, and the bar managed to send a tolerable bottle of white wine and a roast chicken to their room. They sprawled naked under the ceiling fan until Zouzou went to sleep.

Pierre watched her chest rise and fall. One of her hands rested on her belly, as if to protect the child. She had what she wanted. Perhaps she'd settle now, calm the mysterious storm that had disquieted her in recent months.

As for himself, he'd welcome a child. Pierre Farag, family man.

If he were the father.

He sat up in surprise. Where had that idea come from? He pushed it away, but it pushed back. The idea took shape, insistent and ugly. Perhaps it had hidden in his heart. Perhaps he knew, but denied the knowledge. *Something for the baby*, Kerry had said.

Should he ask her, gently, in a round-about way? But how would she react? Zouzou, who had survived as an actress among rich, grasping old men on the maxim 'why tell the truth when an untruth will suffice?'. She would swear the child was his, but what would the value of her declaration be? Better not to know. Not asking would be an act of love, an act of love by a man 'turned in on himself'.

Two sides of a coin, they were—as close to one another as they were distant.

When his wife awoke, he said nothing to her.

On the trip home, the clouds gave up all the water in the world, perhaps God throwing a final tantrum before the Dry began. God? Pierre had lived a life without faith, but his belief in blind destiny had been shaken. Was it remotely possible that some unseen hand had rescued them from certain death and set them down in their own rain-lashed paradise?

Joseph drove bolt upright in the cab, peering through the dark torrent that lashed the windscreen. Zouzou gripped Pierre's arm like a vice, wincing at each slashing wave of wind and water.

"What about the diesel?" Pierre shouted as they approached Mossman, hours later.

"Too wet, mate."

Wet indeed. Was there a wetter place on earth?

* * *

The next morning Pierre woke to a rap on the door of the residence. Joseph's cousin William stood on the veranda against an eggshell blue sky. An azure ocean smiled up at the firmament.

"What's wrong?"

"It's old Eyebrows. He's crook."

You didn't want a sick croc with the tourist season warming up.

Pierre followed William along the path to where the flat-bottomed boat was tied up. They pushed off into the brown tributary creek and puttered two hundred metres upstream.

"He was right here."

They scanned the bank. There the monster was, stock still. Suddenly it made a vile sneezing sound and wrenched its neck from side to side, snapping its jaws open and shut. A clod of something viscous flopped into the water at the edge of the mud. The clod spread out in the water and became a torn scrap of cloth, shreds of green and red around a white rabbit, now grey with crocodile bile. A great black bird swooped to pick it up, and flapped high above the trees before descending to settle on an unseen bough.

"Looked like a Bunnies jersey, boss."

"No, just a bit of rag, William. Let's go back."

* * *

The sun stayed out all morning. Zouzou paddled on the edge of the sea in a faded kaftan. Her hair was a chaos of black. Pierre looked down at his brown legs sticking out of ripped shorts. His mop of hair seemed to belong to someone else. Perhaps it was time for a shave. Perhaps not. He sat on the verandah and drew a plan of a lean-to shelter he would add to the residence. He'd ask

Joseph to teach him carpentry, perhaps think about lining the walls of the residence with varnished planks. After lunch he and Zouzou took a siesta. At some point, Pierre was awoken by a clap of thunder, the clatter of rain on the tin roof, and the aroma of wet vegetation. He pulled a sheet over them and went back to sleep.

"Pierre, somebody is outside."

He opened his eyes to see Zouzou stretch like a cat.

There was a knock on the flyscreen door.

"Wait, I'm coming."

The rain had gone away. A luscious sunset of pinks and purples filled the sky. Pierre squinted to make out the haloed figure who stood in the doorway.

"Who are you?"

"It's me."

"Mark?"

"Yes. Any chance of a bed for the night? Goodness, you look like a *khunfus*."

"Yes, I suppose I could be described as a hippy," Pierre chuckled. "My house is your house, *habibi*. Sit down out here."

Pierre's old friend settled into a cane chair. All trace of the bumbling drunk was gone.

Zouzou came outside dressed in a wrap. She rolled her eyes.

"I guessed you'd turn up. *'aawiz shaay*?"

"Thank you, Zouzou. Tea would be splendid," Mark replied. He passed a cigarette packet to Pierre and they both lit up.

"How did you get here?"

"We came by motorbike." He pointed to a bike parked back long the access road.

"We?"

He nodded. Zouzou brought out a mug of tea.

"And what have you and your companion been up to, Mark?"

"This and that. A bit of boating. There was a nasty accident last night."

"So I understand."

They sipped their tea.

"And your plans?"

"Plans, Pierre? A bit like you, I suppose. Hide out somewhere for a while, get a new ID, find a way to get back to Britain. Take it from there."

"And the explosion that night, the Hilton. Was that Clem's work? Was that part of the plan."

"Good Lord, no. Clem was led up the garden path by someone—God knows who, but he underestimated how rough these Australians play. Ealing told him to clean up the mess and get out of Australia."

"And Zouzou and I were part of the trash?"

"The last bits. Well, almost the last. That would have been me except for your alligator."

"Crocodile," Zouzou said.

* * *

Mark Bellamy and the motorbike were gone when Pierre awoke the next morning. He walked down to the beach, turned and looked back at the residence. Yes, he'd build the extension just there, on the right.

Something had changed: A lightness in his soul, an absence of tension, a chain swinging free from an unbearable load. The last link with Ealing broken. He'd make a sign to hang above the door. It would say *'adan* in Arabic. Or *yedem* in Armenian. No, plain Eden would do for John Smith.

THE END

I love to get feedback on my novels. Readers' comments motivate me to keep writing, and help me to spread the word about my work. If you enjoyed *The Sunset Assassin*, scan the QR code below to tell me what you liked. You can write an essay or just a few words! Thank you very much – Stuart.

You can find out about Books One and Two of the trilogy *Cairo Mon Amour* and *Bury me in Valletta* at my website.

www.stuartcampbellauthor.com

About the author

Stuart Campbell was a university Pro-Vice Chancellor and a Professor of Linguistics before he took up writing fiction in 2011. His other books include the novels *An Englishman's Guide to Infidelity*, *Bury me in Valletta*, *The Sunset Assassin* and *The True History of Jude*, as well as the novella *Ash on the Tongue*. He is also the author of numerous academic works on Arabic-English translation, and on the Arabic component in Malay and Indonesian. Stuart lives at Manly Beach in Australia.